SWAPPED by a KiSS
Luisa Plaja

www.**rbooks**.co.uk

Also by Luisa Plaja:

Split by a Kiss
Extreme Kissing

SWAPPED by a KiSS
Luisa Plaja

CORGI BOOKS

SWAPPED BY A KISS
A CORGI BOOK 978 0 552 56096 2

Published in Great Britain by Corgi Books,
an imprint of Random House Children's Books
A Random House Group Company

This edition published 2010

1 3 5 7 9 10 8 6 4 2

The Random House Group Limited supports the Forest Stewardship
Council (FSC), the leading international forest certification organization.
All our titles that are printed on Greenpeace-approved FSC-certified paper carry
the FSC logo. Our paper procurement policy can be found
at www.rbooks.co.uk/environment.

Set in Palatino and Kievit

Corgi Books are published by Random House Children's Books,
61–63 Uxbridge Road, London W5 5SA

www.kidsatrandomhouse.co.uk
www.rbooks.co.uk

Addresses for companies within The Random House Group Limited
can be found at: www.randomhouse.co.uk/offices.htm

THE RANDOM HOUSE GROUP Limited Reg. No. 954009

A CIP catalogue record for this book is available from the British Library.

Printed and bound in Great Britain by
CPI Bookmarque, Croydon, CR0 4TD

To Rocco and Isabella

Special thanks to: Lauren Buckland, Rosemary Canter, Kelly Hurst, Jodie Marsh and Jane Willis for bookish brilliance; Emily Gale, Caroline Green, Alexandra Fouracres, Keris Stainton and all my writing and book-blogging friends for encouragement and support; and an extra-special thank-you to Jenny Davies, aka prophecygirl.

THE KISS

I am in the doorway of a dance tent and my boyfriend is inside, kissing a girl who is not me.

And the freakiest thing is, I can't think of a single thing to say. This is really something, coming from me. (Or, you know, *not* coming from me.) I can curse in five different languages. Six, if you count British English as well as the regular American variety, which I pretty much have done ever since I met David.

I calculated this impressive total just yesterday at the airport, when Mom made me go through my entire multi-lingual dictionary of what she calls 'colourful language' under my breath. (OK, *mostly* under my breath.)

Also, you know, she didn't exactly *make* me drop the word-bombs – I mean, she didn't say, *Now, Rachel, if you could just be really rude to me before you leave for England, I'll get your father to give you a raise in your allowance when you get back.*

No, that didn't happen (and anyway, getting money out of Dad is pretty easy, for all kinds of majorly wrong reasons). Upsetting my mother was totally voluntary on my part, and not something I'm particularly proud of, even if she makes it her mission in life to drive me crazy.

But I'm way less proud of the way I'm *not* swearing at David, who drives me crazy in a different way. In a good way – usually. I was really looking forward to surprising him here too. I can't believe I'm the one who got the surprise.

Still, that's me. Rachel Glassman, seventeen years old, oversized, gothically inclined (though not an actual Goth – there's a difference) and eternally kind of doomed.

And I don't mean doomed in a deep and sparkly vampire-love sort of way, either. Right now I am definitely in a damp and muddy boyfriend-fail scenario. The only thing this situation has in common with vampire-love is the way it completely sucks.

Also, the only way this almost-deserted English festival ground could be any damper would be if it was officially in the ocean. The mud-splats on my black clothes camouflage me against the flaps of the tent doorway. My boots are so caked in mud that the silver caricature I drew of me and David on the side is fully obliterated. Yeah – ironic much?

Anyway, none of that is even the worst thing.

Because I'm standing here, all uncharacteristically quiet and non-cursing (and thinking about the *weather*!), and my friends haven't even noticed.

Yes, my *friends*. Both of them. I can only see the back of her right now, but I know who that girl is.

And that is the worst thing.

It's Jo.

Jo.

Insert curse-word here. Insert a whole stream of them, except I can't seem to do that right now.

I think the reason they don't see me isn't that I'm silent and match the tent. I think it's because they're so involved in each other. They're not kissing now – I only caught the end of the kiss, a tiny moment. (Enough.) But she's leaning her normal-sized body into him and he's not moving away. Her natural brown curls are everywhere, hiding David's face from me and cascading over her soft-looking powder-blue sweater.

That's what Jo's like. She's normal, natural and soft-looking, and liking her is effortless. Even the most evil girls in our school, Chelsea Cook and her clones, wanted to be friends with her when she landed in the States last fall and descended on The Mill's junior class like some exotic, un-made-up British angel.

I knew back then that David wanted her. On Jo's first day he called her 'too cute', and it made me so jealous that I swear even my *hair* shone green. (Though my cheap black dye helped with that.) Yeah, David and Jo had some kind of instant British connection. (Or 'Limey connection', as I'd say if I was trying to annoy David, ever since he made the mistake of telling me that 'Limey' was some historical insult meaning 'British person'. Trying to annoy David used to be kind of a hobby.)

But then me and David got together and I stopped worrying about Jo, eventually. (I never really stopped the annoyance efforts, but David mostly shoots cool insults right back.)

I also thought Jo was pretty serious with Albie, her gonna-be rock-star boyfriend.

Well, clearly not.

Would this have happened if I'd got here even sooner? Or if David and I hadn't had that argument before he left for England?

Or was it always going to happen? Has it been going on for ages?

I stand there for about two more seconds, thinking, *It's OK. I've half expected something like this would happen for months – I'm ready. I can deal with it.*

And then I find myself thinking crazy thoughts instead. Wishing I was over there with him right now.

But not as me. As *her*.

I wish I was Jo.

Yeah, that would solve everything. I could be with David without even having to be me. People would stop looking at me that way – the way they have since seventh grade. Even Chelsea would begrudgingly kind-of-not-entirely-hate me. I'd make people laugh instead of scaring them with what David calls my 'intense intensity'. I'd lose my history and my reputation. I'd lose my nagging mother. I wouldn't lose my father because there's nothing much to lose, but everything would be perfect. *I'd* be perfect.

I'd be Jo.

And I'd still have David.

It's a freaky thought.

I step back out of the tent. Everything blurs as I turn and run and run, through field after tent-filled field, past the security guards at the entrance, under the flapping banner that says ENCHANTMENT. The wilderness of the moor stretches out in front of me. I vaguely thought England would be some kind of ancient miniature village in the middle of a big pond, but I was wrong. The space here is vast.

I reach a group of grungy-looking people sitting in a circle, passing roll-ups and bottles around and laughing – obviously strays from the festival site. The view from here is amazing, right down onto the main stage, but I don't stop for long. The festival strays look up but don't say anything as I heave myself past them, panting from the uphill struggle. I am so not a runner. I'm oversized. I'm unfit. I'm nothing like Jo.

Just beyond the people there's some kind of stone structure and I collapse inside it. It looks like it used to be a house or maybe even a tiny castle, but now it's a crumbling mess. It looks how I feel.

OK, that's it. I refuse to feel like this.

I take a black Sharpie from my jacket pocket, where I always carry my drawing stuff. I scratch at the rubble, marking the outline of my enemies in the ancient stone. It's symbolic. I found out about sites like this in the teen witchcraft books I used to read. The books were really just fun, and kind of garbage. But who knows – maybe this time I'm going to unleash some long-buried mystical powers, the kind that Jo seems to think I already have. She once told me she'd seen a double-faced voodoo doll of herself in my locker, but of course it was just a little statuette I'd brought in for my Still Life art elective. I joked for a while about having made it after her first day of school, after David called her 'too cute', but she looked so spooked that I spent ages reassuring her I'd never used it. Not long after that, I gave up trying to make fun of my feelings, or mentioning them at all. They're not so much a joking matter.

Part of the stone I touched crumbles and falls apart, and now I'm not even sure whether the girl I drew next to David was Jo – or me.

6

If I was Jo, life would be better. Jo doesn't get all angry the way I do. Jo can do relationships.

If I was Jo, I wouldn't have to deal with Mom, and Dad would be completely out of my life, and Chelsea Cook wouldn't be a problem.

If I was Jo, I'd be normal-looking, I'd be easy-going, I'd be lovable.

If I was Jo, he'd still be with me.

I've had enough of being me.

I want to be Jo.

I look up. The rest of my graffiti disintegrates slowly until it's dust; a pile of dust at my feet. I can't bring myself to care.

I wish I wasn't myself any more.

I wish I was *her.*

I wish I was Jo.

The sky goes dark.

ENCHANTMENT

We were in the middle of an awesome date, me and David, when he first mentioned Enchantment. (Ingredients for the perfect date: *X-Men* off-shoot movie, popcorn, David's house, his family miles away. David. Me. Mix together, watch sparks fly, don't necessarily watch much movie.)

I was in a kind of trance when David started talking instead of kissing, so it took me a while to tune in to what he was saying.

'It's a pretty minor British music festival,' he explained. 'But Jo told me the other week that Madison Rat got a gig there.'

'Oh, right. Great,' I said, shifting a little, if we were going to talk now. During the movie I'd somehow ended up completely entwined with David on the couch, though I don't exactly remember half of it. The movie, or how I'd gotten so entangled.

Then he said he'd been dying to tell me something

since late that morning, but first his family (that afternoon) and then an urgent need to kiss me (that evening)
had got in the way. But here was the thing: a while ago
he'd emailed a British music magazine and begged for a
summer work placement, telling them he knew one of
the bands playing at a minor British music festival,
which he did. He knew Madison Rat, Jo's boyfriend
Albie's band, who had been getting some international
attention recently through online music sites. So the
magazine had just contacted him and offered him an
internship – unpaid, four days in the summer (three at
the festival and a setup day), blogging some band interviews and providing an in-depth piece on Madison Rat.
He was going to be in England all summer anyway, like
he was every year with his half-British family. It was
perfect. He sounded really excited about it.

'Loads of people are going. Albie's whole family, for a
start,' he told me. 'They're dying to hear Madison Rat's
British debut.'

'Can you imagine Tori in England?' I laughed and did
my impression of Tori Windsor. *Like, omigod, everything
here is so totally old.* I was supposed to like Tori because
she was Albie's sister, and also now Jo's best friend, but
it was hard to forgive the fact that she used to hang
around with Chelsea Cook, the most popular and
incredibly evil girl in school. Besides, Tori was also a
total airhead.

David reached over and did something melty to my neck, possibly to shut me up. It worked. I gulped.

'My family's not going, though.' His breath tickled me, made me shiver and crane closer to him. It never felt close enough.

'I'll be there by myself,' he told my neck, his voice low and throaty. 'I'll borrow Dad's one-man tent.'

I turned and kissed his shoulder blade, made him sigh, got my own back. He smelled like coconut soap and something else. Some extra, irresistible David ingredient.

He cleared his throat and continued. 'But if Albie's family are there, it will seem all respectable, you know. To other parent-types.' I had an idea what David was going to say next, because I knew he was referring to my over-protective mother. (My father probably wouldn't even notice I'd gone.)

'So I was wondering . . .' He nibbled my neck again. 'You wanna come too?' He took a breath, sat back and waited.

Oh, wow. Me and David? Alone? In a tent? For a whole weekend? I couldn't think of anything I wanted more than that. Well, maybe an end to inequality and social injustice worldwide. But, you know. It was a close thing.

It could never work, though. In fact, it was terrifying. I'd be blurting out undying love for him by the end of the first night, and that would so not be a good look for me.

I laughed nervously. 'England in August? Isn't it worse than that Forks place out of *Twilight*?'

David smiled. 'Yeah, it'll probably rain. It's a festival – it's practically a legal requirement. But it means you'll get to hear English people say things like "brolly" and "wellies".'

Oh, wow, that was tempting too. I loved British. I was learning it from David, and I spoke it at every opportunity.

'And what if my hay fever flares up with all that out-doorsy stuff?' David said. 'You can take my mind off it.'

He kissed me properly then, to demonstrate. It took my mind off the planet.

When we re-entered the earth's atmosphere he said, 'Actually, I'm sort of nervous about it, Ray. I really want it to go well.'

'It will. You'll be great – you rock.' I didn't mind say-ing things like that. But there was a whole lot of other stuff about my feelings for him – and about me – that I was too scared to say. This was one reason David and I were not the perfect couple, not like Jo and Albie. Jo didn't seem unsure of Albie at all, ever. There was no way either of those two kept stomach-churning secrets from each other.

I kissed David again, but he stopped quickly to tell

me more. 'The festival's called Enchantment, Ray! It's exactly your cup of tea – or rather "non-fat mocha hold the sprinkles". You know, with all your witchcraft stuff.'

I laughed at the way he remembered the fake coffee order we'd invented in ninth grade, but I said, 'David, you know the Wicca thing was just something I loved reading about. But I love reading about everything.'

He shrugged.

'Anyway, if I go to Europe, I want to see famous arty stuff, not muddy fields. Even ones with "brollies" and "wellies" in them. Plus, you know, Madison Rat? Not my thing. I like music to move mountains, not sulk around in the valleys complaining.'

He laughed at my joke but his eyes didn't sparkle the way they usually did. I was totally talking myself out of going to the festival and he knew it.

'Also, I have plans for the summer,' I continued, wanting him to smile properly again. 'I'm going to research a new heroine for when I finish the RachGrrl book. A Greek goddess or something.'

'Oh. Cool.' He looked genuinely pleased. David loves the fact that I write and draw graphic novels. A lot of it was his idea to start with, when he was trying to stop me getting into trouble for drawing graffiti at school. RachGrrl is a character we came up with together, loosely based on me.

'Well, anyway, think about it, Ray. Oh yeah, and

Jo's probably going.' He smiled. 'To be with Albie.'

'Yeah?' OK, well, honestly? *That* didn't help at all. In fact, I wished he hadn't said it, even if he did add the last part. I'd never really gotten over the 'too cute' comment. I hated my raging jealousy but I couldn't seem to stop it. Especially because it wasn't founded on nothing. David liked Jo. It was obvious.

There was a commotion at the front door: David's parents and little brother were back from the movies. David's mom made a great show of clattering around outside before she came into the den to say hi, even though David and I were pretty much completely disentangled by then anyway. David's British dad and American mom are both amazingly cool. David complains about them, but really he has no idea how terrible parents can be.

David had a chat with his mom where everything he said meant *Go away*, and everything she said implied, *We're back now so don't even think about it, son*. It could have been excruciating, but my thoughts were elsewhere.

I was thinking about Jo. The way David acted around her. He talked to her so easily – way more than I ever could. I was terrible at female friendships; I had been ever since seventh grade. I wasn't great at being friends with boys either, not platonic friends, anyway. Except David, who'd been my best friend since ninth grade and then thrillingly more-than-friends for the last few months.

But David was great with everyone. Especially girls. And especially Jo. I had trouble dealing with it, even though I knew she had a perfect relationship with someone else.

Then I thought about the festival. Jo would be there, and so would so many other girls. David would like them all, and smile at them all. He just would – it was what David did. So we wouldn't be alone at all. We'd be with *them* – Jo and all the girls – and I wouldn't be able to stand it. If he was going to flirt with other girls, I'd prefer not to know about it, to pretend it wasn't happening. There was no way I could accept David's invitation.

When his mom left the room, David kissed me but it wasn't the same. He clearly thought so too because he said, 'Sorry they're back already. I wish I had a car. And possibly also a driving licence. I wish we could go somewhere together, just you and me.' He wrapped his arms around me and kissed me deeper.

'Mmm,' I said, warming up a little after all. 'I mean, yeah. Me too.' God, yeah.

'So come to Enchantment.'

'Mmm? No. No, I can't go. I'm not going. Sorry.'

He shrugged and kept kissing me, acting like he

understood, the way he almost always did, though I really didn't think he possibly could.

It was a week or so before we had the argument.

JUDGEMENT

After the argument, David went to England with his family for the summer. I didn't say goodbye before he left.

I threw myself into the graphic novel research and I did OK at first. It was pretty fun. I looked at Greek myths and found the perfect female god for my novel: Eris. Eris was the Goddess of Discord, kind of like the evil fairy in *Sleeping Beauty*, only cooler and way more powerful. In the myth, she didn't get invited to some lame wedding, so she got revenge by making three other goddesses fight over who was the best. They asked a mortal guy called Paris to decide, bribing him with various things, and he made a typical guy choice: he went after the promise of a really hot girl. This ended up bringing down the whole of Troy, his city. The whole Trojan War thing was because he'd thought with, you know, the wrong part of his anatomy.

Typical guy.

I respected Eris for highlighting guys' failings like that. Eris was definitely my kind of character. So I was ready to start my new novel, *ErisGrrl: Birth of a Female Superhero*. I thought I could even illustrate the Judgement of Paris story, but up to date and in high school, with those bitchy goddesses looking a lot like Chelsea Cook.

The trouble was, I couldn't seem to write about Eris at all. I couldn't concentrate because I was missing David too much. All my serious research faded into nothing as I doodled panel after panel depicting me and David as a crusading duo, avenging social evils in high school. The strips always ended with the two of us together in a heart-shaped bubble.

I could *not* believe myself.

Then, a couple of days ago, Jo's best friend Tori, the sister of Albie 'Madison Rat' Windsor himself, called to say her mom was sick and did I want to go to the festival with her?

Well, she actually said all of the following, in very few breaths and in about two minutes flat:

Her mom had injured her leg playing croquet in their back yard (though Tori called it a 'lawn') and the doctor advised her to rest it as much as possible for at least a week. Tori's dad was going to stay and look after her, even though they were heartbroken about missing their son's British debut. But Tori said that Albie had totally put his foot down and insisted their olds shouldn't go; in fact he'd been saying this for the last few weeks anyway, and she absolutely agreed with him. After all, there was no way Tori's parents would be anything less than embarrassing at a music festival. I mean, I'd met them, right? Omigod! Besides, Tori had to prove she could go it alone. As she knew I knew, Tori was enrolled in a British school for part of the next semester and her parents had already made Albie move his pre-college internship so that he was close enough to visit with her. Now her olds were talking like they wanted to transfer *their* jobs to England as well. Which, Tori emphasized, was *totally not the point*.

Besides, it was unfair! Albie had already flown to England without parental supervision, to do some sightseeing with his band before the festival. Why were they fine with Albie travelling and not her, when she was only six months younger than her brother? Yes, *six months*, I'd heard her correctly. I knew about how Albie was adopted and she wasn't, right? Anyway, she was digressing ... The point was I had to understand how wrong it was to have one rule for a boy and another for a girl, what with my feminist leanings or whatever. And also her parents had to learn to let go, and this festival would be a good place to start.

At this point Tori paused for a moment and I rubbed my phone ear. Within seconds she'd started again.

So, but get this! Her twenty-year-old cousin Brad, who was studying in Britain and staying in his London apartment through the summer, would use one of the parental festival tickets and help Tori with British travel, accommodation, etc. (She did go into details – the 'etc.' there is mine.) But there was still one spare festival ticket, and Tori and her boyfriend Topher were so *over* that she couldn't ask *him*, but her dad knew for a fact that Tori's flight wasn't full and he desperately wanted *someone* to fly to Europe with Tori and make sure she met Brad at the correct terminal of the correct London airport. *As if* she couldn't do it alone! It was so annoying, but he was still her dad after all, and he might not let her go if she didn't find anyone to travel with and she couldn't think of anyone else to ask. She was dying to see her big brother and her BFF Josie – and, oh, wouldn't it be great for me to see David, and please please please would I consider getting a last-minute plane ticket and helping her out?

Then she took a really big breath and waited for me to speak. Her hopefulness bounced off the cell-phone masts and into my super-sore ear.

And, you know, much as I didn't want to sit with a style princess in the confined space of an airplane cabin – probably discussing shopping malls and the failings of preppy ex-boyfriends for six hours – it sounded kind of perfect. I could get away from Mom, whose ridiculous

19

nagging had been getting steadily worse all summer. And Dad ... Dad knew all about last-minute long-distance travel. I could easily get him to buy me a ticket for the same flight as Tori. We'd arrive in England before the festival officially started and I'd surprise David, who was sure to be there early too as he'd be dying for a break from the summer vacation with his parents. He'd smile at me the way only he can. We'd fall into each other's arms and forget all about our stupid argument. I might even try to control my temper more next time.

After all, we'd had arguments like that a lot. There was no reason to think this one was any different.

Though, clearly, it was.

THE ARGUMENT

It was nearly the end of the semester and I'd just finished some comics I'd borrowed from David. They were all about a Batman offshoot called 'the Huntress'. She's fantastically tough and it's not even clear whether she's on the side of good or evil, but the main thing is that no one, but *no one*, messes with her.

I found David by his locker and handed the books back.

He flicked through the one on top and settled on a particularly ass-kicking, no-nonsense image. The artist was a woman, and the character didn't even have the exaggerated boy-fantasy curves and/or skin-tight outfit that would make any regular female overbalance with the weight of her boobs and/or contract cystitis mid-battle. She was just a woman. Awesome.

'She always reminds me of you,' David told me, and the look he gave me made my cheeks burn.

We made out for several minutes right there against

the cold metal of his locker. I loved that he saw me that way. I'd worked hard at that image. No way would I ever let the world know what a super-softie I really am – not after what happened in seventh grade. Luckily David started at our school two years after that.

'I bet RachGrrl could fight Gotham's evil gangsters, just like the Huntress,' David continued when we finally paused. 'She's such a cool heroine.'

'RachGrrl's a *hero*,' I said when I'd got my breath back. 'A hero who happens to be female. And you know I don't want to write about imaginary gangsters. I want to write about *real* evil. You know, like the oppression that goes on in high school.' I gestured around us, although at that point the halls were just filled with zombie-like students, shuffling to class with blank expressions on their faces. Still, I guess zombies can be kind of oppressed. 'Like how wrong it is that school is ruled by boys. Oh, and girls like Chelsea Cook, who are basically serving the boys.'

David smiled. He has this awesome smile, all dimples and wickedness like he's laughing at you and telling you you're special to him, all at the same time. It's unnerving. It's also unbelievably hot.

'Why do you keep saying school's ruled by boys? I think you rule way more than I do,' he said. 'No, actually, I think you chuffing *rule* full-stop.'

I melt inside when he talks like that, all 'actually' and

'full-stop', and that adorable British almost-cursing. In Britain they have about ten semi-bad words for every one of ours, and they all sound completely cute to my American ears.

I tried hard to focus on what he was saying instead of the way he said it. 'Yeah, but you don't even notice the injustice. Because you're a boy. It's different for you. You never have to worry about nineteenth-century concepts that still exist today, like "reputation", and what people will say if you go out with loads of guys.'

He gave me a look.

I back-tracked, flustered. 'Yeah, obviously, I mean *girls*. Because if you went out with guys, it would be a total problem with the jock boys that run the school, which is just so wrong.' I nodded triumphantly. 'You see what I mean? High school is full of injustice.' It really is. I can't stand that kind of thing, and I'll fight it if I can.

Yeah, and I'll especially fight Chelsea Cook.

David ran a hand down the side of my dress, which made me breathe in sharply. 'Don't you think RachGrrl needs a sidekick?' he asked.

I laughed, but only to steady my knees.

He let go of me – *aw!*– and clutched both hands to his chest. 'The wonderful, charming, supercool—'

I called him a few curse words – lightly, just to shut him up.

He grinned. 'Yeah, those sound like great sidekick

names. Original. But how are you going to reach high-school girls if your comic's rated eighteen?'

I went to give him a shove but he caught my hand and held it, making my heart thump even faster than before. I tried to cover it up by grunting, 'Do you mean it's rated *R*, Limey Boy?'

'Call me *Dastard* Boy. It rhymes with one of the things you just called me anyway, and it sounds wicked.' His thumb stroked my palm. He looked at me so intensely that I shut my eyes for a second, but that just increased the whirling sensation. Did he know what he was doing to me? What he *always* did to me?

Of course he did. He was Dastard Boy.

He held my hand and talked about superheroes and sidekicks all the way to the cafeteria, and he was still talking as we sat down with our trays of lunch gloop.

In the distance I saw Jo and Albie weaving through the tables towards us. By their side was Albie's sister Tori, dressed like a Chelsea Cook clone.

I knew that, the minute they reached us, our *brilliant* graphic novel conversation would be over and David would start flirting with Tori, and probably also Jo. He couldn't seem to help himself around most girls. And most girls couldn't help themselves right back.

'Yeah, it's perfect!' David finished at last. 'RachGrrl and Dastard Boy, fighting injustice in high school!' He punched the air heroically and then looked at me solemnly, taking my hand again. 'United in the lunch-room and in love,' he added.

'Jesus, David. Stop' – I thought of the British way of saying 'kidding around' – 'taking the piss, OK?'

'But I'm not,' David said simply. He noticed our friends and let go of my hand. He waved at them. 'Uh-oh, here come Lady Too-Cute, Sir Singalot and Maid of All Fashion.' He clearly meant Jo, Albie and Tori, in that order, and I tried to smile. He'd just said he was in love with me. Sort of.

He'd also called Jo 'too cute'. Again. And he'd dropped my hand.

They reached us, and David smiled a lot at Jo and Tori, laughed at stuff they said, totally turned towards them.

I kept quiet and tried not to stare at Albie's hand, which was clasping Jo's the whole time. Jo and Albie: the perfect couple. Albie didn't even seem to mind that David was flirting with Jo. He probably trusted Jo with his life.

David didn't reach for my hand again. He barely even looked at me. And I *did* mind. A lot. And I did not trust him. We were nothing like Jo and Albie. We were not the perfect couple.

After they left, David tried to put his arm around me but it was too late. I'd crossed over to the dark side. I was angry. Huntress-angry, RachGrrl-angry, seeking

25

revenge. As usual I couldn't even begin to tell David how I was feeling, or why. And, as usual, he either didn't notice or pretended he didn't. Which made it worse.

He moved his arm away, bit into his apple and said lightly, 'So, about RachGrrl! I was thinking, how about giving her a superpower?'

I was not in the mood for this at all. 'You know I don't go for that macho stuff,' I replied.

'It doesn't have to be macho. What about invisibility, or the ability to fly? Tinkerbell did it, and she wasn't exactly butch.' He shrugged. 'Or what about super-strength?'

'RachGrrl should fight with her *words*,' I said tightly. 'I don't want girls to think they have to fall in a vat of acid or be bitten by a spider before they can stand up for themselves.'

David absolutely wasn't going to stop. 'What about shape-shifting?' He gripped his stomach. 'Or the ability to eat school food without getting gas.' He belched. 'Super-gut.'

'You're disgusting.'

'You're right.' He smiled. 'Well, what about in real life? What superpower would you have? What if you could breathe fire? Or ice?' He looked at me sideways. 'Oh, wait, you're already quite good at blowing hot and cold.'

I told him what I thought of that. I know I can be moody, but still. I did not appreciate David making fun of me when it was his fault I felt like this in the first place.

'I'm kidding, Ray! Anyway, I know what power I'd want. I'd like to be an elementalist. You know how I'm a total veggie nature-hugging freak' – he was quoting me, trying to make me laugh – 'but I can barely go outside in the summer because of my hay fever? Well, I could solve all that if I was an elementalist who controls the weather, like Storm from the X-Men. Or I could just kind of rule over vegetation, like Swamp Thing.'

'Figures,' I said, wafting my hand around as if he smelled bad, although he totally didn't. He smelled like David: kissable. Irresistible.

'Yeah, and if I'm an *elementalist*, you could just be a *mentalist*.' He laughed.

I repeated my complaint from before, but louder. If he'd been annoying before, he was really super-annoying now.

'Hey, relax! I just meant you could have mental powers, like telekinesis or telepathy. You know, ESP and stuff.'

His eyes sparkled and I knew he didn't mean that. He was the one who'd taught me what 'mentalist' meant in British. It meant 'crazy'.

Yeah, he'd forgotten me as soon as some other girls

had come along, he'd called me moody and, seconds later, he'd called me crazy.

And he was still acting like it was no big deal.

It was infuriating.

'So go on,' he insisted. 'If you could have any super-power, what would it be?'

I could not believe him.

I glared at him. 'The power to make you stay away from me for ever.'

He laughed. 'Rachel, would you lighten up?'

No, I wouldn't. If there was one thing I was seriously *over*, it was people calling me crazy. I was *not* going to take it from him.

I cursed at him. I told him to leave me alone.

A shadow crossed his face. He'd finally stopped pretending everything was fine.

'Rachel,' he said in a low voice. 'Come on, you know I didn't mean—'

'Yes, you did.'

'OK, but I was kidding.' His voice was quiet, firm. 'I don't understand why you're so upset.'

'I'm not upset,' I hissed. I was *angry*. It was worse.

'Yes, you are. Tell me why,' David said. 'Explain it to me.'

I couldn't. 'I don't owe you an explanation.' I stood up. 'I don't owe you anything.'

'Rachel, hey. Sit down.'

'Don't tell *me* what to do!'

David's eyes hardened. This was a new look for him but I didn't care. 'Fine. I won't.'

'Great.'

He reached for my hand. Too late, too late. 'Rachel—'

I pulled away. 'No, that's it. I've had enough. You're . . . You're like . . . I can't stand the way you . . . because you . . .' But I couldn't finish any of those sentences. I gave up and strode away, calling behind me, 'Just forget it, David. We are *through*, OK!'

But I didn't mean it. Any more than I meant it after all the other similar arguments we'd had before, which all started with David flirting with other girls and me getting out-of-control, pit-of-my-stomach angry. And always ended when we were drawn back together with a powerful electromagnetic force that neither of us could ever resist.

A couple of days after that last argument David left for summer vacation. He called me from England a few times. He asked me how I was. I told him I was doing great, implying *without him*, because I was still angry even though I'd spent all day thinking about him. Our long silences echoed back and forth across the Atlantic.

I guess we were still officially broken up when we had these non-conversations, but I think the fact that we had them at all proved we were basically still together, in a bad patch. I was sure that, as soon as I saw him, the

Magneto-like forces would kick in and reunite us. Besides, this time he'd kind of just said he loved me. He can't have thought it was really over between us.

He can't have thought it would be OK to hook up with sweet and lovely, perfect Jo.

SWAPPED BY A KISS

It's all I think about as the sky goes dark –

I wish I was Jo.

– and something compels me to touch my head. But when I do, it's weird because it feels wet, and what could possibly have caused that?

I wish I was Jo.

And now I'm pretty sure I'm lying on the hard, cold ground, and I must be looking up but I can't see the grey clouds that filled the sky before. I can't see anything. For a second I'm scared –

I wish I was Jo.

– until I realize that the darkness isn't outside; it's inside my mind and it's swallowing me whole. I'm disappearing into a whirl of black and red, and now I want to laugh: the only colours I ever wear (black clothes, red lipstick). And they're all around me now; they *are* me. It figures.

I wish I was Jo.

The colours are swirling like a Munch painting, but there's no sound. Only stillness. Nothing.

Oh my God, this is it. I've really lost it. All those Personal Relationship classes Mom makes me take at school, which I pretend to my friends are detentions so I won't have to admit my mother thinks I'm crazy ... and now it turns out she was right. And David was right. I'm a proper mentalist after all.

I thought going totally, no-way-back crazy would be worse than this – I thought it would feel more like literally falling apart, for a start. But I feel quite together because I'm thinking it so clearly –

I wish I was Jo.

– and the swirling stops.

I open my eyes.

AT THE AIRPORT

'Rachel, are you sure you have everything you need?'

'Mom. For the *tenth* time.' We shuffle forward in the slow-snaking line for British Airways. '*Yes*, I have everything. I am absolutely the girl who has everything. People the world over wish they were me. They leave notes for Santa – *All I want for Christmas is to be Rachel Glassman*. But all *I'd* want is a lump of coal, because I *am* Rachel Glassman and I *have* everything.'

Yeah. If only.

Mom sighs. 'I can't help worrying about you.'

OK, I've decided I don't need a plane – teleporting would be quicker and more effective. I draw it in my head – a faint picture of myself surrounded by wobbly lines as I dematerialize.

'I mean, where is Victoria, anyway? Are you sure she's coming? I don't like the thought of you travelling without her, you know. Any more than Hank and Felicity Windsor want their daughter flying alone. Hank called again last night to say how happy he was you decided to go; how you'd be well taken care of.'

I stifle a groan.

She does this annoying head-on-one-side chicken impression, clucking at me. 'We're parents, Rachel. Hank and Felicity and I – we worry.'

Yeah, great. Let's not notice the missing detail in what she just said. Tori's mom *and dad* worry. My mom worries. I've always been way better at math than my ex-high-school-airhead mom, but even she can do a subtraction like that.

'Mom, we're early. Tori's probably still doing her evening travel makeup. Popular girls take hours to trowel on their barely-there look. I bet you used to be the same.'

Mom ignores that. She doesn't like being reminded that she was basically a Chelsea Cook type in high school – in fact, her best friend was Chelsea's mom. 'You need extra check-in time for transatlantic flights,' she says. 'Are the Windsors aware of that? I wish I'd checked.'

'I'm sure they know about it. Albie and the band left for Britain last week.'

She sniffs as we turn into the next fold of the snake. 'I should have offered Victoria a ride, then I wouldn't have this worry. Besides, her mom can't drive right now.'

'Mom, Tori will be here. I'm sure *her dad* wanted to bring her.'

It's sort of like picking a scab, saying that kind of thing.

Mom ignores that too. 'And that cousin of hers – Brad? I don't know much about him. How old did you say he was? Twenty? College students aren't always all that mature, Rachel. Be careful. If he offers you any . . . illegal substances, you should be sure to turn them down—'

'*Jesus*, Mom!'

She gives me a worried look. Well, really, she just gives me a look. She's always worried. 'Are you sure you can handle this? Because it's not too late to turn back. I can explain it to the Windsors.'

I kick hard at my carry-on luggage to shift it forward, even though it's a large holdall on wheels and a light tap would have been enough.

'Rachel, I asked you a question.'

'Mom, for f—' I swallow the curse words I was about to use. Sometimes I can't bear to make the eternally heartbroken look on my mom's face any worse. 'Of course I can handle it.'

'It's a pretty long time to be away from home, honey.'

'It's five nights, Mom.' I smile to myself. Yeah, it's five nights to start with, but with Dad's guilt money I could afford the expensive ticket with the open return. He also gave me enough spending money to buy a small mall. It should be easy to change my ticket in England; stay a bit longer, visit art museums, see paintings. Take David with me, though he doesn't know it yet. I can't wait to tell him. I also can't wait to announce to Mom that I'm planning on spending what's left of the summer vacation in Europe. She will *freak*, but she'll be too far away to do anything about it.

'Make sure you nap on the plane to help with the jet lag,' she continues. 'The right amount of sleep is so important for your mental health. Don't sleep too *much*, though. I'm glad you'll be staying with Victoria – she can keep an eye on you. Plus I didn't approve of you sleeping in a field.'

That's another thing I spent Dad's money on – a twin-bed hotel room in the town nearest the festival, sharing with Tori, who 'cannot survive without adequate shower facilities'. Her dad changed the booking he'd previously made for the whole Windsor family – except Albie, who is sharing a tent with his band – and my dad paid half. I accepted it for a quiet life, but when I get there, who knows? Maybe I'll room with Tori. Maybe not. David has a one-man tent. That thought used to scare me, but now it kind of thrills me. It's amazing what missing him has done to me.

Mom's frowning, and for a second I think she's reading my mind. But she's not a mentalist; at least not in the superpower sense. Probably in the crazy sense, because she asks, 'Did you pack your meds?'

'Jesus, Mom!' I hiss, starting to lose it now. I don't mean to – it just happens. 'I don't take any *meds*.'

'You know what I mean. The herbal therapy. The special drinks. I put some extra ones in your holdall this morning.'

I roll my eyes and curse under my breath. The words threaten to burst out.

'Rachel?' My mom's voice gets high-pitched and extra grating. 'You *have* been taking them, haven't you?'

Taking them? 'Of course I have.' I've been taking them to school and throwing them in the garbage, or occasionally emptying the sachets into the pot plant outside Principal Harwood's office between classes so that I can bring the empty wrapper home in case Mom asks. I now have conclusive evidence that the therapy doesn't work, as the plant has gotten decidedly droopier in the last month or so. Or maybe they just don't work on plants, because they come from plants. Maybe plants need 'people therapy'. I should ask David – he'd know, being such a plant-hugging elementalist.

We move forward again, though Mom's stuck on the same track. 'You do have your medical card, don't you? You should keep it with you at all times.'

Will she *ever* stop? 'Yes, Mom, but I will *not* need

medical insurance in England. I am perfectly healthy. I swear.'

'You're on the greatest plan, honey. All thanks to your father.'

Then she sees my face and adds quickly, 'Now, Rachel, don't be selfish. You know how hard he works for us. You can tell him all about Europe when he gets back from his business trip.' She sniffs and stands up straighter, switching right back to her previous, safer subject. 'You know, recently I read about some cognitive psychologists who suggest diary-keeping for mental health purposes. They recommend it for anger management and fighting anxiety. Won't you consider it?'

And then I release the expletives. I promise I really tried not to. But there are only so many ways my mother can be in total denial about my father's latest so-called business trip and then suggest *I'm* crazy before I feel like she's driven me to the gates of bedlam and given me an access-all-areas freedom pass.

At the end of my string of words I add, 'I. Am. Sane.'

But I sure don't sound it. People are staring at us, and I know what they're thinking. I'm an out-of-control teen, a freaky Goth with an attitude problem, accompanied by a caring mother with impeccable taste in designer fashions and incredible patience. I am loved, spoiled, ungrateful; the black-clad black sheep of the family.

No one sees a regular girl who feels so let down by

her parents – again – that giving in and checking into the funny farm almost seems like a plan.

Mom's mouth tightens, but no way is she shocked – she's heard it all before. Then she says in a small but triumphant voice, 'You see, Rachel? You have anger issues—'

'I don't have *anger issues*, Mom. I'm *angry*. There's a difference.'

'– and unresolved issues with your father. I think you should try the diary-keeping therapy.' She opens her purse and pulls out two white envelopes. Herbal sachets. 'And have more of these,' she says, shoving them into the side pocket of my holdall where I keep my favourite lipstick.

I would love to storm away at that point but we're nearly at the head of the line. I keep myself rooted to the spot with thoughts of travelling thousands of miles away from her. And seeing David again.

In the distance, the automatic doors open and shut repeatedly and Tori appears. She waves to me as she rushes over, followed by her smiling, supportive father who gave up a trip to his favourite country to stay with *his* wife when she needed him.

The rest is kind of a blur. Tori reaches us and tries to make me join her in a screechy jumping-up-and-down thing that doesn't work well with my plus size, not to mention my supreme and chronic lack of perkiness, but at least I manage to smile at her. Tori checks in with me even though it makes three people behind us grumble in British about Americans having 'no concept of queuing'.

Tori's dad and my mom exchange worries and cross-question us all the way to the security check. Mom actually cries when she says goodbye, which makes me angry for ten seconds before the guilt floods in and I tell her I love her and give her a hug. Tori does the same with her dad, combined with promises to call and text and send Albie and Brad his love.

Past security, Tori drags me around what must surely be the most boring collection of stores in the history of commercialism. And then we're on the plane, and I don't even care that I was totally right about Tori's incessant chattering.

I'm on my way to surprise David.

FREAKY THURSDAY

I open my eyes because I don't seem to be lying down any more, and that's weird because I don't remember moving. I *couldn't* move. Did I imagine all that?

I reach up to the wetness on my face, but it seems to have shifted downward. Now it's all around my eyes. And when I rub them and hold out my hand I can see it's just water; most likely tears. Strange – I don't remember crying either. But hey, at least I ran up to the ruins first, and David and Jo didn't see me lose it.

My heart sinks – there's a *David and Jo* now – but I squash those thoughts down and look around and—

It's all wrong.

The stones are gone. I'm surrounded by straw, mud and canvas.

It's the dance tent. I'm back where I was when I saw David and Jo kissing, before I ran away.

What's going on? I *did* run away, didn't I?

There were the stones . . . and the blackness. How did I get *here*?

And then my heart lurches. Because walking towards me is David himself. He's holding a paper cup and he's not looking surprised to see me, or happy to see me, or anything much, really, except slightly concerned.

He's looking totally hot, though. And I can't believe I'm thinking that when I am furious with him.

I'm too stunned to say anything, so he gets to speak first. And then I'm even more stunned. It's been weeks since I've seen him – weeks when I've ached for him and he has said he missed me too.

Yeah, he's said that, and yet he's made out with another girl. *At least* one other girl – what do I know? Plus there's still that argument, hovering behind us like a black cloud gearing up for a tropical storm.

All this, and the first thing he says to me is: 'Here, I found you some tea.'

I stare at him. Tori's cousin Brad told me, just after he met us at the airport, that the rumours about British people and their tea obsession are all true. But the David *I* know has always been a strong-black-coffee type of guy. And he knows that I'm a coffee person too.

Well, maybe he's a different person in Britain. A tea fan who kisses British girls.

My brain kicks into action. 'Tea? *Tea?*' I kind of spit the words at him, and they come out warped and alien-sounding. What's wrong with my voice?

'And listen, Jo . . . about what happened—'

'Yeah! About what happened! Oh my God, David! *What* did you call me?' My voice sounds totally weird. It must be stress. But I'm too angry to think about it. 'I cannot believe you!' I wish I had a weapon. Or super-powers. I'd totally use them on him right now!

It's his turn to look stunned. Well, good. I've barely started, really. Though I'm a little distracted by having just wished for superpowers, which is kind of ironic given that argument we had.

He clutches the cup he's still holding out to me. 'But, Jo, I . . . We . . . You . . .'

I briefly wonder about grabbing the drink off him and throwing it at his feet – would it stop him mumbling streams of pronouns and/or wipe that annoying look of confusion off his face? What is the *matter* with him? How can he stand there and call me by her name? *Twice?*

But before I can do anything like that, I hear a familiar squeal. It's high-pitched and perky and I heard it when our plane touched down. And there were similar squeals all the way to the festival site, punctuating Cousin Brad's tour-guide impression on the long drive from the airport in his super-old and tiny car, although it was the middle of the night for us. Even in British time it was still early morning, and the roads were full of these freakish double rotary systems with

43

everyone driving around them the wrong way. I had to shut my eyes to avoid thinking about that, but nothing stopped Tori. *Squeal! Squeal!*

Squeal! 'Omigod! Omigod, it's so great to see you guys!'

Tori bounds up to us even though I'm beaming evil rays at her. Yeah, great. So she's happy to see David. This is clearly the best time for her to have a cheery, over-dramatic reunion with my boyfriend. With my *ex*-boyfriend: Can't she see we need our privacy right now?

Then, instead of hugging David, she totally goes for me. *Me!* Unbelievable! As if we hadn't been together for the last however many hours, and she didn't desert me as soon as she humanly could. We had a brief stop at the hotel first, where Tori unpacked ('I hate creases, don't you?') and I shoved a few of my things into a bedside drawer. But as soon as Brad brought us to the festival, Tori told him we didn't need a babysitter, and he disappeared into the beer hut nearest the entrance. Tori ran off to find her brother, who she hadn't tried to call when we landed because Brad told us there was no cell-phone reception at the festival site, and Albie had already been there for a day.

That's when I went David-hunting to get my heart broken.

And now Tori hugs me as if she hasn't seen me for weeks. *Squeal! Squeal!* Then she says, 'At last! I was beginning to think everyone was hiding from me. I can't find Albie anywhere! It's so good to see you! How've you been? Listen, I cannot wait to tell you about the awesome Dolce and Gabbana accessories at the airport store . . .'

And it goes on. I totally know all this – I mean, you know, I've *lived* it! I heard this for six hours and twenty minutes at thirty-three thousand feet with a headwind (or was it without one?). But that's not why I stop listening.

I stop because I look down at myself and nearly fall over in shock.

My clothes! Where are my clothes?

Not that I'm naked or anything, like in some freaky dream.

But actually, in some ways, it's worse than that. Worse than any freaky dream, I mean. Because I'm fully awake and . . . my black clothes are gone.

Instead, I'm wearing a skirt. A long purple skirt – not totally horrible, but not remotely me. It's the sort that Jo buys from that thrift shop she loves.

The sort that Jo wears.

No, scratch that.

It's the exact skirt that Jo was wearing before, when I saw her with David.

I stretch my arms out. They're covered in powder-blue sweater, which totally clashes with the skirt –

which I didn't notice before, when I saw them on Jo. I expect colours like that on Jo, but not on me. I wear black all the time.

Except that clearly I don't, because right now I'm wearing powder-blue and purple. Together.

These are not my clothes.

Why am I even thinking about clothes? I turn my super-thin wrists. These are not my *arms*! And how *small* are my hands? Not to mention my top. I've shrunk. I've lost my boobs . . . and gained a waist. I do not believe this.

David puts the tea down on the speaker and says something to Tori about how great it is to see her and did she have a good flight? Tori answers, but she sounds kind of cagey, like she's hiding something from him. I remember that everyone knew Tori was coming, but not me. I'm supposed to be a surprise. And yet, when he brought me that tea, David didn't look at all surprised. I stare at my strangely clothed thin arms.

Jo's arms.

'Hey, are you OK?' Tori looks at me in concern.

'I don't know . . .' I mutter, stunned, and my voice doesn't sound like me at all. It's all wrong. And I've worked out what's wrong with it. It's . . . British!

Oh. My. God.

Did I get my wish?

Am I Jo?

No WAY!

But the clothes . . . the lack of boobs . . . the accent . . .

'Actually, I'm feeling a bit dodgy,' I say, testing out my new voice. It's true! I sound British! I trawl my mind for more British phrases to test. 'It's half-one! Or maybe quarter to one! I'm the dog's bollocks! I just came from the *car park*. I like watching *films* at the *cinema*.' I sound exactly like her! Like Jo! 'Ladies and gentlemen, *queue up*! I'll be here all *fortnight*!' Wow. Wow wow wow. I'm Jo. I'm *Jo*! I got my wish!

Oh my God. This is the freakiest thing *ever*!

Tori's staring at me, horrified. 'Josie?' she says – and I know she always calls Jo 'Josie'. 'Omigod, what's wrong with you?'

'She's . . . She's had a bit of a shock,' David says quickly.

Yeah, the shock of kissing you, I think.

But – wait – I'm Jo! So he just kissed *me*!

This is incredible.

This is terrifying! Now what? How can I be angry with David if he's just kissed me? Am I *with* him now, as Jo?

Oh my God!

How could this possibly have happened?

It can't have. It's impossible. *What's going on?*

'What happened?' Tori asks me.

I don't know. It can't be what I think it is. This can't be real.

'Look, I'll leave you two to catch up,' David mumbles,

backing nervously out of the tent. 'I've got to get to the press office.'

I glare at him. Where does he think he's going?

But before I can figure out what to say, he's left and Tori's frowning at me.

'So what's up, Josie?'

She called me 'Josie' again. But I still don't believe it. I need to see it for myself. I need a mirror.

'Where are the restrooms?' I remember to be British. 'I mean the *loos*?'

Tori gives me a strange look. 'Weren't you getting here early this morning? Haven't you already, like, set up your tent and stuff?'

'Yeah, but I . . . haven't needed the *loo* yet,' I say, sounding totally lame.

'Ri-ight. Well, I *really* only just got here, but I think there are some in the far field.' She leads me out of the tent, frowning. After a minute she looks at me sternly and takes a deep breath. 'OK. Josie . . . Have you taken something? Is that what David's talking about?' She shakes her head. 'Because, seriously, I'm surprised at you. It's so not a good idea. One time in ninth grade this guy offered me and Chelsea some—'

Oh, I am *not* listening to the Perilous Adventures of Popular Girls! 'I haven't taken anything! I'm not even . . . pissed. As in drunk, not angry. It's British!' I learned that from David.

48

'Omigod, Josie. Please quit acting weird now.'

Acting weird? But that's something Rachel would do. I'm Jo now. I'm totally normal. I'm a girl everyone instantly likes.

I'm Jo! I'm Jo!

I decide to keep my mouth shut until I've figured this out. I feel suddenly tired, but in a strange way, like it's all in my head and not in my body. My body is trotting along after Tori like it hasn't just missed a full night's sleep on the plane. Because, of course, it hasn't. I'm in Jo's body, and Jo hasn't travelled half as far to get here.

And then it hits me.

Where's *my* body? If I'm Jo, then is Jo me?

She can't be, though, because if I made this happen by wishing it, well . . . there is *no way* she wished to be me. I mean, let's face it: who would want to be Rachel Glassman – who'd want my life? Especially when you're Jo Reilly and you're perfect, and you have everything. Including David, who has just kissed you.

Or me. David has just kissed me, Jo.

I realize something else. If David thinks I'm Jo, this could be interesting. I can cause all kinds of problems for him. I could be a total trouble-maker, like Eris, Goddess of Discord. Or rather, ErisGrrl, my new super-hero. In the shape of perfect Jo, I can probably get away with anything.

I gaze at my slim Jo arms, brush them over my cute Jo skirt and do a little hop. I feel lighter.

Of course. Because I *am* lighter!

Tori rolls her eyes. 'Omigod, Josie,' she says, 'I cannot believe you . . .'

'I can't believe me either,' I mumble. And then I start worrying again. Me? Who's *me*? Where am I? I mean, where's my body? Jo must be in it – it's the only explanation. Where is she? Still up at the ruins? I need to go there! Am I – is she – are we OK?

Help, what if I'm not OK?

Tori cuts through my increasing panic. 'Soon as you've used the restrooms, we'll go find Albie, OK?'

She links her arm through mine like it's a natural thing to do, and I have to resist the temptation to shake her off. She thinks I'm her friend, after all. She thinks I'm Jo. I look like Jo! I *am* Jo!

Jesus, though. Tori's words sink in.

Albie?

If I'm Jo, then Albie's my boyfriend. And I've just cheated on him with David.

Tori says, 'My brother will know what to do with you.'

RAT BOYS

I have to get out of this. I can't see Albie – not if I'm Jo. I also need to go back to the ruins, see if my body is there. How much would Tori freak if I said those words? Then again, how freaky is this whole situation?

'Listen, Tori, after the restrooms I need to go . . . outside the site. I need to check something,' I try. 'I mean, by myself.'

She shakes her head and tightens her arm's hold on mine. 'Nuh-uh. No way. You're going nowhere on your own. Seriously, I'm keeping you *way* out of trouble until we find Albie and he takes over.'

I give up. My head hurts as I trudge along with Tori. She shows me to a row of hideous-looking and stinky plastic portable cubicles and stands as far away as possible, fanning her nose. I remind myself why I wanted to come here in the first place: I want a mirror. I want to see my face. Jo's face. On Jo's body. That I'm in.

But after ten seconds I'm back at her side, announcing

that I've changed my mind and I don't need 'the loo' after all. It wasn't only the stink; it was just too dark once I shut that plastic door. I couldn't figure out where the light might be, and I didn't want to touch anything.

I should ask Tori for a compact – I bet she has at least one with her at all times – but she instantly gets wrapped up in hunting for her brother. She dips in and out of quiet tents and run-down wooden shacks that are doubling as snack bars, pulling her phone out of her pocket at intervals and grumbling about how it's not working in this strange country. In her single-minded focus on finding Albie, she seems to have forgotten what Brad told us about the lack of reception here on the moor.

I remind her, but at the last second I manage to stop myself mentioning Brad. *Rachel* heard Brad say that, not Jo. Not *me*. Jo has never even met Brad.

But maybe Tori wouldn't have noticed anyway. She's getting more panicky the more she searches through the debris of what looks like some heavy partying. I kind of know how she's feeling. Not that long ago I was on a similar hunt for David. I knew he was supposed to have arrived first thing today, but most of the bands and their roadies had an extra setup day and they clearly spent it getting wasted. Everything on the festival site is quiet and morning-after-ish, and the dance tents are empty and naked, as if they shouldn't be seen without a night-time atmosphere and a swelling crowd of moving bodies filling them. When I was looking for David, I felt like I would be searching for ever.

But, of course, I *did* find him – *shudder*. There really seems to be no sign of Albie anywhere.

It's weird, though. The more worried Tori gets, the more I relax in contrast. I stare at the legs that aren't my legs, the feet that aren't my feet. But when I tell them to move, they do, and I'm walking, putting one of Jo's feet in front of the other over and over. It's mesmerizing.

Are they my legs and feet now? Will they always be mine? Will I be Jo for ever? Is she me? Will she always be me? Would I mind? I don't think so. It's what I wanted, after all. But it's so freaky, my brain can't contain it. I fall into a daze, more drifting than walking.

We pass various signs of the festival's 'enchanted' theme. There's a play area filled with giant plastic mushrooms and a bunch of wild-looking children running about completely unsupervised. To the left of this is a gazebo surrounded by plastic-looking trees in front of a backdrop covered in white stuck-on stars. The whole place is like a low budget, run-down Disneyland. I stare at it in my out-of-body trance.

'Josie, come on!' Tori links arms with me again, pulling me urgently. 'This way!'

'Hey!' I say, suddenly fighting the urge to do something Rachel-ish like storm off in the opposite direction.

'I mean, hey, have you found him?' I struggle to keep the dread out of my voice. Help help help! What am I going to say to Albie?

'No, but there are the others. Under that weird ivy!' She nearly splits my eardrum with her screeching. 'Clyde! Tamber! Hey!'

She runs over to two boys I've seen millions of times but never exactly noticed. The members of Albie's band aren't on my radar. They're too normal to hang out with my friends, but too nice to cause trouble for us. I like them well enough; I just don't really know them. I'm not even sure what their real names are – Tamber's a nickname from playing percussion, I think, and Clyde is Clyde's last name, which I know because the Clydes live at the end of my street. Tamber's mostly famous for his red hair and his height – he towers over most teachers and regularly hits his red-topped head on door frames. Clyde has amazing long dreadlocks and is kind of outsized in the other direction – widthways, I mean, like me-Rachel. Even so, I'm not sure I'd have spotted them here at all if Tori hadn't pointed them out. As we get closer, I can see why I didn't recognize them – they both have woollen beanies hiding their identifying hair. They also look half asleep, slumped against the foam base of the gazebo's pillars.

In fact, as we get closer, it becomes obvious that they're fully asleep. Clyde is snoring with his mouth open.

'Ew, gross,' I remark, and then I correct myself. 'I mean, how utterly revolting.'

But Tori's not really listening to whether I sound British or not. 'They'll tell us where Albie is. We should wake them.' Before I can say anything to stall for time, she's shaking Tamber by the shoulder.

He stirs and opens his eyes, mumbling, 'For the last time, it's not in C!' Then he sits up straighter, stares at me and Tori and gasps, 'Am I dreaming?'

This wakes up Clyde, who shuffles about mumbling, 'Man, that was some night.' He nods at me, then at Tori, totally unfazed by our presence. 'Hey, girls. When did you get here? Train go OK, Jo? Flight go OK, Tor?'

I nod, though I have no idea what Jo's journey to the festival was like. I expect Tori to go into detail about the airport purchases she made so I'm shocked when she gives a quick answer and cuts straight to, 'So where's Albie?'

Tamber and Clyde give each other a look that's almost guilty. Neither of them says anything.

'You guys, what's going on? Is there something I should know about my brother?' Tori squeaks. 'You *have* to tell me.'

Tamber speaks first. 'He told Clyde he had to go somewhere. He said he'd be leaving today. I guess he's already gone.'

'Gone? Where?' Tori's voice gets even squeakier, which is saying something.

'Don't know,' Clyde says. 'I'm sure it's nothing to worry about.'

'Yeah, except that we don't know where he is or when he'll be back,' Tamber says. 'You're so dense! You should have asked where he was going! Tori's clearly worried. I'm worried that she's worried.'

Clyde straightens up. 'Listen, man, the guy's an adult. He can look after himself. He's probably gone to see that mystery chick— Ow!' Clyde rubs his leg where Tamber kicked him. 'What was that for?'

Tamber stage-whispers through clenched teeth, 'Dude!'

'What? You know! The one in that photo I told you about – the groupie with the vintage smiley-face T-shirt. She was hot. It's so unfair that lead singers get all the chicks.'

Tamber shakes his head desperately. 'Quit it! Do I have to spell it out? Albie's betrothed is standing right there!' Then, to me, 'Sorry, Jo, don't listen to him. He's talking complete bull.' He glares at Clyde.

Clyde gives me a guilty glance and sniffs. 'Man, talk about bull. You're using words from two centuries ago. What is "betrothed"?'

'And you want to major in English? Dude, you're a loser!'

'I've changed my mind. I want to major in music production and you can major in English on your own! And you're the loser! You've lost the lead singer of our band!'

'*You* lost him! I wasn't even there when he told us he was leaving. I was totally out of it.'

'I was totally out of it first!'

'Yeah? How would you know that, if you were totally out of it?'

'Guys! Guys, stop it!' Tori sounds like she's used to speaking to Tamber and Clyde like this. 'Just tell me what you know about Albie. What exactly did he say to you?'

'He said he might be gone a couple of days,' Clyde admits.

'A couple of *days*?' Tori gasps. 'And you didn't think to ask—'

'He said he was going to do a thing. His thing, you know. When a guy has a thing, you don't ask about it,' Clyde explains slowly and carefully. 'It's a guy thing. You gotta respect us guys.'

'Tori's right, you should have asked,' Tamber says. 'Us guys are playing on Sunday – what if he's not back by then? What about the gig?'

'He'll be back, man. It's the greatest gig of our career. He wouldn't miss it.'

Tamber's lost in thought. 'We can work it so we get by

without his guitar part, but who's gonna sing? You can't hold a note. You can barely hold a note on the keyboard.'

'Yeah? Well, you can barely hit a drum. You got less rhythm than a drunken slow-worm staggering home after a night out at the slug bar.'

Tamber shakes his head. 'You're mixing up reptiles and gastropods, dude.'

'Yeah? Well, you're mixing up your ass—'

'Stop it!' Tori shrieks.

There's a dazed silence.

When she speaks again, her voice has finally come down an octave or two, but is still super-squeaky. 'What am I going to tell Mom and Dad?' she says. 'And Brad, if he ever leaves that bar. Where has my brother gone?' She looks at me, obviously expecting me to be as upset as she is.

But seriously I think that Clyde, dense and zoo-logically challenged though he clearly is, has a point. Albie is eighteen, and he told his friends he was going somewhere. It doesn't really matter where. He's not exactly a missing child. And I have bigger things to worry about, anyway. It's kind of a relief that I don't have to figure out what to do with Jo's boyfriend on top of everything else.

Tori is still looking at me, so I pretend to care. 'Bummer,' I try.

Tori frowns.

'I mean, ooh, what an appalling pity.'

'He said he couldn't leave until he'd talked to Jo,' Clyde says accusingly. 'He said he was going to find her after she arrived this morning.'

This hangs in the air for a few seconds. None of us are too sure what to do with it, least of all me.

Then Tori asks, 'Did he talk to you, Jo? What happened? Is this anything to do with what David said before, when he said you'd had a shock? Was it about Albie?'

Oh, I was sure David meant the kiss. Kissing David is always a shock. A whole-body shock. Jo must have felt it too. I feel a massive surge of pure jealousy.

'Omigod, Jo, your face!' Tori's fully panicking now. 'What is it? You gotta tell me!'

Tamber adds, 'Yeah, tell her, Jo. And us too. It's not like Albie not to tell his buddies stuff.'

Clyde shrugs but doesn't add anything about guys and their 'things' this time.

'So what's going on?' Tori demands.

Three pairs of eyes are on me – all equally bloodshot, which Tori would be upset about. She was applying eye drops every half-hour on the plane.

What should I say? Where *could* Albie have gone?

Maybe he took off because he figured out that Jo and David were together, before I did? I almost want to find him now. We can get our revenge together. We can cause double the trouble.

Except that he'd think I was Jo, and he probably wouldn't want to see me right now. And as if Albie would cause trouble anyway. He's too nice. He'd most likely just . . . leave.

'Jo, come on,' Tori pleads. 'You have to tell me. What's wrong?'

Do I tell them? Do I say Jo cheated on their brother/bandmate and Albie might know about it, and then wait for them to tear me-Jo apart? How did this turn into *my* problem, anyway? I've been cheated on too! Life was supposed to be better as Jo. This is so unfair!

And then something – maybe the thought of Albie knowing about Jo and David, or my relationship with David being over, or the jet lag (of my mind), or the general weirdness (of my body), or Tori, Clyde and Tamber staring at me, or all of it – makes this really freaky thing happen. It's almost stranger than being in Jo's body in the first place.

I start crying in front of everyone. It's like my worst nightmare.

'I . . . I don't know!' I sob in that voice that's not mine.

I'm so shocked at myself that my tears dry up instantly. There's a silence.

Then Tori grabs my arm and pulls me away as Clyde

60

and Tamber shift nervously, looking oddly concerned, for boys, but not too surprised. After all, Jo doesn't have the super-tough reputation that Rachel does. Maybe they even *expect* me to cry. Weird. I almost feel like bursting into tears again, just to test it out.

Tori's voice goes all commanding. 'Jo, come with me,' she says. And as soon as the boys are out of earshot, she adds, 'OK, what has my brother done? You are going to tell me everything.'

FREAKY AMBULANCE

Luckily for me, Tori is the girliest girl in the known universe. Telling her everything isn't something that can happen just anywhere, immediately. It needs to be scheduled and catering needs to be called, and she has to go back to the hotel first to change into an outfit specially picked out for a telling-of-everything occasion.

Well, really she tells me she 'needs to visit the hotel to wash up' because she 'cannot believe how muddy English fields are' and now she gets why 'the royal guys in Dad's favourite portraits always wear those ugly green rubber boots'. Plus she wants to call Albie's cell or send him a message and she thinks her phone will work from the hotel (and she's probably right because I ignored three incoming messages from Mom while we were there before, but I don't tell her that).

But she says she won't call Albie until she's heard what I have to tell her, just in case her brother has 'done something stupid' and I'm about to tell her about it. She thinks she should hear my side of the story because even though he's her brother she 'has to put the sisterhood first'.

As if Albie would ever 'do anything stupid'. The only thing more perfect than Jo herself is Albie, the perfect guy, and their perfect relationship with each other.

Apart from the whole David-kissing-Jo thing, of course.

We walk towards the security gates – the same ones I ran through earlier when I just wanted to get away. Who'd have thought I'd be back so quickly, in someone else's body? This is just so twisted. And sort of cool. In a super-twisted way.

In the distance you can just see the top of the ruins, and I desperately want to go over to see if Rachel (me?) is still there and if I (Rachel?) am OK. I just need to figure out how to get away from Tori.

But when I glance back from the ruins, Tori's gaping at an ambulance just by the entrance. There's a couple of grungy and vaguely familiar-looking people around it, and some green-jacketed types saying brisk official-sounding things to the security guards.

'Rachel!' Tori says.

'Yeah?' I reply instinctively.

But Tori's still staring, frowning, and I get this chill when I remember I'm not Rachel.

'I thought I saw her,' Tori says. 'Rachel. Like, sitting in

that ambulance. But it's not possible. She was fine! She'll be with David by now.'

Bile rises in my throat. 'She will not be with *David*!' I spit his name out.

Tori looks confused. 'But where else would she be? We arrived and she went to find him. But down there – it looked like her.'

'Are you sure?'

I don't wait for an answer. I run down to the entrance. I recognize the kids now – they were with the crowd who were smoking and drinking near the stones earlier, when I was myself. They look a lot more polished close up, like their grungy look is very carefully put together. They're staring openly at the green-jacketed paramedics fussing around. One of the Green Jackets is closing the ambulance doors on—

Me. It's definitely me.

I'm sitting in the corner of an ambulance with my head in my hands.

The world stops turning. My head takes over the spinning duties of the whole planet.

Within seconds the doors slam shut and the ambulance is speeding away, with me inside it.

Tori rushes over. 'Did you see? Was it Rachel?'

Was it? I don't know anything any more.

I nod.

'Omigod, what happened?' She turns to the onlookers

64

as the security guards start to wander off, talking into their radios. 'Is she OK?'

'No idea, mate,' a dark-skinned boy with heavy-lidded eyes mumbles. 'We were up by those ruins, just getting away from it all, and she ran past us. Then she popped out again later in a bit of a state, so we took her down to security and they got an ambulance as a precaution, like.'

The girl giggles, shaking her stumpy blonde braids. 'Yeah, 'cept we ignored her for ages 'cos we were busy.'

I feel like hitting her.

'It wasn't that long,' the boy insists. 'Besides, she seemed totally out of it. What difference does it make?'

I feel like hitting him.

'So, wait, they called an ambulance? Do their phones, like, work here?' Tori asks, holding up her own blank phone.

And now I feel like hitting *her* too. How can Tori think about her phone when I'm in an ambulance! Or, at least, my body is. What am I going to do? Why did they think I needed the ambulance? What's *wrong* with me?

'Security have got special phones or something,' the heavy-lidded boy says. 'Short-wave radios.'

Never mind that! 'What was wrong with her?' I sound panicky.

Tori gives me a concerned look and mumbles, 'Oh

God, yeah, Rachel.' So at least she's stopped thinking about her cell for ten seconds.

'She your friend?' Heavy Lids asks casually. 'You two don't look like Goths.'

'Rachel's not a Goth,' I tell him. 'She's *gothically inclined*. She's an individual who doesn't believe in labels and refuses to be branded by—'

'Yeah, we're her friends,' Tori cuts in.

'Right. Only they wanted to check her name. Kept asking us. She gave them a name, then she changed her mind. Seemed really confused. Maybe you should go to the hospital and talk to them.'

Heavy Lids and Stumpy Braids start to wander away.

'Should we go, Josie? I could ask Brad to bring us, but I bet he's started drinking already. I could find—'

I leave Tori rambling and run after Stumpy Braids and Heavy Lids. 'Hey, hold on!' I say when I catch up with them, and they stop, exchanging a bored glance.

'Yeah, what? You want an autograph?'

Are they for real? 'No, thanks. But . . . so you're saying she didn't know who she was?' I mean, I know the feeling. But still. This is worrying.

'Nope. She was too out of it to know her own name,' Stumpy Braids giggles.

I narrow my eyes at her.

'She had some kind of ID card and she was acting all weird, checking it a lot and reading it out,' Heavy Lids says. 'She kept saying that name you called her before. Ruth?'

'Rachel.'

'That's it. She was rambling on about her name actually being Joanna?'

'Josephine. Jo.'

'Yeah – Jo.'

My head spins. We definitely have swapped bodies. This is crazy.

Stumpy Braids laughs like a woodpecker. 'Fake ID, I bet. Fancy forgetting about it! She was on something strong!'

'She wasn't on anything,' I hiss. Not even the herbal sachets, no thanks to Mom.

'Oh. Well, then you should probably tell them that too. I heard them say something about testing her blood and maybe pumping her stomach as well as checking for head injury because of some small cut on her head—'

'Pumping her stomach? Head injury? What happened?' I remember the blackness. Did I hit my head? How bad is this?

'I don't know, but she was in the old Temple of Diana. As in Diana, Goddess of the Hunt, you know,' Stumpy Braids says, and then she puts on a woo-woo voice. 'It's a mystical place. We get a lot of inspiration from being near it.'

'It's also unsafe,' Heavy Lids adds self-righteously. 'Everyone knows not to go inside, except the newbies. Now they'll probably threaten to shut down the festival or something.'

'They wouldn't do that,' Stumpy Braids soothes. 'Not with us here.'

OK, is there no limit to the arrogance of these guys? Who do they think they are?

'Still, newbie festival-goers get my goat. If they can't handle it, they should stay home. Or at least stay on the site. She shouldn't have been up there in the first place.'

Huh! 'But you didn't stop her going in!' I point out. 'And you were off the site too!'

'Yeah, course we were.' Stumpy Braids shrugs in an entitled kind of way. 'We don't like confines.'

'Confines are bad,' Heavy Lids agrees. 'They stifle our creativity.'

'Way bad,' Stumpy Braids adds meaningfully. 'Way stifling. We gotta go.'

'But she was conscious all the time, right? She was walking about OK?' I ask them as they head towards the Temple of Doom, or whatever it's called. They pretend not to hear me, acting like they've had enough now and I'm stifling their creativity.

I turn back to Tori. 'Help me out here!'

But Tori's not there and possibly hasn't been for

a while. And I realize why almost immediately, when a small blue car pulls up.

Tori's in back. She gives me a little shrug and a wave through the open window.

In the driver's seat is an auburn-haired girl in a sporty-looking hooded top. I vaguely recognize her. Then I remember everything's back to front in Britain and this girl is actually in the passenger seat. There's someone else at the wheel of the car. A boy with messy hair and a leather jacket and the hottest looks in the world.

David.

Tori must have found him and told him where we needed to go. He's staring right through me, his eyes full of concern.

I didn't know he had a car here. Or a driving licence. He didn't tell me any of that when he called me from England.

Tori went to get him. She must have known he was a driver. Someone must have told her. Most likely Jo. Why does Jo know things about David that I don't?

'Josie, get in!' Tori calls.

I hesitate.

But I should probably get to the hospital. If I'm not already there.

I get in.

BOYFRIEND OF RACHEL
GLASSMAN

Everyone says a quick 'Hi,' and then Tori puts her hand on mine and says, 'Rachel's going to be fine, Josie. Don't worry. It will all be OK.' I feel soothed for about ten seconds, until I glance at what I can see of David, and my anger and confusion come flooding back.

He's acting weirdly – shoving the stick-shift around impatiently, revving his foot on the gas pedal at every red light. He's putting on a very good show of being worried about Rachel.

But maybe it's just the way he always behaves behind the wheel. How would I know, when I didn't even know he could drive?

And anyway, there are more important things to think about right now. Am I – is Rachel – OK?

Things at the hospital are better, but also worse, than I thought they would be. First of all Tori and the other girl take command and stride up to a desk, practically shoving each other out of the way in the process. Then, instead of finding anything out, they start arguing about who's going to talk to the receptionist, a tired-looking woman with a streak of grey in her long wild hair. She kind of looks like Rogue from the X-Men, if Rogue were as old as my Great-Nana Glassman. Tori and the girl keep elbowing each other in front of Great-Nana Rogue until David takes over in this masterful, unsmiling kind of way that really isn't him at all.

I hang back, stressing but unsure of what to do, and my worry must be obvious because Tori and the other girl come over and stand on either side of me, taking it in turns to tell me, in sugary voices, that everything will be fine. Though first Tori does mumble, 'I didn't realize you were *that* close with Rachel,' and the other girl tells her off for being insensitive and that I – Jo – probably relate better to someone like Rachel than to someone who dresses entirely in marshmallow colours. By which I'm pretty sure she means Tori. But Tori doesn't take offence because she's too busy consoling me.

I end up sandwiched between the two girls while they practically compete with each other over who can comfort me the most. If I wasn't so worried I'd be rolling my eyes – I mean, how pathetic is Jo that everyone wants to look after her? I can take care of myself! On the other hand, it feels pretty nice to have all this attention.

After a while I tune out their reassurances and try to focus on what the receptionist is saying to David. All I can work out is that she's probably a ventriloquist in her spare time because her lips are barely moving. Whenever she does speak, she seems to choose that moment to shuffle a stack of papers behind a huge sign that depicts a crossed-out cell phone, so I can't hear a word she says. I can't hear David either, as he has his back to us.

Finally he comes towards us, running a hand through his gorgeous hair and looking defeated. I stare right at him but he's avoiding my eyes.

'It's definitely Rachel,' David tells us grimly. 'Her pockets were full of all that medical ID her mum makes her carry.'

'Is she OK?' Tori asks.

David glares at her as if she has something to do with what happened. 'Why didn't you tell me before that Rachel was with you? That she travelled with you? I didn't even know she was here!'

Tori looks affronted. 'She didn't want me to tell you.'

David sort of slumps and looks at the ground. Yeah, work that guilt, dude. If he'd known I (Rachel) was coming, would he have been more careful about his public displays of affection with other girls?

'So is she OK?' Tori asks.

'They didn't tell me much,' he tells his black leather boots, which usually match mine. But not any more. Now I am wearing some kind of canvas Jo-footwear.

'They said her condition is stable, but she seems a bit confused. They think she's fine but they haven't ruled out a head injury, so she's having tests and scans.'

'Oh yay, she's OK!' Tori squeaks.

Oh yay, I'm OK! But ugh, I don't like the sound of tests and scans.

'She'll hate the tests and scans,' David says. 'I asked if I could go with her, but they won't let me. It doesn't even count that I'm her boyfriend.'

My heart leaps for a second. Then it drops like a stone. Dastard.

'But I thought you and Rachel had split up?' the girl with the hooded jacket says bluntly. Who *is* she and how does she know anything about any of us?

Tori looks shocked. 'No way, Hailey!'

Ah-ha, it figures. Hailey! No wonder she seemed familiar. I vaguely remember her as Jo's best friend from England, who visited Boston at the end of last year and acted like she was too good for any of us. I only met her once, at a Christmas party Tori and Albie held, and I didn't exactly speak to her, not because she was acting all stuck up, which she was. But mostly because I was kind of busy, you know, making out with David.

I drift into a quick daydream about that. Then I quickly bring myself back down to earth with this thought: *Why hasn't David told Hailey she's wrong about him and Rachel?*

He's studying the ground again like he's expecting a quiz on it later and won't graduate if he gets a failing grade. It's a weird look for him, as he practically never studies for anything – he's naturally gifted. He's also plainly not interested in academic stuff. The teaching faculty are always lecturing him about 'wasted talent'. He's so stubborn, though. It's like he refuses to be good at stuff on purpose, the same way he pretends his family aren't mega-wealthy and one of their houses isn't on the same street as Chelsea Cook's. I really like him for that too. Denying a connection with Chelsea Cook is just fine by me.

I mean, I *used* to really like him for that.

He still hasn't told Hailey she's wrong, so Tori does it for him. She fills the silence with, 'I mean, yeah, I know you and Rachel fight sometimes, but you're together for ever, I can totally tell. Hailey, where did you get that crazy gossip from?'

'Hey, it's not gossip,' Hailey protests. 'It's the truth. David told us, didn't he, Jo? When we were pitching our tent, first thing this morning.'

I look at her in amazement. David told Hailey *and* Jo? They had some cosy chat about his personal life while they were settling in? And all this time I didn't tell anyone at all that me and David were broken up. I didn't tell anyone because *I didn't think we were broken up at all*. But David . . . David thought we were, despite all those calls

74

to me-Rachel, and that comment just now about being Rachel's boyfriend. And he told Hailey.

And Jo.

Or did he just say it because he wanted to hook up with her?

'Um . . . yeah,' David mumbles, still looking at the ground.

'Josie, you OK?' Tori gives me a questioning look.

'Hey, Jo?' Hailey says softly. 'Listen, me and you should go somewhere and talk.'

Tori pulls me towards her, eyeing Hailey suspiciously. 'Leave her alone. She's been acting real weird. She's obviously had a hard day.'

Hailey pulls me the other way. 'Yeah, I know, and she needs her *friends* right now. Come on, Jo, let's get back to the festival. We can talk about Albie on the way.'

I curse absent-mindedly. Everyone stares at me for a second, all shocked. Oops. Jo doesn't really use that kind of language, does she? She's way too perfect for that.

I cough. 'I mean . . . f— *hell*, oh . . . kay? Yes, fl-oh-k. Uh . . . *flock*?' Yeah, that could work – it's a nice, innocent word, like 'shoot' or 'heck'. I practise it. '*Flock!*'

Luckily Tori and Hailey have started fighting again and no one's paying any attention to my pathetic attempts to transform Rachel-ish into Jo-ish.

'No, she's coming back to the hotel with me,' Tori says. 'She has to talk to *me* about it. Isn't that right, Josie?'

'She's called Jo,' Hailey snaps. 'And she's going back to the festival with me.'

'*I* call her Josie – I always have.'

'What do you mean "always"?' Hailey glares at Tori. 'You've only known her a year.'

Oh, Jesus! Though this is vaguely cool. No one ever fought over Rachel.

'Anyway, Jo needs to be at Enchantment with me,' Hailey insists. 'Like I say, we need a chat. And besides, she wanted to help me track down Topaz. Jo adores Topaz.'

Jo's standing right here, I think. Except that, in a way, she isn't. I mean, you know, who the *flock* is Topaz?

'Jo has important stuff to talk to me about,' Tori says.

Hailey sniffs. 'She can talk to *me*. And I can take her mind off things. Topaz are headlining, you know. You can't get more important than that. I've spent the last hour or so hanging around with David just in case they visit the press area.'

I think I detect David grimacing as if he hasn't exactly enjoyed Hailey hanging around with him, but it must be my imagination because that would be totally unlike him. He loves the company of girls – all of them.

Tori and Hailey bicker some more, until David cuts through it with, 'Sorry, guys, I'm staying here. I want to see Rachel.'

I almost cheer. Except that the traitor 'wants to see Rachel'.

Though really I kind of want to see Rachel too. Not that I want to be her (me?), but just to check she's (I'm?) OK.

'So did they say you could visit with her after the tests?' I ask him.

'I don't think so. That Rogue-lookalike over there wouldn't even tell me exactly where she is.' David nods in the direction of the receptionist, and I can't believe he thinks she looks like Rogue too. 'But she let slip that Rachel's parents were arriving on the earliest plane they could manage, so I'm going to wait and talk to them.' He looks determined. 'You can find your own way back, can't you?'

I stifle a gasp. How can they have called my parents? Then I remember the contact details on my medical insurance card. But I don't want Mom here! Or Dad. Though if he turns up there will be an entire flock of topaz-coloured sheep flying through the sky.

'David, come on,' Tori says gently. 'There's no way they can make it before tomorrow some time, at the earliest. You can't stay here.'

David juts his chin out. 'I'm not leaving until I see Rachel.'

I nearly roll my eyes. *Yeah, great impression of someone who cares, David, but are you forgetting you've been kissing*

77

another girl? Who exactly is he trying to kid? I decide it's probably Tori, because she's Albie's sister. Right now David and me-Jo clearly have a secret relationship. Ick.

Great-Nana Glassman/Rogue finishes a phone call and notices us looking at her. She calls over, her voice cutting through our collective nervous silence. 'Hey, you over there? Boyfriend of Rachel Glassman?'

Or not, I think.

David walks over to Great-Nana Rogue, but this time we all hear her clearly.

'Sorry, love, but you may as well go home now. Your girlfriend's been transferred to another hospital.' She adds the next bit quickly, as if she thinks David will panic. 'Nothing serious – don't worry a bit. She's fit and healthy and chances were we were going to discharge her sooner rather than later anyway.' She lowers her voice. 'Between you and me, some kind of private medicine strings have been pulled all the way from America, and she's off for a luxury stay at The Clarence.'

'The Clarence?'

'Sounds like a hotel, doesn't it? Well, it's not far off! It's the nearest private hospital. Don't worry about her, love, she's going to be swanning about in the lap of luxury. She'll be totally fine. I'm sure she'll contact you as soon as she can.' She turns away to take another call, dismissing David with a wave of her hand.

CUCKOO IN THE NEST

Hailey loses the fight-over-perfect-Jo but Tori doesn't exactly win either, and at my suggestion all four of us end up back at the hotel together. The presence of David means there's no chance of making the Albie-related confession that Tori's expecting from me, which is good. But I wish I could have thought of a way of leaving David out of this weird gathering. I've got to work out what I'm going to do about him. I need to cause some trouble for him, ErisGrrl style, but I can't exactly put any revenge plans in motion when all four of us are crammed into one hotel room.

By 'hotel room', I mean the tiny space I was supposed to be sharing with Tori when I was Rachel. Clearly me-Rachel is now at a much classier joint – some luxury hospital. But we don't even know where it is, which doesn't stop David asking everyone in a five-mile radius, including Mrs Pernickety, or whatever English-sounding name the hotel owner goes by. She introduced herself to me-Rachel and Tori earlier and I forgot her name within ten seconds, because I'd already decided I was going to stay with David in his one-man tent instead of rooming with Tori.

Huh.

Anyway, Mrs Pernickety has recently retired here from Manchester and isn't completely sure where the private hospital is; she thinks it might be in the nearest city, which is about forty miles away. And, by the way, she hopes we know that if we're *all* planning on staying here, we need to book another room. No, actually, *two* extra rooms. (At this, Mrs Pernickety stares pointedly at David.) Unless *this young man* is planning to share a twin with the young American – Mrs P pauses to consult something behind the counter – 'Bradley Windsor'.

'My cousin's name is Bradford,' Tori tells her. This seems to stun Mrs P into silence long enough for Tori to explain that her friends are just visiting for a short while. 'Not enough time for, you know, anything like *that*,' she adds in a sweet, sincere voice. Mrs P looks like she's eaten ten lemons.

Then we go up to the room, where Tori laughs about Mrs P clearly having 'sex on the brain'. She then spends about a year talking David out of making the journey to the city. 'You really don't want to hang around all night in a waiting room,' she's telling him.

I tune them out and look at the bed where I dumped

my holdall when I arrived and could only be bothered to unpack a couple of things. When I was still Rachel. I contemplate the ever-increasing weirdness of my life since arriving at the Enchantment festival, not to mention this so-called 'hotel'. The name on the outside of the building says LITTLE HILLSIDE HOTEL and the first two words are accurate enough, but I'm sure you could sue for use of the third. I've clearly been spoiled by my rolling-in-money lawyer father after all. The family vacations we managed – *before* – were in hotels that looked like palaces, all newly renovated and glistening and full of Tiffany glass mosaics and facilities that catered for your every need, with cabana boys I was too young (and already a bit too 'alternative') to appreciate. I just stayed out of the sun reading books and making my mom tut and worry about me. (No change there, then.)

This place? Our room is clean enough, but it's tiny and super-cluttered. The lobby was crammed with old-fashioned furniture, and though there was an 'Internet point' in the corner, the computer there was massive and cream-coloured, like something from the last century. In our room there's a cuckoo clock on the wall and miniature ceramic animal ornaments in dangerous clusters on every available surface – wolves close to rabbits, eagles near field mice, lions with guinea pigs. If these animals came to life, half of them would be snacks for the other half within seconds.

There are also paper circles with cut-out shapes that look kind of crocheted. Hailey sees me staring and laughs at them a little, calling them 'doilies'. They are everywhere – under the fluffy-animal-and-wild-predator combos, and even prominently displayed on their own as if they're some kind of works of art.

Hailey, I'm starting to notice, is a lot more like Jo than Tori is. She's not the kind of girl to know the first thing about crochet and doilies except in a super-factual, Jo kind of way. No wonder they're friends. They must have out-nerded some serious nerds in their British school.

She nods at a doily and proves me right: 'I heard their patterns are based on the Cartesian co-ordinate system. Can you see it?' Her volume increases. 'You know more about it than I do, with all the extra *math* classes you took in the States.'

I'm sure she's trying to make a point here, but I'm not sure what it is. I feel a swell of panic. Could she suspect that I'm not really Jo – is she testing me? I hope she's not planning on asking me about the Whedonverse, or anything Jo-ish like that. I have read *Buffy* Season 8 now, after Jo recommended it. But my knowledge of the TV show is not encyclopaedic like Jo's or Albie's.

I was in a lot of the same classes as Jo for the last two semesters, though, so I can smile and make small talk about geometry when required. Who knew it would ever be a handy life skill?

82

After I do this, it's instantly clear that Hailey is trying to upset Tori and not to catch me out. Phew. I know this because Tori stops talking to David and bounds over, all threatened, staring at us and then at the doily.

'That sure is . . . geometrical!' Tori says, putting her head on one side. 'And kind of . . . *Cartesian* all right. Now, Hailey, sorry, but can you and David just excuse us a second? Josie and I need to talk about my brother. Don't we, Jose?'

My instant reaction to this is, *Noooooo!* but I can't think of a Jo-like way to say it, and judging by the way Hailey glares at both of us, my silence is taken as a yes.

'I'll talk to you real soon, OK?' I tell Hailey, and she brightens a little.

'Don't forget we're doing the Topaz thing,' she says, waving as she leaves the room, followed by David, who says something about asking to use the computer in the lobby.

After they've left there's the longest silence. Tori lies back on her bed so I mirror her, lying back on mine (Rachel's). I wait for her to fire questions at me as I nudge my holdall out of the way and stifle a longing to change out of Jo clothes and into my (Rachel's) black stuff, some of which I can see sticking messily out of the top zipper. I push the holdall onto the ground, out of temptation's way, and it lands with a muffled thud.

Tori yawns. 'What a day! It's so great to see you

again at last.' She sighs. 'Hey, I hope Rachel's OK.'

'It sure sounds like she is,' I mumble, marvelling at how uncomfortable this bed is, with so many craters and lumpy bits that I think the surface of the moon must be smooth in comparison. But I'd rather be here than where the real Jo probably is (in my body), with the threat of tests and scans and my mom's arrival hanging over me/her, no matter how luxurious the hospital room might be. Luxury's way overrated anyway. Luxury's for people like my dad and Chelsea Cook.

'Yeah.' Tori takes a deep breath. 'And I hope my brother's OK too. So, Josie, what's the deal? I have to know before I call him. I can tell it's something big.'

I sigh, which seems to be the right thing to do.

Tori says more super-sympathetic things and I fill in all the gaps she leaves with more sighs. She's just being so *nice*; the tone of her voice is like a flowery comforter wrapped around me, and I love it. No one has ever spoken to me-Rachel like this – they all think I'm too tough to need word-blankets. Except Mom, who over-does it in the other direction and makes it hard to breathe.

'Believe me,' Tori's saying in her earnest, sugary manner, 'you guys are just made for each other. Not like me and Christopher Rendell.'

'Who?'

She laughs. 'Topher, dummy! You may remember him

as my most recent, most annoying ex. Oh, wow, I can finally tell you all the details of the Topher thing, now that you don't have your mom telling you she needs the laptop every two minutes, making you rush off in the middle of a chat.' Her voice goes all quiet. 'Seriously though, Josie, where have you been the last few weeks?'

Good question. 'Uh . . . England?'

Tori frowns. 'Sure. You know, your mom is a total computer-hog. It's good that I'm studying in England soon and we'll at least be in the same time zone. When your mum kicks you off the computer I'll totally turn up on your doorstep. Anyway, so . . . remember I told you about when Topher said . . .'

I've actually heard this entire story already, more than once, during that everlasting flight. (Here's a summary, cutting out all the arguments, several chat sessions which Tori reported word-for-word, and her shopping list of Things Tori Looks for in a Guy, None of Which Topher Possesses. So Topher told Tori last-minute that he couldn't go to junior prom with her because he had some 'family problems', and Tori was all understanding and good-girlfriendy about it, which was, like, so super-*nice* of her because she only had one more shot at prom before graduation. But then he started having more and more 'family problems' on Saturday nights, until she got suspicious and accused him of cheating. But it turned out he wasn't; he just wanted to be out with his college guy friends doing college guy things, and couldn't he and Tori 'cool it but still sleep together', which Tori can't believe he would even ask because the answer is, like, no, *obviously*. The rat.)

Believe me, that was the short version. The other one goes on so long that my moon-surface bed starts to feel oddly inviting and my eyelids droop.

Tori's storytelling gets slower and the pauses between 'like, totally's get longer, so I think she's even putting *herself* to sleep this time.

'All guys are basically assholes,' I tell her through a dreamy fog when I realize she hasn't said anything for a while.

'Hey, that's just what Rachel said,' Tori mumbles. 'She made me feel better too.'

It makes me open my eyes for long enough to glance at her bed and see that she's sound asleep even though the sun's still streaming through the weird white crocheted drapes.

Tori clearly has jet lag. I guess we did miss a whole night's sleep.

Well, jet lag must be entirely a body thing and not a mind thing, because I'm in no way as tired as—

A banging sound at the door wakes me up. Tori has gone.

And David walks in.

Room 121, The Clarence
Friday

Rachel's Diary Therapy

Hello. My name is Rachel.

Except for one small detail.

Which is that it's actually not.

Look, I'm going to trust Rachel's mum when she told me that no one is going to read this. This diary-keeping is for my own mental health benefit, she said.

Only she has no idea just how right she is, in a completely warped way, as it looks like this is the only place where I can actually tell the truth.

And the truth is that my name is Josephine Reilly and something extremely weird is going on.

Because I'm Jo, but I look like Rachel. And everyone thinks I'm Rachel.

Oh God, oh God, oh God! Why do freaky things always happen to me?

So yesterday everything went swirly and I woke up in some kind of stone circle all dressed in black,

Rachel-ish clothes, and I have no idea how I got there, and my first thought was: *What's happened this time?*

Except I vaguely knew, really.

Rachel happened. Again. I think.

And it's kind of my own fault, because of all that stuff with Albie, and there was that stuff with David, and ... I wished I could live Rachel's life instead of mine. I wished I could be tough like her, I wished I could have the uncomplicated relationship she has with David. I wished I was her, and then I *was*. Her. So really I only have myself to blame.

Nah, I'm still blaming her.

You know, Rachel and I are good friends and everything, but I swear that girl has some kind of terrifying powers. Luckily I mostly only swear it to myself so that no one thinks I'm mad.

Although of course, right now they do think I'm mad. They've thought it ever since I woke up in Rachel's body and freaked out. They finished testing me for head trauma (clear) and dodgy substances (clear – phew! I mean, *I* didn't even manage to get a cup of tea before it happened, but who knows what Rachel might have done?). But I was still rambling on about not being myself. (Look – my mind hadn't had a cup of tea yet, right? Plus I was *not* myself. And there was the Albie thing and the

David thing and I was just not thinking straight.)

Then I made it all worse today by not instantly recognizing my own mother. Because she wasn't my own mother. My own mother is in Paris with her Frenchman and she doesn't even know that her daughter is going through all kinds of nutsville trauma in a posh hospital.

Whereas Rachel's mother turned up this morning with Dr Boxtree (who I've already nicknamed Foxy Boxy behind his back – he looks like one of those TV doctors with that whole sexy chin-stubble, seventy-two-hour-shift chic going on). My so-called mother was wearing a crumpled trouser suit and looking like one of those admin types off a hospital drama called something like *Stat!* – you know, the posh battleaxe who makes budget cuts and is hated by all the lovely male nurses. So I thought she was sniffing about how many sheets of loo roll I was allowed in my en-suite shower room or something, and I basically ignored her. I ignored my own mother. Which is probably pretty Rachel-ish, come to think of it. But Foxy Boxy didn't know that and he said, 'I'm getting the feeling you don't recognize this person. Am I right?' He had this smugly sympathetic look on his face that seemed to say *See? Crazy!* It was the doctor equivalent of twirling his index finger at his temple, school play-ground style.

Luckily, at that moment I twigged who the woman was (I've actually met her a couple of times, but she looked different out of context). So I went all hyper-enthusiastic to make up for my mistake. I gushed, 'Oh, Mum, it's so great to see you. I've really missed you. How have you been? And how's Dad?'

I really wasn't thinking. Rachel would never talk to anyone in such an upbeat way, let alone her mother, and if she ever says the word 'Dad', her lips go all mega-snarly. So every word I said after 'Mum' increased the freaked-out expression on Rachel's mum's face, until she looked like she was the one in need of hospitalization.

The grown-ups left the room and there were hushed words outside the door. Then Foxy Boxy gave me this diary, which apparently Rachel's mum had brought all the way from the States specifically for loony-daughter therapy purposes. It actually has swirly stencilling on the front that says:

My feelings
In black and white
Written down
To make things right.

And it thoughtfully has a pen attached, which by

the way contains blue ink and makes a mockery of the whole poem.

Seriously, now I see where Rachel gets her, er, *individuality* from. I thought MY mum was weird, but Rachel's mum makes my mum's tie-dyed sun-hats look like normal headgear, if you know what I mean. (If you don't, I mean she's a loon.) (Er, and who's 'you', anyway? I'm talking to a diary. Uh-oh. Looks like Foxy Boxy could have a point about me.)

So now here I am. In a posh hospital, in Rachel's body. Working out my 'feelings of anxiety' in this private (and it had better be) diary. Wondering where my body is and – what – is Rachel in it? Did we swap? She must have come to the festival after all – we can't have swapped bodies across the Atlantic or Rachel's mum would be a lot more freaked that I'm here. But why did Rachel come here if she's broken up with David? (David. Oh God, oh God, oh God. No, I'm NOT going to think about it.)

Anyway, there's no one tougher than Rachel. I'm sure Rachel could live my life better than I can, and she couldn't possibly make things any worse. At least I don't have to face anyone here. Maybe I can stay away for ever. Be Rachel for ever. Rachel's body could be the perfect place to hide.

Uh-oh, Rachel's mum seems to have interrupted her hushed chat with Foxy Boxy and I can hear someone else's voice now. It's a male voice, a weird accent that's a mix of American and English.

Oh my God.

It's David. David has come to see me.

No, he's come to see *Rachel*.

Why am I even surprised about that?

Oh my God, this is a right bloody mess.

SUNSHINE AND UNICORNS AND SUGAR LUMPS

When the banging at the door wakes me up, and before David walks in, I quickly notice these things, in this order:

1) The sunlight is streaming in so maybe I only slept for ten seconds;
2) I've been sleeping on top of a flowery comforter in a room with lacy paper circles everywhere;
3) I'm in Jo's colourful clothes;
4) For that matter, I also seem to be in Jo's body, which manages to freak me out all over again when I look at my tiny hands;
5) Tori has disappeared; and
6) So has my holdall – Rachel's holdall, I mean.

Then David walks in with a large, rainbow-coloured cloth bag in his hands and mumbles, 'Oh. Hi. When no one answered, I tried the door. I thought I could just pop in for a second.'

OK, this is all so crazy that it can only add up to one thing.

'I'm still asleep,' I say out loud to test my theory. 'I'm dreaming. You're not here.'

David doesn't look at me, but I notice his eyes are all red so his hay fever must be flaring up.

'Bollocks,' he says under his breath, but I still catch it because I have special radar for David's cute British cursing. 'Isn't Tori here?' he asks at normal volume.

I shake my head and shrug. 'I don't know where she's gone. I just woke up . . . maybe.'

'Oh. Sorry,' he says awkwardly. He sets the rainbow bag down at the end of my bed. Then he shifts about from foot to foot. For someone who was kissing me yesterday (well, Jo, but as far as he knows that's me) he sure isn't taking advantage of being alone with me in a bedroom.

Not that I'd want him to.

Would I?

'So . . . are you OK?' he asks. 'You know, after . . . yesterday . . .'

I blink. 'Yeah, I'm good. I guess. How long have I been asleep?'

'I don't know,' David answers, folding and unfolding his arms.

I stare at him. It's like he doesn't know how to act around me.

I don't know how to act around him either. I'm so angry with him. I'm also thinking he looks totally hot.

I feel this surge of longing for him that is hard to stifle. It mixes like oil and water with my other more murderous and more welcome thoughts.

'Hailey and I left you and Tori sleeping,' David explains. 'We thought she must have jet lag and you . . . Well, you had a really weird morning yesterday.'

'*Yesterday?*' So much for ten seconds! I must have slept for the rest of the day and right through the night. And I woke up in the same freaky state that I fell asleep in.

'Yeah. It's Friday afternoon. I took Hailey back to the festival yesterday and then I . . .' He shifts about again. 'I went to find the hospital. I thought I should take Rachel her bag.'

'You took the holdall! Without asking!' He took my stuff!

He gives me a strange look. 'It's Rachel's.' He nods at the colourful cloth creation at the end of the bed. 'Hailey gave me yours today. Oh, and she said you should remember to meet her later.'

'Oh, OK.' I should have known the rainbow bag was Jo's. It's probably filled with Jo-ish things, like sunshine and unicorns and sugar lumps.

Then David's words sink in.

'You went to see Rachel!'

His eyes go kind of cloudy. 'I didn't see her. By the

time I got there last night it was too late, you know, for visitors.' He stares at the floor. 'And today her mum said she . . .' He takes a deep breath. 'Rachel didn't want to see me.'

Oh, well, that's kind of a relief. Though I wonder why. Jo must be really embarrassed that she's me. Or maybe she doesn't want to see David if she's Rachel and he's all broken up with her. Yeah, he's with *me* now. Kind of.

'Is Mom – *her* mom – OK?' I ask. 'And her dad . . .' I take a breath. 'Was he there?' Then I can't believe I asked that. How dumb can I be?

'No, just her mum.'

Super-mega-*dumb*.

'She looked pretty knackered. She'd been travelling all night, I suppose. But anyway, she told me that Rachel's physically in good shape. She's passed every single test, or whatever.'

'Great.' That's a weird kind of relief.

'But her mum wants her to stay in a bit longer, for observation. She says she's worried about Rachel's mental state.'

It figures. I knew Mom would love this. I can't believe she's here, ruining my European vacation so soon.

Then I remember it was already ruined, thanks to the boy standing in front of me, and the girl whose body I'm in. Yeah, I'm not Rachel anyway. It's so much better to be Jo, and here, than be Rachel in that hospital room with

Mom. I need to concentrate. Focus on the main show. I'm Jo, and I can think of a way to get revenge on my cheating boyfriend. Who's standing right in front of me. And cheated . . . with me.

He sighs. 'I still can't believe Rachel didn't tell me she was coming.'

'Well, she didn't come to see *you*,' I snap.

'Yeah, I'm starting to get that.' His voice is tight.

I bite back my irritation because it's not very Jo-like. I'm behaving more like Rachel. What would Jo say next? Something perfect and understanding, no doubt. But I can't quite manage it, not after what he's done. The closest I can manage is: 'You know, if she doesn't want to see you, you should respect that.'

David frowns. That's when I realize I haven't seen him smile even once since I arrived in England, or heard him make any stupid jokes. I miss it like crazy. It's like, without that stuff, he's only half here. He's only half David.

He looks so pained that I suddenly, irrationally, feel sorry for him. I walk over to him. Then I catch my breath because being close to him has always had a powerful effect on me and nothing has changed, even now I know he's the enemy. I mean, clearly I want revenge, and I'm going to get it.

But I also want David.

And I'm in Jo's body, so I know he wants me too.

I reach over and touch his hand. It makes my heartbeat race. I make a soothing noise and squeeze his fingers in my palm, as if I'm just consoling a friend and what I'm doing is completely platonic. But we both know it isn't. I linger too long, and there's a moment when I can tell he's thinking what I'm thinking. The lying cheat.

He turns those gorgeous grey-green eyes on me and I take a step closer to him.

The door bursts open and David jumps away from me.

Tori blares, oblivious, 'Omigod, Josie, you're awake at last, yay! I have to talk to you! They have, like, zero fresh fruit over at that British pub! I mean, no wonder Brits have all got lyme disease, or whatever Rachel goes on about when she wants to insult you.' Then she seems to notice David and quietens down a little. 'Oh, hey, David. Don't you Brits believe in five servings of fruit a day?'

David half smiles. 'Tori, it's a pub. It doesn't even seem like one of those foodie ones,' he says. 'The most you can hope for at this time of day is some crisps. That's *chips* to you.'

Tori pouts. 'But I totally missed the hotel breakfast! So I told them, and they were all, like, *Have a packet of pork scratchings*. I mean, what even *is* that?'

Yeah, what *is* that?

David goes to catch my eye, as a fellow Brit and

someone who clearly knows all about eating itchy pigs as a breakfast substitute. I make a little 'ha' noise, but inside I'm steaming about David and Jo and their British connection.

'The only good thing about the pub is that the cell signal's good there,' Tori says. 'I can't believe there's no reception at the festival! It's like living in ancient times – like the twentieth century or something!'

'Yeah, I know what you mean,' David says. 'I can't even get online to send my work posts. They're all on my memory stick because I can't save onto the press office computers. I sent some from here yesterday.' He taps the sole of one boot absent-mindedly against the floor as he explains all this, and I drift into a daydream, thinking about his boots. They're illustrated by me, and they're special Goth ones with a coffin-shaped hollow space in the sole that comes as standard. I have the same ones, which I'm desperately missing right about now. Sometimes we sneak notes into each other's boots when we have the same phys ed period. I usually draw him cartoons, but David writes stuff, and it's always romantic and sometimes hot and it is awesome.

Was awesome.

David's still talking enthusiastically about his work. 'And I'm writing a special article about Madison Rat and—'

I cut him off. 'Yeah, David, we know.' He told me

before our argument that the Madison Rat piece would make him into a music-reporting star. He said it a lot more modestly than that, but I know it's what he meant.

David looks surprised. Oops.

'I mean, I heard it from Albie,' I explain in the same bored voice.

'Oh, yeah, of course,' David says. Then he adds tentatively, 'So . . . has he been in touch, Jo?'

Honestly, if I were really Jo, would I want to talk about Albie to him? And in front of his sister too?

Before I can think of an answer, Tori goes all weird and extra-loud. 'Yeah, so, Josie, England's pretty cool, isn't it?'

'Uh . . . yes?' I say, wondering what's got into her.

'Yeah, it's OK,' David says. 'I like the US too. Both places are . . . good.' Then, after a silence, he babbles nervously, 'Anyway, Jo, you've got your bag so . . . I was just leaving. I've got to see if Topaz are still up for an interview after their gig on Sunday. Oh no, that's a secret – don't tell Hailey or she'll never leave me alone. Topaz almost never give interviews.'

At the word 'Topaz', Tori gives me a look and I try half-heartedly to look as impressed as she expects me to. But all I can think about is David. If Tori hadn't burst in before, would he have kissed me?

Would I really have wanted him to?

Yes no yes no.

'Bye, guys,' says my cheating (ex-)boyfriend. 'See you at the festival.'

As soon as he's gone, Tori waves her phone in the air. 'So did you hear from Albie?'

'No, I ... my cell ...' Does Jo even have a cell? I wouldn't know. Mine – Rachel's – is in my jacket pocket. Which is in some hospital somewhere.

'I did!' Tori sits on her bed and bounces in excitement. 'He said not to tell anyone but I figure he didn't mean you. Anyway, he's totally OK. Kind of mysterious-sounding, but definitely alive.' She holds her phone out to show me the text, but she won't sit still so it's hard to read it.

Eventually I make out: Sorry, had to get away a while. Pls don't tell anyone I wrote you – need to think and will explain later. Nothing to worry about.

Tori bounces onto the edge of the bed, puts her chin in her hands and says, 'So, OK. About you and Albie. Spill.'

Room 121, The Clarence
Friday

Rachel's Diary Therapy
by Jo in Rachel's body (THIS HAD BETTER BE PRIVATE!!!)

Oh, yay! Rachel's mum has left me alone for some 'diary time' and I flippin' need it. Honestly, she's so attentive, it's doing my head in. She's trying to meet my every need, waiting on me in ways that would make my mum bleat, 'What did your last slave die of?'

But Rachel's mum is all, 'What else can I get you, darling? Anything at all, just ask!' I've already permanently borrowed some of her clothes because Rachel's – brought here thoughtfully by David, aargh! – aren't exactly my thing. I've also ordered a non-stop stream of tea. I'm getting sort of tempted to test Rachel's mum by requesting some unusual stuff, like pointy-toed slippers or unicorns or a limited edition *Buffy* box set signed by the entire cast, but I've managed to resist it so far. (Hmm, actually, I think that last one is worth a try.)

The biggest thing I've asked her for so far, though, was to tell David I couldn't see him. And she did. Phew. Apparently he's been here twice already. I bet he's coming back too. Oh my God, oh my God. I don't even want to think how much he cares about Rachel. I just know it's *immense* amounts. Rachel and David completely belong together – they are the perfect couple. They're always so fiery and passionate, and they banter constantly and finish each other's thoughts. It's like they exist in their own little world. It's really cute and occasionally kind of sickening.

Oh, but I mean it *was*, of course. I cannot believe those two have broken up. I suppose you never really know what's going on with other people.

Like me and Albie. Even I am not too clear what exactly happened there. I just know it bloody hurts. Yeah, I've ended up in hospital with a broken heart – ha not-very ha.

Well, I suppose now I do have an idea where it started. I just don't know why.

It was a couple of months ago, at a time when I was still bouncing along on cloud nine, plus a whole skyful of other numbered, fluffy clouds. I was wrapped up in Albie in a way that made me want to hug myself, or hug the whole world, or preferably hug *him*, the whole time. He was constantly in my mind, brightening the most boring lessons at school, making lunch-time confrontations with girls like Chelsea Cook bearable. He was Albie, he was my boyfriend, he was amazing.

And then, one Sunday afternoon, he called to say he couldn't come round like we'd planned. He said that Chelsea's mum had called him: there was some kind of family problem, and she'd asked Albie whether he could run the ice-resurfacer for them or something.

It wasn't all that unusual, really. Albie used to work for the Cooks, back when Mr Cook had a breakdown and Mrs Cook needed help with the family business, which included running the ice rink. He hadn't really worked for them since Mr Cook got out of hospital, but I know that Mrs Cook had come to really depend on Albie before, and I bet she didn't think twice about ringing him again. She used to call him at all kinds of times, and she'd got used to relying on him for more than practical support – I mean, she kind of leaned on him emotionally too for a while. Albie's just that kind of guy.

I told Albie I could go with him but he said that wasn't a good idea – he had to go round to the Cooks' house first for keys and instructions, and things weren't always easy there. I think he meant that Mr Cook wasn't as stable as he could be, but it made me realize how little I wanted to visit mean girl Chelsea anyway. I agreed with Albie that he should go alone.

So I said, *OK, see you tomorrow*, and I didn't think any more of it. But then, at school on Monday, I spotted Chelsea whispering to Albie in a quiet bit of the corridor.

She stopped instantly when she saw me – on purpose to upset me, I reckon. Chelsea's only happy when she's stirring things up for someone. Especially Rachel – she really has it in for Rachel, but luckily Rachel gives as good as she gets.

Anyway, I kept my face all blank and went over and said hi to Albie and I wasn't really worried.

Yet.

Chelsea gave me one of her usual disdainful looks, said bye to Albie and left.

I kissed Albie hello and held his hand all the way to the lunch room. I waited until we were sitting down with our lunch before I said, 'So what was all that about? With you and Chelsea?'

He said, 'Oh. Yeah.' He chewed his food for quite a long time. 'Some bad family stuff went down yesterday. A huge argument. She was upset, but don't worry, I think she's OK now.'

I rolled my eyes. 'Er, I think Chelsea can look after herself.' I laughed.

He didn't. 'I know what you mean about her, Jo, but also . . . I don't know. I think things are really hard for her.'

'Oh,' I said, starting to feel a tiny bit panicky.

'Yeah, and yesterday was pretty bad.' He rubbed his brow at the memory.

'So what happened?' I asked. 'What was the argument about?'

A weird, pained look crossed his face. 'Chelsea asked me not to talk about it,' he said. He said it gently, but still. He said it.

I knew he cared about Chelsea's family. He was Albie – he cared about everyone.

I also knew that Chelsea's family life wasn't perfect. I remember finding out that when her dad had his breakdown, Chelsea had gone to live with the school heartthrob (my ex, ha ha!), Jake Matthews, for a while because things were so bad at home (though I think she probably loved that). I'm not completely sure her family crises excused her being a total bitch at every opportunity, but still. I had some brilliant friends by that time – I didn't really care about that.

What I cared about was that Chelsea and Albie had some kind of secret together. It felt weird.

But I had every confidence in Albie so I bit my lip and changed the subject until Tori came over with some exciting news about a dance. Then Rachel and David landed at our table too, and David pretended to be mega-interested in what Tori was saying, and he kept smiling his gorgeous smile at me, but everyone could tell that all he really wanted to do was drag Rachel into a corner and snog her face off. As usual.

Albie held my hand tightly the whole time – too tightly. I thought he was worried about my reaction to the Chelsea-secret thing, so I made a point of showing him it was no big deal. And it really wasn't. We didn't mention it again and I pretty much forgot about it because Albie was being his usual wonderful self. Though now I think about it, he was a bit quieter than normal, on and off, like he was worrying about something. And it happened more and more, the closer we got to the end of the school year. At the time, I put it down to graduation nerves – Albie was in his final year of high school, after all – and maybe also the fact that he'd be away from me in the summer, after I went back to England with Mum. I didn't really think it was anything to worry about. I knew we'd work things out.

I was back in England, having what started off as a normal conversation with him on the phone, when suddenly he confessed that he'd been sneaking around in a way I never, ever suspected he was capable of. He told me it had all started on the day he went to Chelsea's house, though he still didn't explain what had happened that day or tell me exactly what part Chelsea had played in it all; what she'd said

107

to stir things up like this. He still insisted on keeping Chelsea's secret, whatever it was. And then he expected me to keep *his*. When he told me about it, I was confused; I was hurt that he'd been keeping something like that from me; I couldn't believe he was surprised that I was upset.

After that, it was downhill all the way for us. Albie and his band came to England a week early but he didn't even try to see me before the festival. I travelled down with Hailey, listening to her boy troubles all the way and not knowing how to begin to tell her mine. Still, a little part of me thought that when I saw Albie in person, we'd sort everything out. Everything would be OK.

I arrived at the festival on Thursday morning and I finally saw Albie. I also saw David. And nothing was OK.

Wow, dearest loon-diary. Dear little blue markings on white paper. What a relief it is not to be me any more. If I was still me, I'd be so miserable.

But I'm not, and you know what? I'm not going to write like this any more because I can't make any sense of it. Maybe I'll just scribble down odd things, like the conversations I've been having with Rachel's mother. Yes, some of those are *very* odd.

Oh, Rachel's mum is at the door right now.

I think I'm going to ask her for that *Buffy* box set.

COMMUNICATING IN NERDISH

In the end, I fob Tori off with some story about Albie not telling me what he had to do, but saying he wouldn't be gone long and we shouldn't worry about him. I'm mostly borrowing it from the text she waggled in front of me, but it seems to get her off my case.

'Yeah,' she says, patting her cell. 'That's kind of what he said to me too.'

Yeah, that's kind of why I said it, I think. Then I add that I was upset yesterday because everyone was reminding me about his absence and I was missing him so much already. Aw, aren't we adorable?

'Aw, Josie, you guys are adorable,' Tori coos. 'I guess he'll be back real soon and he'll explain everything. You know Albie – he'll have a good reason for leaving like this.'

I give a little shrug. I'm still thinking that he left because he found out about David and Jo, but now does not seem like the right time to mention it to Tori. Really,

I'd rather not be in Jo's body at all when she hears it. Despite all her talk of putting friends first, I know how protective Tori is of her brother, and I do not want to be on the receiving end of that.

That's weird. I stand up to any amount of crap from Chelsea Cook, and here I am worrying about being called out by Chelsea's ex-sidekick Tori?

Except that Tori would have a real reason to be upset, whereas Chelsea is always one hundred per cent trouble-making. And, yeah, I just don't want Tori to be mad at me.

She gives me an uncertain look. 'So what exactly did David mean about you having a shock yesterday? And why were you were acting so freaky when I arrived? It seemed bigger than just missing your boyfriend.'

Tori, kind of annoyingly, seems a lot smarter than I imagined. I should have known that she'd finally grown more than one brain cell from the way she abandoned the Chelsea Cook crowd pretty dramatically last year.

'Oh . . . uh.' I try to think fast. 'I'd only just found out Topaz were headlining at the festival. I lost it for a while. I'm, you know' – I take a deep breath – '*such* a huge fan.'

She looks at me and laughs. 'You and your passion for weird music. I've never even heard of them!'

Yeah, that makes two of us, I don't say.

'Don't tell me – they sound a bit like Madison Rat, only their lyrics are influenced by *Twilight* instead of *Buffy*.'

110

Actually, that guess makes a lot of sense, so I nod. 'They're totally awesome – I mean *brilliant* – but they're not as good as the Rat,' I say, because I think Jo would.

Tori gives me a knowing look. 'You know, it's kind of a relief to hear that you still have it bad. With my brother missing and Hailey saying you needed to talk to her about him, I was starting to wonder.'

I laugh as lightly as I can manage. 'Oh, what does Hailey know?' I ask. I mean this way more literally than she thinks. What *does* Hailey know?

Tori smiles. 'You're right. So anyway, I think it's time we hit that festival!'

'Sure.' It sounds good to me. Maybe I could start putting some revenge-on-David plans in motion; spreading some ErisGrrl discord as I hide in my perfect Jo disguise. Well, really I need to think of some good plans in the first place. I wonder when superheroes have time to devise their strategy; they always seem so busy when they're in the thick of the action. I guess they don't sleep for nearly twenty-four hours like I did.

I'm at the door when I realize that Tori hasn't followed me. She's looking at me strangely.

'Uh, Josie, are you going like that?' she asks. 'I mean, no offence, you always look great and all, but didn't you just sleep in those clothes? You'd be welcome to take a shower here if you wanted to. In fact, you'd be welcome to stay here with me while Rachel's in the hospital – I don't think she'd care, and Hailey won't mind, will she? I mean, I know you guys were sharing a tent . . .'

'I guess not,' I mumble, though I suspect Tori knows that Hailey absolutely *will* mind. But, to be honest, I'd rather stay here than sleep in a tent next to a total stranger, which Hailey basically is. And Rachel definitely won't care. Ha.

'You know what?' Tori makes a conspiratorial face. 'I never thought Rachel was going to stay here with me anyway. She mentioned David's tent more than once on the plane!'

I try not to look indignant. I did not! I barely managed to say a word, the amount she was trash-talking Topher the Terrible Traitor.

'Poor Rachel. It's so great that she's basically OK, though.' Tori gestures towards the bathroom. 'Anyway, Josie, go right ahead. I felt loads better after taking a shower, even though it took me nearly an hour to work out that the water comes out of a curly tube thing stuck to the faucet on the tub and you have to hold it up yourself, which is kind of dumb.' She makes a face at me. 'Uh, sorry. Is that, like, a typical British shower?'

I don't know, so I just smile, which could be interpreted either way.

'Wait till I tell Dad about this!' Tori chirps. 'He's always saying how much more civilized British people are than us! I'm going to tell him we've beaten you in the shower department. No offence.' She looks at her phone. 'Think I'll call Dad right now. He called a couple of times when we were asleep, you know, and he probably tried Brad too, but that sex-crazed hotel woman said Brad didn't come back here last night. And you should have heard the way she said it!' She laughs. 'Anyway, Dad's voicemail mentioned Rachel and stuff, but he didn't say anything about Albie, which proves that Albie really is OK, because he'd so tell Mom and Dad if there was a problem, wouldn't he?' She waits for me to nod. 'So . . .' She starts pressing buttons on her phone.

I pick up Jo's rainbow bag and hesitate for a second by the nightstand, wondering about the things I stuffed in the drawer, like my black eyeliner and red lipstick, and possibly even my black dress. But Tori would definitely notice, and anyway, if I'm going to be Jo, I should do this properly. I can't exactly go around dressed like Rachel.

In the bathroom I immediately see what Tori means about the tub and the strange shower contraption, though it's not exactly hard to figure out.

Much harder is going through someone else's stuff and choosing what to wear, especially when I keep getting freaked out by my reflection in the semi-steamed-up mirror. I wrap myself tighter in a rough hotel towel that probably wouldn't even go around Rachel's body at all, and I rifle through the crumpled mass of Jo-ish clothes. In the end I settle for a knit-style mini sundress that's three different shades of purple with lacy short sleeves and pockets that are embroidered patches. It isn't a million miles away from something I'd wear, if it was black, or at least darker purple. Although I'd definitely heap several layers all around it – no way would I leave all that skin exposed. And it's so short! I remind myself that it's technically summer (even though no one told England), and that I need to be Jo to complete my mission: take revenge on my cheating ex-boyfriend. All avenging superheroes wear a costume. Mine just happens to mean covering up less rather than more. And that includes my face, which feels twenty kinds of naked without lipstick and eyeliner.

I glance in the mirror again, where the steam has mostly cleared now.

Yeah, and it's gone straight to my hair, by the looks of it.

Well, it's not exactly hair – more untamed plant life with tendrils all over the place. What does Jo do with it?

I spot some straighteners in her bag and I pull them out. I've never used anything like that, though. Even with all the black dye I use, my hair looks like something out of a 'before' picture in a bring-your-hair-to-life shampoo ad (though David calls it 'silky' when he has his hands buried in it, which – stop! – I did *not* just think). I normally wear it over at least one eye, like drapes I can hide behind, which can be particularly useful when I'm bored in class or want to stare at people without them knowing. Yeah, I have the hair equivalent of mirrored shades.

But Jo's hair is frizzing all over, and when it goes in my eyes it's kind of spiky and hurts. I push it away, taking out the straighteners and staring at them for a while. They have an adaptor thing stuck to them which ends in a plug that's far too huge for any socket I've ever seen, including the one in this bathroom. I decide to go for the ultra-natural look after all.

As I put the straighteners back, I notice Jo's cell phone rattling next to the books at the bottom of the bag. So that's where she keeps it. Wow, Jo might be perfect but she's messier than me, and that's saying something.

A rush of curiosity makes me pick up the phone. The screen reads: 1 NEW MESSAGE. I press a few unfamiliar buttons until I reach the text inbox. The display says the message is from Albie and it was sent yesterday at around the time Tori and I arrived at the festival. I guess Jo was already at the site – and then in hospital, being me – so she didn't get a chance to see it.

It's weird; I'm in Jo's body and in her life, but I still feel like I'm spying on her by doing this. But, all the same, I click to open it. In a way the message is mine, right?

115

Wrong. Albie's text is utterly meaningless to me. It says: **S5 E2? S5 E13. Sorry.**

I groan to myself. Trust those two to communicate in Nerdish. I have no idea what the first part means. And why would Albie be apologizing to Jo and not the other way around?

As I've started this anyway, I decide to look through some older messages. There are a couple from Jo's kind and down-to-earth mom, who talks about being in Paris with some guy called 'R'. They're from yesterday morning and she's asking Jo how her and Hailey's journey to the festival is going, but not in a pushy way – not like my mom would. It's like she was really interested or something, and not just checking up on her. She even ends with: **OK, Jo. Tell me all about the festival on Monday!** Jo's mom is so cool.

Then there are a couple of messages headed DAD, but they're a scramble of numbers and symbols, even less meaningful than Albie's text, so I guess they could be from the cute half-sister Jo talks about a lot. Jo's so perfect that even her half-sister is adorable.

Then I stop. There's another text from Albie, sent some time on Tuesday, which is the day before Albie and his band arrived at the festival.

It says: **Sorry yes am seeing her.**

I exit the screen quickly, feeling weird about intruding on this personal stuff between Jo and Albie. And my mind is racing. Could my hunch about why Albie left be wrong? Maybe it wasn't because he found out David and Jo were together. Maybe he didn't walk away all hurt and innocent, like I pictured.

Wasn't Clyde talking about Albie having a picture of 'a hot chick'?

Am seeing her. Maybe Albie's not so perfect after all.

Maybe Albie was cheating on Jo.

Yeah, once or twice I've wondered about Albie. I thought he didn't fit the profile of a typical lead singer, as featured on Perez Hilton – the big ego, the prima-donna attitude they're famous for.

Well, now I suspect he's more like that than I realized.

And why wouldn't he be? He's male. It's what they do. Cheat and run. Or not. Some of them cheat and stay. But they all cheat. I've known it for years now.

I put the phone back in the bag, take a deep breath and open the bathroom door, half expecting Tori to gasp and recoil in horror at my bare arms and face, combined with my massively big hair.

But she just smiles at me and keeps talking to her dad, a conversation which seems to consist of his booming voice calling her 'princess', which I can hear clearly from across the Atlantic. In response, she's laughing, rolling her eyes and saying, 'Da-aad, quit it' every five seconds.

It's been so long since my father and I spoke to each other like that. Or spoke to each other at all, really, except through my mom, when strictly necessary and/or I want extra money.

'Oh, uh, sure, Albie's good, I think. He hasn't called you?' Tori's saying into her phone, twisting a lock of her blonde hair around one finger and biting her lip. I can tell that, unlike me, she's not used to almost-lying to her parents. She's doing it for her brother. So sweet. When I was in elementary school, I used to fantasize about having a sibling – no, actually, a sister. I thought it'd be fun; I thought she'd be on my side the way I can see Tori is with Albie. Albie doesn't deserve her loyalty.

Tori chirps, 'Sure, I'll tell him . . . when I see him. Yeah, Brad's having fun . . . You can't use cell phones at the festival site, like, at *all*. Da-aad, not *everything* is better in Europe, you know! OK, uh-huh, if you say so, Daddy . . .'

I sit on the end of the bed, pulling at the hemline of my dress and waiting for the father–daughter cute-fest to finish. I try to use the time to hatch my superhero revenge plan on David, but I don't really manage it because my thoughts are all in the wrong place.

Room 121, The Clarence
Friday

Rachel's Diary Therapy
by Jo in Rachel's body (IF THIS ISN'T PRIVATE
I'M DENYING IT ALL!)
Conversations with my so-called mother, Part 1

Spooky voiceover: *'Captain's Log. I am Jo the
intrepid explorer, lost in the wild tropics of Rachel-
land. I am having serious trouble being as hostile as
the native and I fear this may blow my cover. I am
transcribing this in the hope of making sense of it
later.'*

My So-Called Mother (entering, expression
 concerned): Rachel, honey, how are you?
Jo-in-Rachel's-Body: Oh, fine.
MSCM (*frowning*): Fine?
JIRB: Oh right, yeah. I mean . . . bloody hell, Mother,
 you didn't even knock! I'm so extremely angry with
 you now! (*Self-congratulatory smile*)
MSCM (*touching JIRB's forehead*): Rachel, honey,

I'm worried about you. Have you been keeping that diary like I asked?

JIRB: Oh yeah, it's a right old giggle. (*Sudden look of alarm*) But you can't look at it!

MSCM: Oh no, no, I wouldn't dream of it, darling. It's for you alone. (*Little smile*) I like the way you're using British vocabulary. Is that nice boyfriend of yours teaching you to speak British?

JIRB: Oh, yeah, he did. But I heard we . . . I mean we did, not I heard . . . I mean, we broke up. Mother! Yeah, actually! How could you be so insensitive as to ask me something so . . . er . . . insensitive! (*Note to self: increase Rachel-style vocab.*)

MSCM (*look of genuine concern*): Oh, I'm so sorry, honey. I wondered about that. Why you wouldn't see him when he came to visit, I mean. Do you want to tell me what happened between you and David?

JIRB (*look of genuine horror*): No I bloody don't!

MSCM (*look of genuine hurt*)

JIRB: I mean, God, sorry. I mean, no, not sorry. Mother! You're impossible! Grr! Etc. Though, yeah, actually. Mostly sorry.

MSCM (*confused laugh*): You know, Rachel, I've had a lot of time to think since you left for England. And actually, now I'm away from the pressures of trying to keep everything nice for your father – you know, in case he comes home early from his business trip – I've had a thought. I'm not a very good role model for you, am I?

JIRB: Aren't you? Why not? You seem OK, especially with the whole waiting-on-me thing. Plus your clothes are quite posh and normal-looking, so you look more like a conventional mother than my— Oops, I mean, grr, no! Mother! I wish I could storm out now! Grr, argh! (*Adopts zombie pose like at the end of Buffy*)

MSCM (*looking sad*): I don't want things that happened between me and your father to affect your relationships, Rachel. Promise me you won't let them?

JIRB: Er . . .

MSCM (*sighs*): It's too late, isn't it? I'm right, aren't I? I feel so bad.

JIRB: Oh no! Don't feel bad!

MSCM (*touching JIRB's brow again*): You're a sweet girl, Rachel.

JIRB (*doubtful*): Um, that doesn't really sound like an accurate description of Rach— of *me*.

MSCM: You're a very sweet girl. You feel everything so deeply – you always have. Remember when you were six and you launched that campaign to fight for the rights of your old stuffed toys – the ones I wanted to throw out?

JIRB: Did I? Aw, that *is* cute. Ha ha ha.

MSCM (*thankfully not listening*): No wonder you have anger issues. (*Big pause*) Especially about me and your father.

JIRB: Yeah, I've got anger issues all right. I've got them and then some. I'm often right, though, and I, you know, stand up for my friends a lot, which they think is pretty cool. So . . . (*Clears throat*) Do you think I'm right to be angry about you and your husband . . . er, my father? Just out of curiosity.

MSCM (*about to cry*): Oh, Rachel. Oh, Rachel. I'm so sorry. You're right. I think you're right. (*Beats hasty exit*)

JIRB (*desperately wondering what the deal is with Rachel's dad*)

'End of log. Filed for future analysis.'

FRUITY FRIDAY

The atmosphere at the festival is completely different from yesterday's half-asleep, hung-over vibe. Even from the entrance I can tell there are about five times as many people, and all the ones near us seem fresh and newly-arrived in an eager, bouncy, ready-for-anything way.

Also in a bare-skinned way. The sun's shining but it's no way as stifling as a Boston summer, and it must have been raining because there is mud everywhere. But boys are walking by me all shirtless and gorgeous-chested, and girls have on weird outfits like denim overalls with nothing underneath, and bare feet or flip-flops, or else they're wearing patterned rubber boots with colourful sundresses.

In fact, in Jo's tiny purple dress I kind of blend in. It's strange – no one will look at me and think I'm weird. It makes me feel invisible and like I could get away with anything.

Tori must agree with me because she looks around

and says, 'I'm overdressed.' But really she's looking totally like herself in her pastel-coloured delicate designer clothes and strappy high-heeled sandals. 'I thought you were going out half-naked, you know, though I didn't like to say. But now I think you had the right idea.' She pouts.

I think about what Jo would say in this situation. She doesn't really care too much about clothes. 'It's what's inside that counts,' I try.

'Oh, thanks a bunch,' Tori says sarcastically, but with a laugh in her voice. 'Next you'll say I have a nice personality.'

'You don't . . . I mean . . .'

'Oh, I *don't*? So I have bad dress sense *and* a lousy personality?'

'No, I mean . . .' Argh! I'm terrible at this!

'Forget it, Josie, I'm kidding!' She laughs. Then she rubs her stomach. 'Hungry. Food!' she says. Clearly hunger has made her regress to one-word caveman-speak. 'Now. Starved.'

'Ug,' I grunt in a half-imitation of her, instead of saying what I would have said as Rachel – something about her always looking half starved anyway, with her Chelsea-clone size-zero figure.

I read from the side of a truck in the near distance. '*Fest-Grub: The Home of Locally Sourced Vegetarian Grub.* Over there, Tori!'

Tori's horror takes her to the two-word stage of language development. '*Grubs?* Like worms?' Then she evolves to a full sentence. 'I'm not *that* hungry.'

OK, I can be British. 'It means food. Anyway, it couldn't be worms. It's vegetarian.'

She frowns. 'Could be soy. Linda McCartney worms.'

'I doubt it, Tori. Why don't we try it? Come on.' She still looks worried so I add, 'Look, I'll go first, and if I don't drop dead then you have some.'

She grins. 'Deal.'

The truck has a selection of cafeteria-style non-food on display. It's labelled, but that doesn't really help.

'*Sesame pan-fried swede,*' I read out.

Tori looks like she's going to faint. 'Swede? Like a person from Sweden? Omigod! That's way worse than worms! Are they *cannibals* here?'

'Vegetarian cannibals?' I try to look reassuring but I'm not too clear on this one myself. 'It has to be a vegetable.'

'Yeah, but if *you* don't know it – and you're English – then it could be *anything*!' Her eyes widen. 'It's not *safe*, Josie.'

I bite my lip – Jo's lip. Tori has a point. I should know what all this means. But I guess when I hung out with David we had more fun stuff to do than discuss British vegetable names.

I cover up my ignorance by talking British to the large man in the truck. 'Listen, do you have any, ah, *grub* which is a bit less . . .' I can't think how to finish that sentence.

The man gives me a tired look. 'Less fancy?' He sighs. 'I've got meatless hot dogs.'

Tori nods, looking relieved, and I order two.

We walk away as we eat. Well, I eat and Tori devours, forgetting that I'm supposed to sample it first, acting as if she hasn't eaten in a month. Her entire hot dog is gone in sixty seconds and she goes, 'More!' so I give her mine. When she finishes that, she complains, 'I'm still hungry. I'll get another four. I owe you one anyway.'

So I watch as Tori buys more vegetarian grub and inhales most of it in front of me. I can't believe I had her down as one of Chelsea's non-eating minions.

'OK, what shall we eat next?' Tori announces as she finishes her last mouthful. 'Don't look at me like that! You know I have a naturally high metabolism. Chelsea Cook used to hate me for it.' She laughs. 'Anyway, I think it's gotta be fruit now – my skin's, like, craving it.' She pats her cheeks. 'Think we can eat the apples from those trees?'

I follow her gaze to a cluster of fake green trees dotted with bright red circles, next to some ornamental toadstools and fairies.

'Yeah, if we were made of plastic. You know, like Chelsea Cook.' I'm annoyed with myself for saying that – it's such a Rachel thing to say – but then I remember that Chelsea and Jo aren't exactly friends either. And besides, Tori is laughing again.

'If I'd had surgery, would I look like this?' She wiggles her wide nose and widens her over-large eyes. And I see what she means – she's maybe not conventionally attractive, but I've never noticed before. She just gives out this aura of looking like a standard popular girl. Or I guess I just lumped her in with the others without ever thinking she wasn't exactly like Chelsea.

'Anyway, seems I'm out of luck in the fruit department,' Tori sighs, looking at the edges of the field which, overnight, has become a giant yard sale. There are stalls selling jewellery, T-shirts, shoes, glow-in-the-dark pins, hippie stuff, used books and just about everything anyone could want. Except fruit.

'Maybe they ban fruit from events like this,' I suggest. 'You know, in case people throw it at the acts and stuff.'

'I wouldn't be surprised, if the bands are all like the ones *you* love,' she teases. 'Just kidding. I secretly love that you love Madison Rat.' Her face falls.

'Oh, Tori, don't worry,' I tell her because she looks so upset. 'You know Albie's OK.'

'Yeah, I guess.' She gives this brave smile. 'Sorry. And if you're OK with it, then . . . you know, it must be OK. It's just so weird that he isn't here. I would have totally, like, avoided him anyway, because it's so not cool to be seen with your big brother. But, still, you know . . .'

She tugs at her designer Tori-wear and I know she doesn't mean it about avoiding Albie. She's feeling completely out of place here without him. Let's face it, this isn't exactly Tori's scene – there's far too much dirt and mess, and the makeshift stalls here are nothing like the malls I know she adores.

I have a sudden brainwave.

'We should find Clyde and Tamber,' I say. She's known those guys since she was tiny. They'll make her feel more at home.

Tori bites her lip. 'Oh, I don't know, Josie. Sunday's a big day for Madison Rat. What if the guys ask whether I've heard from my brother since they saw us yesterday? It'll be weird. It was bad enough with Dad earlier.'

It seems so unlike Albie to cause all this worry. Still, I didn't have him down as a typical cheating male before, either.

Obviously I don't say that to Tori. 'Just tell them the truth about the message Albie sent. It's not so different from what he's told them already.' I should stop right there but I'm Rachel, not Jo, and I can't keep this in. 'Why are you covering for Albie, though?'

'What do you mean?' Tori puts her head to one side. 'I don't know. Because he asked me to?'

Well, yeah.

She adds quickly, 'I'm sure he'll call you soon too,' as if she thinks I might be upset that she's heard from him and I haven't. So now we've gone full circle and reassured each other. It's sort of cute, really, this female-friendship cotton-wool wrapping that comes with being Jo.

'Come on,' I say. 'We'll find the guys. Where do you think they'd hang out? Is there a VIP area for bands?'

She shrugs. 'I asked a couple of people about that yesterday when I was looking for Albie, and they just said . . .' She puts on a terrible British accent. *'This ain't bleeding Glastonbury.'* She gives me a confused look.

'That would be a "no",' I guess confidently in my perfect British accent.

'Yeah, that's what I thought.'

We keep trudging across the field, past some huge screens that are showing some crazy-assed dance music video, and approach a dance tent.

'Let's try here,' I say. I step inside and get instantly engulfed by the throbbing beat. It's nothing like the half-deserted tent I saw David and Jo in yesterday – *shudder*. This one is packed with people partying like it was the middle of the night. In fact, the tent is pretty dark and there are strobe lights picking out revellers at random: I spot a couple of Teletubbies, a pirate, a woman who has quite clearly been a man at some recent point in his/her life, a cowboy and various people in wigs. Everything white is glowing eerie ultraviolet.

There's also a guy in the corner wearing a T-shirt that

glows with the words ENCHANTMENT TV: BEAMING FESTIVAL HIGHLIGHTS 2 U! He's holding a large camera and panning around the room, but it has to be a costume – I don't see how you could shoot a movie in here.

Tori stands behind me biting her lip and glancing nervously at the closed flaps of the tent door, like she wants to make an exit.

'I'll just check they're not here!' I yell at Tori, scanning the room.

'What?' she asks.

'I'll just . . .' I try to tell her in gestures instead, miming an exaggerated searching action that looks almost like a salute.

'What?'

'I'll— Oh, never mind, I'll just do it!' I spot a raised platform that could be useful and make my way over. When I get there, I realize it's actually a very large speaker. Well, I can use it anyway.

As I clamber onto it, though, I snag Jo's dress on a sticking-out bit at the side. I spend a while pulling myself free. Then I stand on the speaker and look around.

The guy with the camera gets closer to me, and suddenly the strobe lights pick me out and a ton of crazily dressed people turn towards me.

I shrug, figuring I may as well play up to it. I mean, you can't exactly make a fool of yourself in a room full of waddling Teletubbies, right?

Right?

I dance a bit in front of the camera. It's kind of fun, and even though the light keeps beaming at me, I mostly feel hidden in the darkness and anything-goes vibe around me.

But soon I notice more and more people staring, and then some kids are coming in and actually heading straight for me, calling something out.

I glance over at Tori, who's waving at me frantically in a *let's go* kind of way. Spoilsport. Just because she's too uptight in her preppy clothes to reveal the amount of skin that Jo does! I smooth out my dress and— Oh.

There's way less of it than there was when I put it on.

In fact, when I look down, I can see that it has unravelled. A lot. And I'm showing . . .

A lot.

For example, my underpants are fully on show. Which, of course, because they're Jo's underpants, are actually called 'pants' or 'knickers' or something, and are pure white and plain and Jo-ish. This also means they are glowing like a beacon in the ultraviolet light.

And I have been dancing about in them. With everyone staring at me as I . . . you know.

Glow.

There.

In the pants/knickers/underpants region.

I take a deep breath.

OK, no problem. It's a music festival. There's a guy in the crowd who has Martian antennae on his head with eyes on stalks bobbing about at the end. That's surely way more embarrassing?

I climb down, and now everyone's real eyes seem to be on stalks, all following me. I am the pied piper of pants.

No, I'm imagining it – they have to be too busy dancing to notice some random girl.

'Come on, Tori,' I say, pulling her out of the tent, though she doesn't really need pulling. She's looking horrified and kind of stunned, and is running out all by herself.

'It's not that bad,' I try to reassure her. 'It's not like many people even— Oh.'

The screens outside – the ones I thought were showing a music video – are showing a familiar-looking scene. I recognize Tinky Winky, complete with handbag, a cowboy and a guy with a Martian headset. Eyes on stalks. Pointing at . . .

The picture flickers and a still appears.

. . . me. Well, Jo. Gyrating in an unravelling and very short sundress, underpants beaming enough light to power a small nation state.

The caption flashes *Enchantment TV: Live Festival Highlights!!!*

'Oh,' I say.

'Omigod,' Tori gasps quietly.

'Can they do that? I mean, don't they need my permission or something?'

'Uh . . . I think there was a disclaimer on the back of the tickets. Like, they're allowed to use our images for festival promotion or something. Dad read it out.'

'Oh.'

'Omigod.'

We watch as the caption changes but the picture doesn't, and now Jo is labelled. I've always made such a thing of rejecting labels, to the point where if someone calls me a Goth I snap at them, even though I guess I do kind of dress like a Goth.

Yeah, but not now. Now, as Jo, I'm barely dressed at all, and the caption under my blown-up picture reads: *Enchantment Welcomes . . . GLOW-PANTS GIRL!*

'Oh,' I say.

'Omigod.' Tori's face fills with horror. 'Are you OK?'

'I guess so.' I mean, it's not exactly me up there – although in a way, right now it is.

'Really? You're OK?' Tori's squealing changes pitch. 'Omigod. Omigod! Omigod!' She sounds like a glitchy CD. 'Omigod! *Josie!*' Then I'm stunned when she goes, 'That's fantastic. Way to go!'

'Uh . . .' I say.

'No, seriously,' she says seriously. 'This is great.'

'O . . . K?' I say.

'Yeah, do you realize what this means? Come on! We are *so* finding Tamber and Clyde. Because now I have the best idea! The *best*! You are going to *die*! Seriously, I mean it! *Die!*'

'That's a little worrying,' I mumble, trying to pull what's left of my dress down. 'And anyway, I think I need new clothes first. Like, to die in. So the coroner doesn't see my, uh, pants.'

'Don't be ridiculous, Josie!' Tori laughs. 'A coroner would totally see you *naked*!'

Three random festival-goers give me firm thumbs-up signs as they pass by, complete with cheesy-faced gurning, and one of them shouts, 'Way-hay! Knickers!'

MALL RATS

Tori and I spend a while choosing a suitably long, hippie-style skirt from a stall, and I pull what's left of Jo's dress over it. Then we weave in and out of tents and shacks, *so* not finding Tamber and Clyde.

Word of the 'Glow-Pants Girl' seems to be spreading around the festival, and a few slightly drunken people stop me and slap me on the back, or say bizarre things like, 'Cool knicker stunt!'

Finally Tori announces that she's had an idea. 'T-shirts!' she says.

'T-shirts?' I'm kind of sick of clothing right now, to be honest. Which isn't to say I'd take any (more) of it off or anything.

'T-shirts,' she confirms. 'Tamber owns more T-shirts than The Gap and he's always getting more. That guy likes shopping way more than you do, Josie! We should check out every T-shirt stand we see. It can be like one of our mall trips, only, you know, funkier.'

I give a half-hearted laugh and follow Tori, remembering the last time Mom dragged me to the mall for supplies and half our school was there, including Jo and Tori. Jo didn't seem very happy to be there – but she wasn't as miserable as *I* was. Because Mom and I had just bumped into Chelsea Cook. The memory makes me shudder inside.

'Hey, let's get specially made friendship bands,' Tori chirps, pointing at a stand that's displaying rainbow-coloured chunks of braided thread.

'Hey, let's not,' I say, fully in Rachel-mode after those dark thoughts. She looks like I've kicked her, or told her that Abercrombie is so far out of fashion that it's practically back in again, and I feel terrible. Especially because the way she's staring at my arm reminds me that I'm already wearing one of those cloth bracelets and I get this niggling feeling Hailey had the same one. I've just unwittingly made some kind of middle-school-style declaration that Hailey's a better friend than Tori, which is clearly a big deal.

'F—' I catch myself again. 'I mean, *flock*, I'm sorry, Tori. We can get that shi— I mean *sheep* . . . that sheep by-product . . . woollen bracelet if you like.' I'm pleased at the way I saved the situation – sheep-related cursing has stopped me being a total baa-tch. I link my arm through hers. 'Sorry – really. I'm just kind of, uh, not exactly myself right now.'

She rests her head on my shoulder. 'Omigod, don't apologize. I know you're having a rough time. Anyway, we're like sisters, you and me. We don't need a bracelet to prove it.' She shrugs at the display and keeps walking, but then she gets this slow grin and adds, 'Isn't that right, Glow-Pants Girl?'

'Hey!'

'What? It doesn't even sound that bad in American!' She giggles. 'Glow-*pants*, you know, not underwear. Like a glow-pants suit. Could be useful in a power outage . . . Hey!' She stops walking.

'What?'

'Over there! Didn't I say Tamber would be shopping? I'm so clever!'

'Yup, you're a regular flocking genius.'

She giggles. 'British cursing is so adorable. So I've just come up with this plan to stop the boys worrying about Albie, OK? But I need to ask . . .' She looks at me and reconsiders. 'No, I'm going to surprise you. I think you'll love it.'

I have no idea what she's talking about. 'Uh . . . sure.'

'Great. You're a superstar.' She takes a deep breath and walks over to the clothing stall, calling, 'Hey! Lame boy! Put that geek-wear down!'

When I catch up with her, I notice that Tamber's face is nearly the same colour as his hair. I've never seen a boy blush so deeply. He's putting the Rolling Stones sticking-out-tongue T-shirt back on a rail and looking at a row of David-style boots and then at a rail of sundresses – and, in fact, everywhere except at me or Tori. Then Clyde appears from behind some jackets. He says casually, 'Oh. Hey, girls.'

Tamber looks affronted. 'Don't talk to them like that.'

'What did I say?' Clyde protests, holding out his hands in a gesture of innocence.

'It was the way you said it, dude.'

'What? I just said it the regular way. They're girls, aren't they? And I said hey.'

'Yeah, but you sounded so . . . disrespectful.'

I smile at Tori but she's behind me now, examining some hemp wallets as if they're objects from outer space.

'I'm getting sick of this, man,' Clyde grumbles. 'Why don't you do something about it?' Then, more quietly, 'Why don't you just *tell* her?'

Tamber practically hisses, 'Shut up! I don't know what you're talking about. *You* don't know what you're talking about.'

'The whole festival knows what I'm talking about. It's awesome that we can legally drink here, but that beer makes you *emote*, man. You ruined my chances with that chick last night, the way you went on and on about—'

'Dude, you don't need *me* to ruin your chances with a girl who's way out of your league.'

138

'Yeah, well, you did, because her cute friend wanted to hook up with you, but all you could do was talk to me about someone who's out of *your* league. Until they both left.' Clyde looks over in my direction and then back at Tamber.

Tamber goes all red and mumbles, 'Jesus!'

Oh no.

Oh *no*! Tamber likes Jo? I mean – *me*?

Oh, that's real nice, crushing on his bandmate's girl-friend.

Or – wait – *ex*-girlfriend?

Either way, this is messed up. Does *every* guy in the world love Jo?

And how am I going to handle *this*?

Luckily Tamber seems to want to change the subject as quickly as possible, avoiding my eyes, looking at his watch and saying, 'Hey, don't forget we have that rehearsal shack booked in a half-hour. And isn't that journalist guy from school coming to take notes for his article?'

David's going to their rehearsal? My stupid heart starts hammering, just thinking about him.

'So?' Clyde shrugs. 'I thought you said we can't rehearse without the A-Man.'

At the mention of Albie (well, 'the A-Man') Tori starts raking nervously through the same T-shirt rail she was telling Tamber not to look at earlier.

139

'No, I said we could figure out cover for the guitar part but not the vocals,' Tamber says. 'We need, like, a placeholder for the singing parts – a recording or something, except more flexible. But we have to rehearse. Don't you get it? In two days' time we're supporting the headliners! And Albie said that David dude is putting us in a popular British magazine. It's exposure. It's immense! It's huge! It's immensely *huge*!'

This silences Clyde, who breathes out a long sigh of agreement at its immensely huge immensity and hugeness.

Then both band members spend a while staring into the middle distance, like they're in some old movie and picturing their name in lights.

Tori clears her throat and everyone turns sharply towards her.

'Ah, you need . . . uh, a stand-in singer,' she says.

Clyde groans. 'Well, yeah, duh—'

'Dude! Respect,' Tamber mumbles.

Clyde says, 'We need a stand-in singer, but it's kind of late notice, isn't it? We'd need someone who knows the set.' Then he frowns. 'Wait a minute, you don't mean . . . Do you want to do it, Tori?'

'Yeah, *do* you?' I ask, trying not to notice the way Tamber went bright red again as soon as I spoke.

'No way! Are you crazy?' she practically shouts. Then she adds more quietly, 'I mean, no, no, I couldn't. I don't

140

even know the songs. I learned to tune out Albie's singing at an early age.'

'Then who?' I say, at the same time as all the others stare at me. 'Oh. *Oh*. You mean me?'

Tori gives me a sheepish smile. 'Isn't it perfect?'

'I don't know, man,' Clyde grumbles.

'Why not?' Tamber says.

'Yeah, why not?' I ask. It's not like I exactly want to do it, but I'm offended by Clyde's negativity here.

'You could do it, couldn't you, Josie?' Tori asks excitedly. 'I mean, I wouldn't have thought of it, but then you—'

'I said I don't know, man,' Clyde interrupts, and then he rambles on with some reasons. Tamber and Tori shoot him down at every turn.

Meanwhile I'm thinking hard. This could really work for me. It has given me an idea. No, a revenge plan – one worthy of ErisGrrl the troublemaker, my comic-book alter ego.

David thinks he's with Jo, right? I mean, they haven't gone public or anything, but it's only a matter of time. He'll at least expect to hook up with her again. (At this point I have to take several deep breaths and ignore my boiling blood, in addition to my extra-racing heart. It'll never work if I end up in hospital – you know, next to myself.)

But what if Jo were to suddenly spend time with some

other guy? Someone who's liked her for ages, according to what I've just heard from Clyde?

What if I can show David what it's like to see the person you're dating surrounded by adoring fans? Well, just one adoring fan in this case, but it's a hundred per cent more fandom than I had as Rachel, and I'm sure Jo has lots more waiting in the wings.

I can do this. Tori's right. It's perfect.

'We really need the rehearsal time, dude,' Tamber is saying, sounding like he's won.

I mean, I wouldn't need to hook up with Tamber. (Would I? Argh!) But if he likes Jo that much, then . . . You know, it could be tough for David to take, if he sits in on rehearsals and stuff.

Clyde's still looking doubtful. 'No offence, Jo, but . . . can you even sing?'

Good point. Can I? As Rachel, I can sing OK. In elementary school I was in the chorus for a couple of productions, and I've beaten David at Rock Band a couple of times on his little brother's Wii.

But I don't have Rachel's voice now. I have Jo's.

Still, how hard can it be? And I don't have to be a professional singer, do I? I'm just a placeholder, like Tamber said. Albie might have run off to cheat on Jo, but there's no way he'd miss the big gig.

At least, I hope not.

No, he wouldn't.

142

'Sure I can,' I say.

Tamber straightens up, stretching his long legs, going pale again and frowning like he's just thought of a problem. 'Hey, but . . . would Albie be cool with it?' he says uncertainly.

He seems very concerned, for someone who's been crushing on his bandmate's girlfriend.

Clyde looks even more doubtful, but before he can say anything Tori is practically shouting, 'Listen, you guys! Forget my brother for a second here.'

Everyone stares at her.

'Yeah, I said *forget him*. Let's focus on Josie right now. Do you have any idea how brave she's being? Do you know what it's taking for her to throw you a lifeline like this?' She puts her hands on her hips.

'No.' Tamber is looking at me and going very red in the face again.

'No,' Clyde says.

No! I nearly add. What does Tori mean? Is there something I should know about Jo and singing? And if so, is it, like, a *body* thing or a *mind* thing? Because if it's a body thing, I'd like to know about it in advance.

Tori shakes her head in a really good impression of a disappointed parent. 'Well, she is being *incredibly* brave. I wouldn't even have dreamed of asking her to do something like this if she hadn't just proved she was over it when she . . .' Tori trails off.

'She what?' Tamber asks.

'Over what?' Clyde asks, which is good because that's the part I'd really like to hear about.

'Over her performance phobia. I mean, I know there's no audience in rehearsal, but you did say David would show up.'

I nod. Yeah, that's part of my plan. Wait a minute. Jo has *performance phobia*?

Well, that's a mind thing. I should do OK, though I might have to look a little scared and stuff, just for authenticity. That shouldn't be too hard. I *am* a little scared.

'Anyway, she's about the only person who could do this. She practically knows the lyrics better than you guys. She helped write half of the songs!'

Uh-oh. *Lyrics?* I start to get a panicky feeling in my stomach. Yay! Authentic performance phobia.

'So thanks, Josie. From *me*.' Tori looks pointedly at the guys.

There's a short silence and then Tamber, who's gone an even deeper red now, looks right at me and says, 'Yeah, thanks a lot, Jo. So, uh, welcome to the band.'

'Thanks.' I try to smile at Tamber in a broad and possibly flirty way. I may as well get started. Deep breaths. How hard can it be?

'Is your face OK?' Clyde asks.

'Don't be nervous, Josie. You can totally do this,' Tori reassures me. 'Remember you're Glow-Pants Girl.'

'Remember *what*?' Clyde asks.

Room 121, The Clarence
Friday

Rachel's Diary Therapy
by Jo in Rachel's body (IF THIS ISN'T PRIVATE I'M HIDING UNDER THE BED FOR EVER AND SURVIVING ON A DIET OF FLUFFBALLS!)
Conversations with my so-called mother, Part 2

(*Knock at door.*)
Jo-in-Rachel's-Body: Come in!
My So-Called Mother (*opening door a tiny bit*): You sure?
JIRB: Course I'm sure! God, Mother! Errgh, you're so exasperating! Grr!
MSCM: I thought you'd like to know that David's here.
JIRB: Again? Oh, bloody hell, I can't believe he told me they'd broken up! I should have known it wasn't true. Not that it makes it right either way, but— Oh, I just said all that out loud, didn't I?
MSCM: Rachel, honey, you want me to send him away?
JIRB (*thinking maybe she didn't say it out loud after*

all – phew): Oh, yes! Yes, please! Yes, please, would you, Mother? You're the best! I mean, in a totally annoying way.

MSCM: You're a good kid, Rachel.

JIRB: No way! I can't believe you just said that!

MSCM: Said what?

JIRB (*smiling and dying to call her real mother to tell her some Americans really do say that, like in our favourite TV movies*): Nothing! Go and get rid of David for me. And bring me a fresh cuppa.

MSCM (*perplexed*)

JIRB: It means 'cup of'.

MSCM (*still perplexed*)

JIRB: You know, tea. Cup of tea. White, no sugar. Er, please.

MSCM (*gives JIRB lingering, love-my-daughter look and leaves*)

JIRB (*cursing self for forgetting to ask for a poster of Spike from Buffy. Never mind. Makes mental note to next time.*)

'End of log. Filed for future analysis.'

THE LIST

My first rehearsal with Madison Rat is a disaster.

Clyde goes on about how he can't hear me and Tamber moans that it's because he's playing his guitar too loud and then Clyde slams Tamber's drumming. They argue for about ten minutes out of every fifteen.

Course, the real reason they can't hear me is because I don't know the words. Or where they're supposed to go. I'm dying out here, and the only good thing is that Tamber seems to think it's all about my 'performance phobia' and he's being all sweet and gentle about it.

I look over at the door every five seconds, and every two while Tamber's being super-nice, but David doesn't turn up at all. Where *is* he?

At the end of the rehearsal Clyde is way less encouraging than Tamber. He hands me his iPod and says, 'Here. Madison Rat's greatest hits. You can borrow it tonight and, you know, suck less tomorrow.'

Tori, who has been giving herself a manicure in the

corner throughout this whole thing, looks up in horror. 'Clyde! Take that back!' She looks at the iPod. 'I mean, like, literally! I cannot believe you are treating Josie like this!'

'Well, I cannot believe how much she sucked,' Clyde says, slinging his guitar case over one shoulder. 'I'm going for a walk.'

I sneak the iPod into my pocket – I think I *do* need it – as Tori gets up, shouting, 'You are going nowhere until you apologize to my friend, who is totally helping you out!'

'Bite me,' Clyde says, and it's such a Rachel thing to say that I nearly cheer. I mean, Clyde kind of has a point about me.

But Tori looks appalled on my behalf: 'Josie, don't worry. I'm going to tell him exactly what I think of him!' She stalks out after him.

Totally leaving me alone with Tamber.

The silence echoes around the wooden barn we're using as a rehearsal room. I kick at some damp straw.

Now what?

Well, maybe David will walk in now – late – and see us. I need to make the most of this opportunity. Even if he doesn't, there might be another time soon. I just need to encourage Tamber a little, make sure he acts like a fan around me, the way girls always are with David. I can do this. I am ErisGrrl, taking revenge.

I walk over to where Tamber's sitting behind his drumkit and stand about awkwardly. He glances over and smiles.

I gulp.

'Hey, Tamber, can I ask you something?' I ask sweetly. I beam a huge smile at him and stand closer, and it's really not so hard, flirting with him. It feels nothing like the heart-in-mouth feeling I used to get from doing anything around David that showed I thought of him as more than a friend. Even after we got together, I never stopped having extreme butterflies when I was near him.

Tamber turns to his drums, tapping out a quiet beat, not seeming remotely fazed that he's alone with his crush. 'Sure. What's up, Jo?'

Huh. OK. There's a long and awkward silence while I think of something else to say. Strangely, this is what comes out: 'I'm . . . I'm sorry I wasn't very good today. I'm kind of . . . worried about Rachel.' I gulp. 'You know, my friend. Rachel.'

He grins and says, 'I know who Rachel is,' but he doesn't seem to think what I said is unusual, even though I think it's off the weirdness scale. 'And everyone's been talking about it.' He keeps tapping the drums. 'I heard they've had problems with that temple during the festival before, but they're not allowed to do anything to make it safe. The ruins are under some kind of preservation order. How is Rachel now?'

I shrug. After all, it depends who you mean by 'Rachel'. 'She's good, I guess.'

'Great. We were worried. Especially Clyde.' He smiles meaningfully, like we're sharing an in-joke.

'What do you mean?'

He gives me a sideways glance. 'Come on, you must have heard us getting at Clyde about Rachel. Even though he says it's ancient history.'

'It's . . . what? Clyde has a thing for Rachel?'

'He used to. You didn't hear? You must have heard. He had a massive crush on her when she was a freshman – it was obvious even though he always denied it. He had it bad for ages until she completely cut him down.'

'She did?' I have no memory of this. Then again, cutting boys down is kind of a well-practised skill of mine. I always figure they deserve it – if not right away, then at some point in the future.

'Sure she did. He expected it, though. I think it's kind of what he liked about her – the way she's so outspoken and, you know, passionate about everything. Even if it means she's always rude to everyone.' He smiles like he hasn't just insulted me. I mean, I barely even know this guy; how does he know so much about me? 'It'd never work, though, because Clyde's just like her.'

Hmm, I doubt it. It'd never work because she's never

151

even noticed Clyde and she's still stupidly crazy about someone else, I think. But obviously I don't say any of that.

Anyway, I've got to focus on what I'm trying to do here: make Tamber think I like him so that he'll flirt around me and show David how that feels. I can do this.

I reach over and fiddle with the edge of one of the drums. 'So, Tamber . . .'

'Uh . . . yeah?' He twitches kind of nervously.

I giggle in an over-friendly way and lean closer to him. 'What is your real name, anyway?'

He clears his throat and shifts away from me. 'Uh, listen, sorry, but could you let go of the drum?'

'Oh.' I move and he seems instantly more relaxed. Is it because he can't stand to be close to me, because he likes me so much?

'Thanks. They're, you know, instruments. They're precious.'

Yeah, or maybe he just can't stand me being close to his drums.

'OK, Jo, now I'm getting the picture.'

'What picture?'

'You know,' he says. 'I understand what's going on here.'

'You do?' That's good, because I don't.

He nods. 'This isn't about Rachel, or me.'

'Uh . . . no?' I say hesitantly.

'No,' he says confidently. 'It's about Albie, isn't it?'

'Uh . . .'

'You're acting strangely,' he continues, 'forgetting the lyrics to songs you co-wrote yourself, asking my real name as if you haven't known it for months. Touching my drums! Dancing on speakers with your underwear showing.'

'Uh, yeah.' Tori didn't actually tell them that. They saw it for themselves on the way to the rehearsal barn just now, projected on the giant screens outside the dance tent. Enchantment TV is currently featuring Glow-Pants Girl on a continuous loop. Yay, me!

'You're just not yourself right now,' Tamber finishes.

'Uh . . . yeah.' He has no idea. And, hey, I can't believe Jo knows Tamber's real name when she's been at school with him for about a year. I don't have a clue and he's been a grade above me for *ever*. Yeah, and I barely noticed Clyde at all and it turns out he was crushing on me. I don't remember *his* first name either. At school I never paid all that much attention to anyone outside my immediate circle – which, after seventh grade and before David, pretty much just consisted of one person: me. And after ninth grade, it was just me and David, because there's no way I count the string of boys I hooked up with but never really cared about, or the girls like Kendis and Jo who'd hang out with us and make me jealous. The surplus boys and girls always paired up

153

with other people and left things as they should be: me and David. Exclusively.

Huh. I'm such an idiot.

While I'm agonizing over this, Tamber is filling the silence by drumming quietly. He seems lost in the rhythm until he glances over and seems to remember I'm here.

You know, he doesn't seem like he's crazy in love with me-Jo. Not at all.

'So you want to tell me what's going on?' He slows down the drumming when I still don't answer. 'You're worried about Albie, aren't you? It's so unlike him to go AWOL.'

OK, I think it's official: Tamber is *not* crushing on Jo. How did I manage to misunderstand that?

Tamber changes the beat. Then, not looking at me, he says, 'If this is about the photo . . . you really shouldn't worry. Clyde doesn't know what he's talking about.'

'Oh,' I say. Yeah, the photo. Of the girl Albie's cheating with. I narrow my eyes at the thought of cheating men everywhere.

Tamber says, 'You're not seriously thinking what I think you're thinking, are you? About this girl and Albie?'

I hesitate, because I know I *am* thinking it, and I also think I'm right.

'Jo, come on. Believe me, it's hard for me and Clyde

too, not knowing where Albie is or whether he'll be back in time for the most important gig of our career so far. But I've known Albie all my life, and he'll come through for Madison Rat. And for you.' He shakes his head. 'I don't need to tell you this, do I? I trust him. I know you do too.'

But I really don't, and I doubt Jo does either, not any more. It's hard not to feel sorry for Jo, even if I'm angry about the David thing. The real problem is *guys* – all of them.

Though Tamber seems pretty genuine. And just as I think that, he looks up, smiles sympathetically and says, 'OK?'

I nod. I can't exactly tell him it's not. I'm really not OK.

'Because if it isn't, you can talk to me anytime, you know? I mean, I know you have Tori but . . . he's her brother. And only a moron could talk to Clyde.' He grins. 'So, yeah. Anytime, Jo, I mean it.'

I feel it again – the word-blanket of people who really seem to care about me. Well, Jo. The joy of being Jo. It's not just about wearing glow-in-the-dark underpants by accident and somehow living it down.

There's another silence, an easy one now, and then Tamber says, 'Clyde and . . . uh, Tori are taking a long time.' He shifts nervously. And I realize that, of course, I wasn't the only girl around earlier. Tori was standing

155

right with me for most of it. For the parts when he was blushing, in fact.

I want to be nice to Tamber, who seems like a great guy. 'You know, Tori has split up with Topher, big-time,' I tell him.

He looks startled and then – there it is! The hair-matching blush. So that's definitely it – his crush was Tori all along.

'I, uh, heard.' He looks at the ground, clears his throat and adds, 'I will kill Clyde for saying those things in front of you and Tori.'

I nudge him, totally secure now that I know he's not crushing on me-Jo. 'Want me to say something to her about you?' Deep down, I think I've always loved the idea of being a matchmaker. I even used to tell David about girls who liked him sometimes, before we got together. It was slightly crazy and it didn't help my raging jealousy at all, but it seemed like the right thing to do.

He starts drumming again. 'No way, dude. I mean, seriously, no effing way.' He avoids my eyes. 'I've known her for ever and it is *never* going to happen. Clyde's completely sure of it. I didn't mean to talk about it with him, but I was so wasted I was shooting my mouth off.' He sighs. 'Anyway, Clyde is right. Me and Tori are in different leagues.' He builds up to a drumroll, ending with pretend-hitting of non-existent cymbals with both hands, maybe to save my ears from the real ones. 'Jo, don't tell Tori what I said. Don't tell her anything. Please.'

'OK, I won't.'

He looks at me gratefully.

'Unless I think it will help,' I add quickly, just in case, because I don't want to lie to him. 'Look, I can give you some advice. You know, like the things she looks for in a man.'

A glimmer of hope appears in his eyes. 'No, I . . . Like what?'

I rattle off a rambling shopping list of things, as told to me-Rachel by Tori on that never-ending flight. At last – a use for all this irritating knowledge I have about Tori and guys. Maybe I can forget it myself now.

When I've exhausted my list he says shyly, 'You've pretty much described me anyway. I mean, I'm respectful and stuff, like, normally. I wouldn't let her down.'

'Sure you wouldn't,' I say, and right now I mean it, even if the Rachel part of me is saying, *He's a guy and they're all the same*. I want to believe that things aren't always like that. And now that I'm Jo, I finally can. Well, I can if I don't think about Albie. Or David.

Yeah, being Jo is great. I'm so glad I'm Jo.

I'll bet Jo's not remotely happy being me, though. I wonder how she's doing?

One thing's for sure: I bet my mother is driving her crazy.

Room 121, The Clarence
Friday

Rachel's Diary Therapy
by Jo in Rachel's body (IF THIS ISN'T PRIVATE I'M
GOING UNDERCOVER AND YOU'LL NEVER FIND
ME!)
Conversations with my so-called mother, Part 3

My So-Called Mother: Hey, Rachel? Can I come in?

Jo-in-Rachel's-Body: Like, duh! Of course you can,
duh! (*Rolls eyes and thinks she's getting quite good
at this being-Rachel lark*) Jesus, Mother, I can't
believe you'd even ask! (*Thinking that's a nice
Rachel-ish touch, and sort of fun to say too*)

MSCM: How are you doing?

JIRB: Oh, fine. (*Thinks she's actually enjoying this
quite a lot and wouldn't mind being Rachel for ever,
except . . .*) Has David gone?

MSCM: Yes, he has. (*Sits on chair and looks thoughtful*) You know, Rachel, he looks real upset that you
won't see him.

JIRB (*wondering how she could ever have believed

158

they'd truly split up): Yeah, I thought he might.

MSCM: Rachel, are you conflicted? Are you . . . are you punishing him?

JIRB: Whaaaaat?

MSCM: I think you are. I think you're punishing him. Are you sure it's for something he's done and not for something . . . you know. Your father's done.

JIRB (*unable to hide confusion*): Hey, hold on. What do you mean? What does David have to do with her— I mean, *my* father?

MSCM: I've been thinking, you know. It's not healthy, is it? The way I always forgive him, I mean. The way I always take him back. I thought I was doing it for you, not breaking up our family the way my mother, your Bubbe, did when I was growing up. But I'm wrong, aren't I? I'm wrong.

JIRB (*surprised*): Er . . .

MSCM: I'm shocking you, aren't I?

JIRB (*feeling relatively unshockable right now*): Er . . .

MSCM: I know about your father. I *know*, Rachel. There, are you happy? I've known all along. I've known about all of them. Every single one of the women your father has seen supposedly behind my back over the years. I knew, I knew, but I so desperately wanted to hold our family together! (*Sobs*)

JIRB (*panicking*): Oh no! Oh no! Hey! (*Goes to put arm around MSCM*)
MSCM (*wipes at face and runs out of room*)

'*End of log. Filed for future analysis.*'

SWAMP THING

Tori comes back with a half-eaten carton of fries but without Clyde. This is not because Clyde doesn't want to apologize to me for his attitude – 'He totally does, Josie' – but because, in the line for 'greasy grub', they ran into Tori's cousin Brad. Brad then talked Clyde into joining him in the beer shack with a bunch of his new buddies. Apparently 'Clyde's totally going to grovel in style tomorrow, Josie, I promise.'

Yes – tomorrow. It seems it's turned to evening while we've been in the rehearsal barn, which I guess is what happens when you sleep away half your day.

Tamber goes all red and shifty while Tori talks, but she doesn't notice. I try beaming him glances that say *Smile at her!* but it's no good; he won't even look at either of us.

'So what should we do next?' Tori asks me, picking up three fries at once and waving them in front of her face. 'Tamber, you could go see Clyde and Brad, but Josie and

161

I can't. They're totally checking ID at the door of the beer shack.' She crams the fries into her mouth.

'But Clyde and Tamber aren't twenty-one either,' I protest. Two seconds later I remember that the legal drinking age in Britain is eighteen. David has only mentioned it to me about a hundred times. 'I mean, uh . . . you know, I nearly forgot I wasn't in the States right now.'

Tori laughs. 'Cute. Listen, let's go find the main stage, or whatever. It's a music festival and I haven't even heard any music yet.'

'We were in the dance tent! And you've been listening to us rehearse all afternoon,' I point out.

'Exactly,' she says. 'On both counts.'

Tamber puts his head down and I frown at Tori.

She laughs. 'Omigod, you guys! It was a *joke*! Madison Rat are made of awesome rock-goddage! Well, as much as a band fronted by my nerd-tastic brother ever *could* be. Anyway, who's with me?'

'OK,' I say. 'Tamber?' This could be his chance. I could make some excuse, leave them together. Maybe even go find David or something.

Tamber studies his drumkit and his face is on fire. 'I . . . uh . . . gotta rehearse some more.'

'By yourself?' I ask pointedly.

'Yeah . . . you know.' He still won't look up. This is hopeless!

'Sunday's a big day,' Tori explains to me, slightly too helpfully, and I have to stifle a sigh as she says a bright goodbye to Tamber and almost skips out of the rehearsal barn.

It's surprisingly dark outside. I actually have no sense of time any more at all. I'm drifting in a jet lagged fog.

The festival site is covered in a real fog. The low, damp mist drifts past me and Tori and we can't see much at all, even in those rare moments when the moon manages to poke out and beam light at us from behind thick clouds. They're probably storm clouds, judging by the way we're suddenly hit by a full-on downpour. Giant drops of rain bounce off our heads as we stumble through the darkness, bumping into people and things at regular intervals.

'Oh sorry,' Tori says after her tenth collision.

'Tori, you just apologized to a plastic tree,' I point out. The only reason I know is that I crashed into the same tree myself two seconds ago. I actually gave it the finger before I realized, because I thought it was rude for not apologizing to me. Yeah, I'm as tough on plastic trees as I am on people. Least I'm consistent.

'This is horrible,' Tori complains. 'Omigod, it's so dark! Where are your glow-pants when we need them?'

'Funny.'

'It really is. Anyway, they should issue all

festival-goers with flashlights. I mean, couldn't we, like, sue? It's a basic human right to have enough light.'

'I don't think it is, Tori.'

'Well, it should be,' she declares. 'I can't see where I'm putting my Manolos.'

I can roll my eyes without her seeing, so I do. 'Where's the main stage from here anyway?'

'I don't know any more. I think we got turned around. Maybe we're near the sub-stage, though.' She hesitates and then says, 'I saw your friend Hailey before.'

'Oh, yeah?' Oh no – Hailey! I totally forgot about her. Isn't Jo supposed to be staying with her, sharing a tent? And I haven't seen her since before I fell asleep in Tori's hotel room. I've spent an entire afternoon with Tori at the festival without even looking for her once.

I know enough about Hailey to realize that she is not going to be happy about that.

'She kind of said hey,' Tori continues. 'But I think she was looking for you. When she saw you weren't with me, she disappeared into the crowd near the sub-stage.'

'Oh. Maybe we should look for her?'

'Yeah, I guess.' I detect an odd hurt note in Tori's voice.

Well, hey, I need to remember I'm Jo now. I should be able to sort this out.

'Tori, you and Hailey are both my friends, you know,' I try. We turn into a really quiet area that's even darker

164

than before. Who knew that was possible? 'You can, you know, be friends with each other too. We can all be friends.' Hmm, that sounded kind of elementary-schoolish. I try again as we wander deeper into nothingness. 'I mean, you know – Hailey . . . likes you . . .' And now I sound even younger. I'd place me at around four years old and not particularly gifted. Bah, I have zero social skills.

'I don't think so. She thinks I'm an airhead.'

Oh, yeah. She probably does. 'I'm sure she doesn't. And anyway, maybe it's just because . . . Well, maybe she has issues and . . .' OK, I'd better stop because I am not doing a good job of either reassuring Tori *or* sounding like Jo here. I actually sound a little like my mother.

There's an odd whimpering sound, and then complete silence. I can't see Tori's face to check she's OK. In fact, I can't even hear Tori near me at all.

Oh no – have I upset her so much with my Hailey-talk that she's stormed away, the way *I* would?

Then I hear a yelp coming from somewhere to my left. 'Tori?'

'Down here,' she whimpers, but I can't see a thing. 'Omigod, Josie, help! I'm in quicksand.'

'I don't think they have quicksand in this country.' I don't know for sure, though. I didn't think they had magic temples, either. 'It's probably mud.'

'Help me out, Josie! Please!'

'I can't – I can't even see you.' I take a step forward.

'Oh, Josie, I don't want to die like this! There are too many things I still want to do with my life!'

'Tori, relax.'

'Why are you saying that? Is it because if you struggle in quicksand it makes things worse? Omigod, it is, isn't it? You'd know all about British quicksand too. We don't have it in Massachusetts. I'm totally at the mercy of a foreign land!'

'Tori, you're being ridiculous. It's mud, and we *do* have it in New England. Remember that tropical storm two years ago when the school roof—' I stop myself. Jo wasn't there two years ago.

She's wailing, not listening to me anyway. 'I've never even had a real relationship, Josie! I mean, not with someone I love! Can you believe that? I've been running scared, going out with all the wrong guys for all the wrong reasons! You and Albie are so lucky you've known true love!'

Huh, I think, and I almost want to cry, thinking how that's not true for Jo after all: her relationship is just as messed up as mine, as Mom's. I wish I could wave some kind of superhero cloak and stop everyone hurting.

Tori's voice rings out through the darkness. 'Love is pretty special, Josie! You have to hold onto it, even if my brother is being a total pain in the butt. I mean, seriously, what *is* he playing at right now, disappearing like this? You should totally dump him for being so selfish – though don't really do that, because he'd be so upset and— Aargh!'

'Are you conflicted?'

'No, I'm sinking! I moved, and it's deeper!'

'Hang in there, Tor!'

'I'll try moving again— Nooooo!' There's a squelch. 'This is worse!' Then there's a watery, spluttering sound.

'Are you in a puddle now?'

'It's no puddle,' Tori glugs. 'It's an ocean! Help me!'

The moon peeps out and shines through the raindrops, enough for me to see her outline flailing in a giant puddle that, to be fair, does look a lot like a swamp. Or possibly an ocean. With frogs. Oceanic frogs.

'I'll go get help,' I tell her, and bizarrely my first thought is finding David. Why didn't he come to the rehearsal? Has he looked for me at all?

Wait – do I even want him to look for *Jo*?

And how can I swap places with perfect Jo and feel just as confused and insecure as I did before?

'Josie, where are you? Don't leave me! Don't leeeeave me,' Tori wails, her voice getting smaller, as if she really *is* sinking.

'Tori! Can you swim?'

'Help! Help! Help!' comes the answer, and then there's another splutter and a splash. So I'm guessing it's a no. Honestly, popular girls! All those hours Tori spent perfecting her manicure technique – on herself and on Chelsea Cook, from what I remember – and she could have been learning basic survival in water.

'Relax! I'll pull you out,' I sigh, and in the next burst of moonlight I hold out a hand to her.

But she's panicking so hard that she pulls and pulls on my hand in all the wrong ways until I can't help it. I lose my footing and land right beside her. It barely makes a splash, probably because Tori has churned it all about so much. I can now see why she was panicking. The water clings and smells like wet dog mixed with mouldy cheese.

'Josie?' Tori whimpers from beside me. 'Are we still alive?'

'Nope – looks like paradise to me. The ocean breeze, the cocktails with little umbrellas—'

'What are we going to do now?'

'Wade out.' But how? It's dark; we're muddy; I can't see which way is out. 'Over here a bit.'

We shuffle in a squelchy way till it's definitely shallower. But then the rain turns itself up a notch instead, pouring down on us.

'Omigod, Josie,' Tori says, on the verge of tears. 'Sorry I landed you in it.'

'Hey, it's OK,' I tell her.

'No it's not.' She sniffs. 'This is all my fault.'

'No, no. This is . . .' I remember something I used to

play at summer camp, back when I had girl friends, before the Chelsea stuff happened. It was one of those games where if you laugh, you lose. I can really see it working on Tori.

'This is a very sad and solemn occasion,' I say in a sombre voice. Then, in case she doesn't get it, I add an ultra-long, 'Mmmmmm.' In the proper game, you're supposed to bow as if in prayer when you do that, and call the other person 'sister' first, like in a nunnery, which I guess makes it harder not to laugh.

Even though she can't see my face, Tori gets it right away, just like I expected. She probably used to love camp, sharing rooms with all those girlie girls.

'Sister Josie, this is a sad and solemn occasion,' she says, her voice already lighter. 'Mmmm.'

'A *very* sad and solemn occasion,' I correct her in a serious, booming voice.

'Sister Josie, this is a *very* sad and solemn occasion,' Tori repeats, starting to lose it already. 'Mm – ha! – mmm.'

'Sister Tori, this is a very sad and solemn occasion,' I intone. I was always excellent at this game. Being serious has never been a problem for me. 'Mmmm.'

'Sister Josie—' Tori bursts into fits of giggles. 'This— Omigod! I can't do it! How do you do it? And I'm so miserable!' She laughs. 'It hasn't stopped raining for, like, a second! My hair is *ruined*!'

169

'Hey, d'you think this is better water pressure than the shower at the hotel?'

'Omigod,' she squeaks. 'You're totally right! My hair's not ruined at all! I'm just washing it in the wild, like I'm in one of those celebrity survival shows! No wonder we nearly ate grubs earlier!'

Then even I can't help laughing. Tori's high-pitched giggles are way infectious. We stay like that for a few seconds, not caring about the pouring rain, because how could we possibly get any wetter or muddier? Then I start working on clambering out.

'Hey, Josie?' Tori says through the watery squelching.

'Yeah?'

'Thanks for helping. You're a great friend.'

'No I'm not,' I say, without thinking. Until very recently I was as much a friend to Tori as Hailey is, i.e. not a friend at all. I'd be the first to call Tori an airhead – or worse.

'Shut up, you *are*. Well, yeah, you have been acting kind of weird lately.'

Well, yeah, I guess I have.

But instead of listing Jo's weird behaviour since Thursday, she says, 'I mean, come on, I'm not imagining the way you avoided my calls and messages the last few weeks. Even your mother is not that much of a computer geek that she won't let you message your friends, like, at *all*. You know, I can't believe I told Rachel the story of what happened with Topher before I told you!'

'I . . .' I don't know what to say.

'Yeah, I never thought Rachel would be a better listener than you, but she was, you know!'

'Uh . . . sorry.'

'Well, it's OK, you've been great since I got here. And right now you are *made* of friendage!'

Before I can react (like, *Hey, really, you think?* or *Hey, is 'friendage' a word now?*) there's the sound of chattering in the distance. And lights, dancing through the fog.

'We're saved!' Tori cries. 'Hey, guys! Over here! Over here!'

The voices and lights get closer. Through the dazzle I can make out the outlines of a few girls. Then one of them shines the flashlight on me and says, 'Hey, aren't you Glow-Pants Girl?' and the others get all excited about it, like I'm some kind of celebrity.

After a few seconds of this – though it feels like a year or two – they finally get around to helping us out of the swamp. Tori says I should go first but I insist it should be her because she's been stuck here longer, plus I'm halfway out already.

'Don't grip my hand too tight!' Tori tells her saviour. 'That manicure's fresh!'

You know, Tori *can* be kind of an airhead.

'Hey, get Josie now, quick! She kept my spirits up, you know, throughout this ordeal. I owe her my life! Josie, you know, you can totally have my D&G fragranced lipstick – the one Scarlett Johansson wears in the advert.'

But it doesn't really matter. She's also kind of all right.

GREEN TEA

It's a little past midnight when we reach the hotel. First we stomped and squelched around the site with our rescuers, whose names Tori and I instantly forgot because even our brains were full of mud. We ended up spending loads of time with them around their campfire drinking warming drinks and listening to very bad guitar music. Then we made a getaway, which involved Tori begging the security guys at the main entrance to call us a cab on their short-wave radios, with me biting my tongue all the while and managing not to suggest that we should find David and ask him to give us a ride instead.

Tori's hair-twirling and wheedling failed on the security guards until she told them I was Glow-Pants Girl. Even then, after the cab arrived, we spent well over ten minutes trying to persuade the driver to let two stinking, mud-covered people into his car. He said he'd agreed to this call-out because 'Dave's a mate', but now that he'd seen us he was sure we were 'swampies' and 'our sort' were usually drunk or *on something*, and he couldn't risk having 'sick' on his new upholstery. I nearly made a rude comment about the cheap black vinyl being improved by a splash of colour, which wouldn't have helped, but thankfully Tori spoke first – after she recovered from the offence of the driver's accusation. She offered him an extra-large tip in advance 'to cover cleaning, although you totally won't need it, pinkie-swear'.

Then the driver said he 'couldn't help clocking' Tori's accent, and he suddenly warmed to us. He asked Tori questions about Hollywood and whether she knew Catherine Zeta-Jones. His cousin's friend's son's aunt's brother, or something like that, had once asked her out at primary school in the town he used to live in and he could have been connected to her if she'd said yes. He talked non-stop until we finally made it to the hotel.

Our problems weren't over there, though. Mrs Pernickety was waiting for us at the main desk, ready with a full lecture about festival-goers 'being given an inch and taking a mile'.

We let her talk for a minute and she went on for half an hour, which only meant the rug in reception got increasingly covered in flakes of mud, as Tori and I shed our second skin. In the end Tori threw the promise of extra money at Mrs Pernickety too, at which she bristled and called Tori 'American', which I think was supposed to be an insult, but Tori just nodded and said sweetly, 'Yes, I guess I am, ma'am.'

This seemed to make Mrs Pernickety soften, and she even said she'd give us a key so she didn't need to wait up for us tomorrow if we 'could at least behave decently', because she did believe we were 'nice girls at heart', like that 'lovely American girl' her grand-daughter liked – 'Hannah Banana, or whatever her name is.' (I didn't open my mouth then, in case she remembered that Jo wasn't American. Which seems kind of ironic.)

Now we're in our room. Tori let me use the bathroom first, before heading for what she called 'the shower to end all showers'. Though she might just be mud-wrestling with the shower attachment from what I can hear, which is a whole lot of cursing and splashing noises.

I dry myself off with a hotel towel that's been left neatly folded on my bed, and find a pair of *Buffy* pyjamas in Jo's bag. After I've put them on this strangely unpadded body, I sit on the bed listening to the water running and wondering what to do. I'm actually not all that sleepy, which is probably the jet lag talking, as it's been a hell of a day.

I really feel like sketching, but I don't have any paper or my favourite pens, and anyway, what if Tori sees my drawings? Jo doesn't draw – it'll just look weird.

Instead, I plug the iPod that Clyde gave me into my ears and listen to Albie crooning *Buffy*-based love lyrics in his intense, geek-god voice. I shut my eyes and lie back on the bed. You know, I'm no expert on Madison Rat, but I could swear he is totally singing to Jo half the time. I can't help thinking how incredible it is that he'd cheat on her. They were the perfect couple – everyone knew it. It makes me feel so sad.

To a background of Madison Rat covering a slushy Snow Patrol song, I let my thoughts drift to David, and me and David together. I don't think anyone thought *we* were the perfect couple – they probably heard me break up with him in the school cafeteria, for a start – but, I don't know. Maybe we were just different from Jo and Albie. We had our own way of being a couple. And, really, we were amazing together. We—

What am I thinking? Why am I thinking about David like this when I know it's over? My thoughts have gone crazy! I switch off the emo machine and pull out the earplugs. Crazy! Mom's right about me!

Thinking about Mom makes me miss her – a sudden, shooting pang. I glance at the nightstand beside my bed. Mom's herbal sachets are in there from when I emptied out the side pocket of my holdall. Mom would so love it if I took one. And you know what? The way I'm feeling, maybe I need it. Maybe anything is worth a try right now.

I reach over and pull out the drawer's contents. The herbal sachets land on the bed, together with one crushed velvet dress (well, more like *crumpled* velvet by now) and my favourite bright red lipstick. What would people say if I wore the lipstick and the Rachel dress tomorrow? And dyed Jo's hair black and straightened it and cut it so it covered my eyes when I needed it to, without spikiness?

Now I'm being ridiculous. The whole point is it's great that I'm *not* myself. I never want to be myself again. I want to be Jo for ever. I stuff my black velvet dress and – with a reluctant sigh – the gorgeous lipstick back in the drawer. Then I sit on the bed and shake Mom's herbal sachet before I read the instructions on the back.

It says the powder can be mixed with yoghurt or added to boiling water. I almost give up right there – I mean, I have nothing to eat, and no access to a stove, or even a microwave oven. But then, on a table at the side of the room, I spot a plastic jug surrounded by cups, spoons and two dishes containing wrapped things labelled TEA, SUGAR, COFFEE and CUSTARD CREAMS, which seem to be pale-yellow rectangular cookies.

I figure the jug must be an electric kettle – how else can you make hot drinks in a hotel room? I've heard of electric kettles, but I don't know anyone who has one – not even David, whose family's part-British. His family are total coffee-drinkers.

It takes me a long time to fill the kettle from the tiny sink in the corner. I can't get the spout under the faucet unless it's almost horizontal, and then the water just sprays everywhere. In the end, I use one of the dainty cups to fill it. Then it takes me a while to figure out how to put the jug back onto its base, slot the enormous three-pinned plug into the socket on the wall and press a red button at the side of the kettle. After that, I sit back on the bed in silence and wait for something to happen.

And wait.

And wait.

And then I notice the switch next to the socket.

Jesus, how complicated is life in Britain? No wonder Jo and David both take so many advanced classes. Figuring out how to boil water must make every British person a total genius.

After I switch the socket on, there's a reassuring whooshing sound, and I feel very proud of myself when eventually there's a click and the kettle switches itself off with a puff of steam. I can definitely add the international boiling of water to my superhero ass-kicking skills.

I mix my sachet with water in the tiny cup, thinking how incredible it is that I'm finally doing something

Mom's been nagging me to do for months. And then I feel it again – that weird homesick pang. I almost wish she were here to nag me.

That's it, then. True insanity has hit me. Time to drink the remedy, as pushed by Mom.

I sip the drink, which doesn't taste so bad. Kind of earthy, like the green tea I tried once in a zanily decorated café in Cambridge, Mass, where I went with David and we pretended to be college students.

I start thinking that maybe Mom isn't so bad either. She's had a tough time, and all that stuff that happened with Dad is not her fault. The fact that she tries to pretend it's not still happening *is* her fault, but right now, while I'm crazily missing her, I can even sort of understand it. When you really want to be with someone, I guess you can gloss over all kinds of bad things about them. I'd probably do it myself if I hadn't spent a lifetime watching Mom lie to herself about Dad's affairs.

I lie back, plug the iPod back into my ears and wait for the herbal sachets to take effect, and pretty soon my stomach's gurgling at the thought of revenge.

THE TRUTH ABOUT PERFORMANCE PHOBIA

My stomach doesn't stop gurgling for most of the night. It keeps waking me up, which isn't helping the jet lag thing at all. Tori sleeps blissfully through, though, and at one point she even snores. I decide to keep that fact in reserve for the next time she bores me about designer accessories.

Luckily, by morning the gurgles are small and polite, and after a great breakfast experience (every major food group covered in dripping fat, and Tori looking like she's in heaven), my stomach is blissfully silent again.

We spend so long over breakfast that we're running late for the next Madison Rat rehearsal. I actually feel jumpy about that – I think I've learned some of the lyrics now and I want to get it right today. Also David should be there. I'm glad Tori kept the business card from last night's cab: she calls and it doesn't take too long for Mr Zeta-Jones to arrive at the hotel.

'You girls look more presentable today,' he comments,

and I cringe, because I feel like something out of a washing-detergent commercial in another of Jo's cheerful sundresses. This one is lime-green and yellow, again kind of short with the big pockets and barely-there sleeves, but I checked the hemline several times for signs of unravelling. It also has the addition of low-cut exposure of Jo's boobage-fail. I sort of miss my curves, though I'm surprised by the way guys' eyes still seem to rest naturally on my chest. (Course, as Glow-Pants Girl, that's really the least of my worries.)

Tori forgot about giving me her D&G fragranced lipstick, but she dressed as Scarlett Johansson at an Oscar ceremony anyway, with a sequinned top she says will 'work as reflective gear at night-time'.

Really, though, we both look like we have incredibly short memories of what happened last night, especially when you look at our shoes, which Tori dried with a hairdryer and did her best to clean on the little brush thing in the hotel corridor, but which still look mud-splattered and totally inappropriate. We should be wearing wet suits, snorkels and flippers.

On the way to the festival Tori's kind of spacey, even for her. A couple of times the driver asks her a question – and it's always *her*, because she's the one with the exotic accent and a presumed knowledge of everything American, from cowboys to tornadoes to Wall Street – and I have to nudge her back into the real world to answer. As we show our passes and walk into the festival site, I ask her if she's OK.

'Something is bugging me,' she replies. 'A thought I had. But . . .' She trails off and doesn't sound like she's going to add anything.

'Is it about Albie?' I take out the cell phone I've put in my pocket just for appearances, my handy Jo accessory. 'Did you hear from him again?' I didn't. I considered replying to his messages to Jo but really, what could I say? So I left it.

'Hmm? Oh.' Tori squints at the miraculously bright sun. 'Clyde had better remember to apologize at the end of rehearsal or I'm so going to be on his case.'

It is the most unsubtle subject change I've ever heard, and it makes me suspect she *was* thinking about Albie. Maybe she's remembered something about him and this other girl? I decide to let it slide for now – we're nearly at the rehearsal barn anyway. We're also about three quarters of an hour late for an hour-long session, so Clyde could actually have a reason to be annoyed with me.

Then I stop thinking about all this stuff because I keep passing people with identical photo-printed T-shirts. Something about the photo looks familiar, so I look closer and— Oh.

Oh no.

It's Jo, mid-writhe, pants aglow. It's the picture from

yesterday, plastered all over people's chests, under the name and year of the festival.

Yay, Rachel! Way to swap into someone's body and totally turn them into an underwear model. I'm so doomed, whichever body I'm in.

Then one of the T-shirt wearers stops me, saying, 'It's you, isn't it? It is! It is!' She turns to her crowd. 'Hey, everyone, what did I tell you? It's Glow-Pants Girl!'

'Wow, it is, it really is! Glow-Pants Girl! You're a star!'

The first one holds a camera phone out and takes a picture of me, even though I'm pretty covered up right now.

'My mate's so putting this all over Facebook on Monday,' another one says. 'You're a minor celebrity! Totally Z-list!'

'Uh . . . thanks,' I say. 'I think.'

Tori's just looking stunned. 'Come on, Josie,' she says, and we leave the T-shirt crowd behind.

The first thing I notice when we walk into the rehearsal barn is an overpowering smell of damp wood and sawdust. The next is that Tamber and Clyde stop rehearsing the minute they see us.

Though really the only thing I notice is that David isn't here.

'Jo! You made it,' Tamber says, getting up from behind his drums.

'So did Tori,' I tell him.

'Hi, guys!' Tori calls, sitting on the wooden bench and taking her manicure kit out of her purse.

Tamber goes bright red, mutters 'Hi,' and sits back down.

'No David?' I ask as casually as I can manage.

'He already left,' Clyde says. 'He said he wrote the article yesterday and he didn't need any more from us after all. He had to go prepare for some secret mega-interview with Topaz.'

Tamber makes a face at Clyde, and then the two of them begin some kind of wordless conversation that mainly consists of glaring at each other and making a variety of little head movements. I think it has some-thing to do with David until Clyde puts down his guitar and moves awkwardly towards me, picking up some-thing from the bench on the way.

It's a box of Fair Trade chocolates, lightly mud-flecked and clearly festival-bought.

'Ah, these are for y-you,' he stutters. 'To say, ah . . . s-s—'

'Sorry,' Tamber prompts him, walking up to Tori and holding out an identical box. 'And these are . . . ah . . . for you because . . . I thought. You know. I thought . . . Chocolates.'

Tori looks up and takes them eagerly. 'Oh, hey! You thought right! Now I don't have to eat all of Josie's.' She smiles at me. 'Just half.'

Tamber stares at the ground and mumbles something about wanting to get flowers too but they didn't sell them and they didn't have time to go off-site. Then he looks up at me and says, 'Hey, I'm sorry about yesterday too. I mean, about what Clyde said.'

Clyde gives him a funny look, but I grin as I remember that 'giving chocolates and flowers' was definitely on Tori's list of what she looks for in a man. And so was 'someone who admits he's made a mistake and apologizes'. Oh, and 'a guy who's kind to my friends'.

Yeah, I see what's going on here.

'I'm going to eat mine right now,' Tori says, oblivious. 'All that describing parts of the States I've never visited to the cab driver has made me hungry.'

Weirdly, the mention of the word 'hungry' makes my stomach rumble again, like it did in the night. It feels like my whole stomach's shifting about. Then it does that loud gurgle thing it was doing all night. I look around sheepishly.

Everyone is pretending they didn't hear – or maybe they really didn't. Tori's sitting on the bench eating chocolates and Clyde and Tamber are back at their instruments, and they're nodding in my direction like I'm suppose to join in.

I ignore my stomach and reach for the microphone. I open my mouth . . . and all that comes out is a giant burp.

And I mean *giant*. It feels like it goes on for ever, in slow motion, amplified by the microphone.

Clyde stops playing his guitar and forgets he's supposed to be nice to me. 'You gotta be kidding me.'

'Uh . . . are you OK, Josie?' Tori asks.

'Guess we can hear Jo over the guitar today,' Tamber comments, and then clamps his mouth shut like he's trying not to laugh.

Clyde just laughs.

'Guys, please,' Tori says sternly. 'Josie is really going out of her way to do this for you.'

Tamber and Clyde straighten their faces.

Tori turns to me. 'Josie, don't worry. You'll be OK,' she says reassuringly. 'You're among friends. It won't be like the . . . you know. The embarrassing incident. The one that started the performance phobia.'

I open my mouth to say thanks, but all that comes out is another burp.

This is all Mom's fault! What is *in* those drinks, and how does having gas improve my mental health?

'What embarrassing incident? What happened?' Tamber asks through gritted teeth.

'She doesn't want to talk about it,' Tori says protectively.

'Or belch about it,' Clyde says, and he and Tamber avoid each other's eyes and make snuffling sounds.

The guys are right. I'm scared to open my mouth right

now, even though I'm starting to see the funny side. I give Tori a look and various hand-signals that I hope say, *Go ahead and tell them, I don't mind*. I don't. I'd kind of like to hear this too.

'You sure?' Tori says, understanding me immediately like the friend it turns out she is, and I nod. 'Well, OK. Guys, Josie was in a school play when she was about twelve and she was, like, a beast or a dog, or whatever. It was some mystery thing called *Hound of the Basket Case*, right?'

I nod again. I know that title's wrong but I don't dare to open my mouth. Then Tamber the wannabe English major steps in for me, saying, '*Hound of the Baskervilles?* Sherlock Holmes?'

Tori clicks her fingers. 'Yeah, that's it. So she has this really important role, being the hound and all, but it involves hanging around in the wings for practically the whole play, which is kind of boring. So she's swinging the long tail of her costume around ... You sure you don't mind?'

I shake my head. This might be good.

'OK, so she swings this tail right into the male lead, this guy she has a massive seventh-grade crush on, and he's not looking because he's busy pretending to smoke a pipe or something. So he trips over it onto the stage and crashes into the rest of the cast, and it's during a crowd scene. It sets off a chain reaction, like dominoes.

187

There's a long line of kids, and some even fall off the stage into the audience.' Tori looks at me. 'Sure I should say the next part?'

I nod. I can just picture Jo causing something like that.

'But the worst thing was the way her teacher totally calls her on it. He shouts, "Josephine Reilly, stop *playing with yourself* back there!" like that, in front of everyone – including, like, a thousand parents and her whole class, not to mention the crush-boy. The whole world laughs, and that's it. She's had stage-fright ever since. Isn't that right, Josie?'

I nod, slightly horrified on behalf of Jo.

'And that's why it's so great that she got over it with the Glow-Pants thing, and why it's so kind of her to do this for you.'

Tori's looking serious, but Clyde and Tamber are like total fourth-graders now, going red in the face and sniffing with stifled laughter.

'It's not funny. Is it, Josie?'

'Errrp,' I say, only it goes on a lot longer than that.

Clyde snorts.

Then my stomach rumbles extremely loudly, and Tori casts her eyes innocently upward. 'Must be thunder.'

Tamber finally explodes with laughter, then he stops himself and says to me, 'I was only laughing at Tori's joke, I swear.'

'It wasn't a joke,' Tori says.

Tamber looks worried.

I smile, because you know what? It was on the list – a boy who laughs at Tori's jokes. Also, come on, this *is* extremely funny. And it's cute the way these guys are trying so hard to be nice.

My stomach rumbles again. 'Bollocks,' I say, drawing on my British vocabulary. Only it comes out as half-burp, half-word, sounding more like 'burp-locks'.

'Oh, you mean like Burp-locks and the Three Bears?' Tamber asks.

'No, like Burp-lock Holmes.' I finish off with another burp.

Clyde snorts. Tamber snuffles and then even Tori joins in. They all laugh in kind of a wave, where they stop themselves, compose their faces, and then one of them starts again and sets the others off. After a while I'm laughing too, interspersed with the occasional burp.

'Stop it, guys, this isn't helping!' I complain, clutching my stomach, though actually I seem to be feeling better and – woo – I managed to say a whole sentence.

'Oh no!' Clyde says, looking at his man-watch and sobering up. 'Rehearsal time's practically over!' He frowns. 'The concert's tomorrow. What are we going to do?'

'We'll get by,' Tamber says, all laughed out at last. 'Jo, dude, you're an inspiration. Half the battle of playing a crowd like that is overcoming the fear of it. We'll get through it, even if Albie doesn't make it back. As long as you don't, uh, have gas like today.' He snickers.

'I'm all better now!' I point out, trying to ignore the fact that the guys seem increasingly resigned to Albie not coming back. I'd better practise in the shower tonight or something. Help!

Tori says earnestly, 'I won't let her eat all that cholesterol at the hotel tomorrow.'

'Hey! I'll eat what I want,' I protest, but I'm loving this really. I feel like I'm one of them. I've never felt this comfortable in a group of kids I barely know.

Clyde turns his laughter into a hound-like howl and Tamber slaps him on the back to shut him up.

The guys pack up and we leave, joking and laughing.

And we run right into Hailey, who is dressed as a fairy, complete with white tutu and glitter wings. It's a look that really doesn't go with her sneakers, or the way she's fuming from head to toe.

Oh no, I totally forgot about Hailey. Again.

'Oh, there you are.' She glares at me. 'David told me you'd be here. So what happened to you yesterday?' It's an accusation, not a question. 'You don't have to tell me, I saw the billboards.' She glances at the others and loses some of the attitude. 'Oh, hi, everyone. Yeah. Anyway, I was just out for a run. Have a nice festival!'

She strides away, breaking into a galloping run that makes her glitter-wings flap like she actually might take off any second. Then she stops by a plastic tree in the distance and starts doing stretches, not looking back at us.

So she tracked me down (through David?) just so she could get mad at me and then leave before I could defend myself? That's really annoying.

It's the kind of thing *I* would do. Rachel, I mean.

We all stare at her and the boys shift about uncomfortably.

'She's just attention-seeking,' Tori says.

'Mmm,' I say, though I hate it when people say things like that about me-Rachel. It's like the way my mom says I have 'anger *issues*', as if I don't have a right to be angry.

'Though it kind of sounds like you had plans with her,' Tori says slowly. 'I mean, that sucks, if she was waiting for you.'

'I guess I . . . forgot.'

Tori shrugs. 'OK. See you later, then.'

'Huh?'

'Duh, Josie.' Tori gives a little smile. 'I think you'd better go after her, don't you? Don't worry about me. I'll hang with the guys.'

She links her arm through Tamber's and he looks like he's going to die.

HAILEY AND HEATHER

'Uh . . . Hailey, hey. I—'

'Oh, hi, celebrity stranger,' Hailey says, putting her weight on one leg and puffing slightly. 'Did you decide I was cool enough to talk to after all? Had enough of Taaah-ri?' She says Tori's name in a squeaky, falsetto voice which I guess is supposed to sound American, though it really doesn't. Her American accent might possibly be as bad as my British one used to be. 'Aaaaaaah-some, you know. It's fine. Don't mind me. Never mind that we said we'd track down Topaz together. You've obviously got more important things to do, like flash your knickers.'

I have to fight real hard not to get angry and storm off. 'Look, Hailey, I'm . . . you know. Things are weird right now.' I take a deep breath. 'I'm s—'

Argh, I'm as bad as Clyde! This shouldn't be so hard. Anyway, she's right to be angry. Even though she's Jo's friend, not mine, it was *me* who totally forgot about her!

'I'm sorry.'

She changes leg and stretches in silence for what feels like ages. Then she jumps up and says, 'Yeah. Well. It's OK. You should still know that you were bang out of order, though.'

'I, ah, know that,' I mumble uncertainly, watching as Tori, Tamber and Clyde wander off into the festival crowds.

'Good.' She starts jogging on the spot, fairy wings shaking. 'Because now you're staying in the lap of B&B luxury and I'm bloody uncomfortable in that tent, and you don't even go Topaz-hunting with me, and I've spent half the time hanging around with your Boston friend David, who I can tell is bloody sick of me—'

'There's no way David's sick of you.'

'He is. He's just too lovely to say so. Or too distracted. You can barely talk to him – it's like his mind's on another planet.'

'Well, yeah, I guess he's working.'

She gives a short laugh. 'Doesn't look like working to me. Looks like full-on moping. Loads of staring into space looking like his true love has dumped him. And that's when he's here! He's been backwards and forwards to that hospital tons of times.'

Oh. 'To see Rachel?'

Her look says, *Well, duh.* 'Except her mum won't let her see him.'

'No, my mom—' Mom likes David. She thinks he's 'good for me', which would put me right off if I didn't mostly agree with her.

'Your mum? Isn't she still in Paris?'

'Uh . . . yeah.'

'You might as well have gone with her after all, the amount I've seen you. Honestly, I wish I'd invited my running club mates, or even bloody Grant – at least I'd have someone to hang around with. I feel like a proper Billy No-Mates.'

'Huh?' Hailey's quick-fire British is starting to give me a headache.

'First I see pictures of you everywhere, dancing half naked, and then David tells me you're singing with Madison Rat! I mean, what the hell, Jo?' Surprisingly, she smirks. 'Have you got over *Baskervilles*-gate at last?'

'Yeah, I guess. Look, I'm real sorry about—'

'God, you sound more American every day.' She breaks into a full-on smile. 'So what have you been up to with Taaah-ri?' she asks. 'Did you talk to *her* about . . . you know. You and Albie?'

'No, not really.'

She looks weirdly relieved. 'Oh, OK then. Well, you can talk to me, you know.'

'I, uh, know.'

Should I tell her about Albie's texts and the photo? But how can I talk about someone else's personal

194

life? I have enough trouble talking about my own.

Jeez, being Jo isn't half as easy as I thought it would be.

'It's just, you know, I get the feeling you're upset, and you can't keep this stuff bottled up for ever, Jo.'

What stuff? I wish she'd tell me what she knows.

'I wish you'd tell me what's going on,' she says.

Wow, it actually sounds like she doesn't know *anything*. It's so weird – I thought Jo would be one of those girls who shares her problems. And yet her two best friends don't seem to know what's going on in her life.

Hailey jumps up and down on the spot. 'OK, fine, I'm here if you change your mind.' She isn't, though, because as soon as she says that, she sprints away. Then she stops dead in her tracks, turns and runs back. 'Sorry, Jo, just warming up. I am absolutely dying for a run! I know it might look weird at a festival but – well, I don't really care. That bloke over there with the papier-mâché horse's head on looks weirder.'

I look. She's right.

'So – want to run with me?'

'No way! I mean, no thanks. I don't really run.'

She gives me a strange look. 'Yes you do. You've only been training with me since you were twelve. Come on, lightweight.'

It turns out she's right. We head straight for the empty fields surrounding the campsite area, and I find that even in Jo's strange canvas pumps I can keep up with Hailey pretty well. I'm barely breaking a sweat. Hey, at this rate, I could run the Boston Marathon! Mom would like that. She's always telling me that exercise is good for mental health. Though, you know, anything has to be better than her herbal sachets, with fewer side-effects.

Hailey's going on and on about someone called Raj T and someone else called Heather T, and it's good that she doesn't expect much in response because it takes me a while just to work out that they're the names of the Topaz band members. We run across the fields to the outskirts of the festival site, where most of the tents are pitched. The festival crowds seem very far away now and we can only hear strains of music in the distance.

Faced with a colourful cluster of tents of different sizes and shapes, I can't help thinking about my plans to stay here with David. Possibly. Even though he didn't know it.

I wonder which of these is David's tent? Hailey should know, judging by what she said back at the hospital, but I can't exactly ask her. I look around, wishing I had superhero X-ray eyes. I would spot his stuff straight away.

Hailey stops by a small orange tent, puffing a little. 'Home! Well, for people who aren't swanning about in hotels.'

She ducks into the tent and takes out a towel and a

bottle of water. 'Festival shower,' she says. 'Though really I'm waiting for the rain. It can't be far away.'

I laugh and tell her about what happened to me and Tori yesterday.

'She really is an airhead,' Hailey remarks.

'I know, but she's OK too,' I say, and then I feel disloyal to Tori for saying 'I know'. And then disloyal to Hailey for saying Tori's OK. Jo never mentioned her friendships were so complicated.

'If you say so.' She shakes the bottle. 'Want some?'

'No, I'm good.'

'Well, I got extra warm in my fairy outfit. And before you say anything, I know it's naff, all right? I bought it yesterday because I fancied being a fairy for the weekend.'

'I don't think it's, uh . . . naff? People should wear whatever they want.'

She talks over me. 'I mean, it's a festival! Everyone here is pretending to be someone they're not.' She towels her hair a little. 'Yeah, and I've decided to be one of those mega-confident girls who don't care that they've split up with their boyfriends. Like I bet your friend Rachel is.'

Yeah, right. I try to focus on being Jo. 'Oh, are you still feeling, uh, sad about that?' I throw her a sympathetic glance.

She grins. 'Bloody hell, Jo, it's like you've had a brain

197

transplant or something! When did I ever feel *sad* about dumping Grant? No, I mean I'm going to stop feeling *guilty* about it. I bet he's trying to text me right now to ask if I've met anyone else – it's as bad as when we were together! He used to go super-sulky whenever I even talked about how fit Raj T is! It's mad. I mean, rock stars aren't exactly in my league! Though I wouldn't mind . . .' Her face goes dreamy.

My expression must be fairly blank right now but she still adds quickly, 'Oops, sorry, I didn't mean to make you think about Albie. Anyway, I've decided to stop worrying about Grant and have fun. You know, if he really loves me like he says he does, he should set me free! *Free! Free!*' She starts crooning some old song about that at the top of her voice, fairy wings bouncing, and I watch her, smiling. Then she stops and looks at me, all disappointed. 'I'm doing an impression of your mum's singing and you're not cringing? God, you used to be a lot easier to embarrass.' She shakes her head.

'Uh, sorry.' I can't imagine my mom singing at *all*.

She laughs. 'Yeah, I suppose you're Glow-Pants Girl now, not to mention a singing sensation. Why did I even think of apologizing to you for my completely non-exhibitionist fairy costume?'

I'm kind of warming to Hailey. 'I could draw a fairy tattoo on your face if you like?' I offer. 'If you have eyeliner.'

'Er, I don't think so. You're a bit rubbish at art, aren't you?'

Oh, yeah. I'm not Rachel.

'So, hey, can we look for Topaz today? Your mate David can't – or won't – tell me a thing about where they hang out, and I know there isn't a VIP area, but the fan site said they were coming for the whole weekend and they have to be here *somewhere*. I've given up sticking around David in the press office waiting for them to walk in and—'

'Sunday,' I say, a split second before I remember I'm not supposed to tell Hailey. I shrug inwardly – too late. Well, I don't owe David anything. 'He's interviewing them tomorrow after the gig.'

'Oh, wow! Oh, wow! Really? They're doing an interview? Topaz and David?' She starts screeching then, sounding a lot more like Tori than I'd ever have imagined she could. 'Omigod! Omigod! I can't believe you didn't tell me sooner!'

'Oh. Ah, I was going to,' I lie. 'I was waiting to ... uh ...'

'Wow, I was hoping, but I didn't really think they would. This is a huge deal! Topaz almost *never* give interviews.' She beams at me. 'They're always going on about the press being the bane of their lives, ever since that time Heather T trashed Lily Allen on Twitter and it got picked up by the *Herald* – remember? Oh no, you

199

missed it because you were busy being Am-aaaah-rican.' Her accent truly is terrible. 'And none of your American friends have any musical taste.'

'Uh, yeah. No musical taste,' and I just can't keep the sarcasm out of my voice.

'Though, don't get me wrong, Madison Rat are grow-ing on me.' She barely pauses for breath. 'Ooh, there was that quote from Raj T last month about how he wanted to help school-leavers – is that why they've agreed to meet David? Because he's not a proper journo, just a student?'

'Uh,' I say, which seems to be all that's required.

'So this interview's secret, right? This is massive! David is so lucky. I'm so lucky he told you.' She frowns. 'Is there . . . ? No, never mind.'

'No, what?'

She looks at me sideways. 'I mean, you and David . . . You seem to be talking to him a lot and, well, I know you used to fancy him . . .'

'What? I *what*?' I thought I was doing OK with this conversation but suddenly my head is spinning. I also feel slightly nauseous.

'Oh, ancient history – forget I said anything!' She throws her towel into the tent. 'So is David ready for this interview? Does he have everything he needs? Can we, like, get them something so he lets us in to see them? I heard Heather's a total diva and expects presents and stuff. And flowers in her dressing room and bottled water. And a copy of the latest *Goss* magazine.' She frowns. 'Though I read that in *Goss* magazine.'

I try to re-focus away from what Hailey asked about Jo and David. 'Uh . . . he did say he was preparing, but I don't know if he knows all that.'

'Heather!' she exclaims suddenly.

'Huh?'

'Heather! You know, the plant. That field behind the tents is full of it. What if we pick a bunch of heather for him to, you know, give to Heather? She'll love it!'

This sounds like a totally crazy idea. I can't believe how many brain cells Hailey loses when she talks about her favourite band.

'We can collect some tomorrow morning and turn up at his tent with it first thing. Then he'll *have* to let us in on the interview. I'm brilliant.'

Oh. David's tent?

I can't explain exactly why, but I really want to see David's tent.

'Hey, Hailey, what if we get it right now?'

She's jumping up and down on the spot again. 'Right now? Won't it go off or whatever?'

'We could . . . leave it for David.' Then Hailey can show me where David's tent is, even though she thinks I already know. 'And he'll have all night to think about how grateful he is and how you should go to the interview.'

I shift nervously, thinking she won't buy it. But she's too excited to think straight.

'OK!' She skips to a nearby gate, unhooking its latch and calling, 'Let's get that heather for Heather!'

I can't believe I thought Jo's best friends were so different from each other. Hailey's sounding exactly like a British version of Tori Windsor.

On second thoughts, Tori's pretty grounded compared to Hailey right now.

'Wrong field!' I tell her. The one Hailey is headed for has a couple of goats in it, gazing at us as they chew.

'God, sorry, yeah!' Hailey skips away from the wildlife and jumps over a fence into the next field instead. She starts grabbing armfuls of flowers, her fairy wings flapping.

Then she jumps back out and says, 'Come on!'

I pretend I know where she's going as she leads me to David's tent, leaving a heather trail as she walks.

'Heather for Heather,' she giggles, over and over. 'Oh, this is so cool!'

Room 121, The Clarence
Saturday

Rachel's Diary Therapy
by Jo in Rachel's body (IF THIS ISN'T PRIVATE I'M
RUNNING AWAY TO GRETNA GREEN AND
MARRYING THE LOCH NESS MONSTER!)
Conversations with my so-called mother, Part 4

Jo-in-Rachel's-Body: You feeling better today?

My So-Called Mother: Rachel, honey, thank you for
asking. (*Fussing around for about a year with bits
and pieces in my posh hospital room*)

JIRB: Um . . .

(*Not actually saying this*) FYI, thanking me and
then shifting tissue boxes around doesn't really
answer my question.

(*Actually saying this*) Just I was a bit worried
about you after yesterday.

MSCM (*shocked to the very core*): Really?

JIRB (*mentally slapping forehead*): Oh, er. Bloody
hell, Mum, you're so embarrassing, grr. (*Giving up*)
Yes, really. I mean, you know, I think I've been

through something like this before . . . (*Mentally slapping forehead so hard that I nearly mentally fall off the mental bed*) I mean, my friend Jo at school—

MSCM: The nice British girl I met a couple of times?

JIRB (*bingo!*): Yes, her. Isn't she truly lovely? Anyway, it sounds like she might have gone through something similar with *her* mother so maybe some of, er, her experiences could help? Like, for example, there's no harm in showing your feelings in front of your kids. Rachel's (*doh!*) *I'm* old enough to handle it, and it's not like she— *I* don't guess what's going on. I might even be able to help. But mostly I think you need to get your feelings out sometimes. You know, for your own sake.

MSCM (*silence*)

JIRB: Or not.

MSCM (*silence*)

JIRB: Hey, Mum, do they have any good shops near here? I've been dying to get a poster of Spike from *Buffy*.

'End of log. Filed for future analysis.'

BOOTS

'Ugh, it's a bit scratchy!' Hailey sniffs the heather, dropping another bunch of it in the process. 'I hope it's classy enough for Heather T.'

I swallow hard. 'I'll ... I'll find somewhere to put it inside the tent. You know, to keep it fresh.'

'OK, if you want.' She shrugs, handing me the flowers. 'I'm just not sure about it after all. I heard she was really picky.'

'Hmm,' I say, distracted by a weird need to look inside David's tent. Alone. 'Maybe we should put them in water. That water you were using earlier would work.'

'That's a good idea.'

I wait. Then I give up. 'Maybe you should get some water from our tent?'

'Oh yeah, OK. Hold on!'

When her footsteps have faded I step inside the tent, squashing the feeling that I'm spying on him. I was planning to stay here, after all. And we're doing him a favour with this heather, aren't we? I look around.

David hasn't unpacked – there's a small bag with some black T-shirts sticking out – and his sleeping bag is rolled up messily. There's a stack of papers next to it – printouts from the web. On the top is a page with a large picture of the skinny, nerd-tastic Albie, who isn't so perfect after all. His looks are so dark; so different from his blonde adoptive sister. He stands out in his family the same way I do in mine. With the difference that, in my case, my hair is dyed to look as different as possible from certain so-called members of my so-called family.

I put down the heather and flick through the papers. There's a Wikipedia printout about Topaz, which is listed as 'an established indie band with a loyal fanbase'. It consists of 'singer Heather T and her guitarist brother Raj T', as I've been told a million times now by Hailey. The photo shows two people who look kind of familiar – a boy with sleepy eyes and a girl with blunt-cut blonde hair. It's weird to think they're also brother and sister. They're yet another example of how you can be related to someone and be nothing like them.

Then I recognize them. It's Heavy Lids and Stumpy Braids, the annoying guys I ran past before the craziness started, the people who 'didn't like confines'. I can't believe they're in a famous band, but it could explain their super-confidence (aka arrogance) on Thursday. It's funny that I've been face-to-face with musicians I supposedly adore and I didn't even realize. It's a good thing they walked off before Hailey turned up in David's car.

David. I put the papers back. This is all completely stupid. What am I doing here? David's not even in my life any more. Not *my* life anyway. Not Rachel's. And there's not all that much evidence that he's in Jo's life, either, despite what happened on Thursday. I'm not even sure how I feel about that. Being Jo is turning out to be one huge let-down – with added complications.

I start to leave, thinking I'll catch up with Hailey and say I've changed my mind about leaving the heather. I can say it's because of David's allergies – in fact, come to think of it, it's probably not a good idea to leave flowers in his tent anyway. He's probably having enough trouble sleeping in the open air as it is. Like I care, though.

I shouldn't care.

I do care.

Hell.

And then I spot David's boots. *The* boots, with the caricature in silver nail polish on the side, drawn by me. They're in a dark corner, one on its side and both look-ing kind of abandoned and forlorn.

Why are they here – why isn't he wearing them? They

are normally welded to his feet – they're like a part of
him.

No.

They're like a part of *us*.

OUT TO LUNCH

The boots were the second thing I noticed about David on the first day I spoke to him.

Well, they weren't exactly the same pair – Goth boots don't last for ever – but they may as well have been, they were so similar. I've customized every single pair he's bought since then.

The first thing I noticed about David was his hotness. He doesn't have the regular kind of boyish good looks – nothing like the jock types Chelsea Cook and her minions swoon over, and not even anything like the string of cute, pale Lost Boys I used to hook up with occasionally. David is completely, unconventionally stunning. He has grey-green eyes, untamed hair and a smile that can (and does) almost knock me down from a distance. Oh, and he is *built* – but even that isn't it.

I take advanced math classes, and last semester our teacher, Werewolf Wilson – some kind of ultra-hairy genius who loves the sound of his own voice – told us about a statistical theory called 'interaction'. No one was even listening except me – the other guys were mostly busy laughing as David kept up a stream of comments and questions that were actually barely hidden jokes about the Werewolf's back hair, nose hair and palm hair.

Normally I wouldn't listen either, but this time it was like the Hairy One was really making sense. He talked about how you can have two completely unrelated things, like: 1) adding a lump of sugar to your coffee, and 2) stirring the coffee. Each one, done all on its own, doesn't alter the coffee too much. I mean, yeah, the sugar lump alone would dissolve eventually, but it would sit in a cloggy lump at the bottom of your cup. But if you do 1 and 2 together, there's this 'interaction', and there it is – instant sweetness. It's a reaction that's more than a sum of its parts.

I recognized it straight away: that's what happened when I met David.

David was *not* instant sweetness, though. From the moment he walked into the squalid mire of the Mill cafeteria, he exuded anger and aggression. I couldn't take my eyes off him. As he scanned the room, all his body language said: *You* dare *mess with me and you will get it*. We were all freshmen then – all on the lowest rung of the thumbtack-dotted ladder of high school – but he was newer than the rest of us by a whole semester.

Everyone knows newbies are fair game, and arriving

in the second half of the first year has to be just about the worst, with the kids practically baying for flesh, dying to get their own back after being bottom of the pile for months. I knew there were guys who'd want to eat him alive. He knew it too. Everything about David said: *Back off or I will bite back. And it won't be pretty.*

But I saw through it. He was balancing a tray of cafeteria gloop casually in one hand as if he did this every day, his other hand clenched like he really did expect some guy to punch his lights out right there and he was ready to defend himself. He glared at each table of clique-ridden Mill kids in turn, and his Adam's apple bobbed up and down in a way that made me look closer at him. I couldn't yet make out whether he was nervous or just plain arrogant. But I knew he was hot.

So that was the first thing.

The second thing was the boots. His boots. They were sturdy, wild-boy boots, but they looked brand-new, like he was a rich kid going for a tough-guy look; like he was trying too hard. He walked on, past a table of raucously laughing freshmen jocks, taking a couple of weird, shuffling steps as if he was trying to scuff the boots; like he wanted them – and himself – to look less shiny, wealthy and new. Yeah, those boots totally gave him away.

Then I noticed Chelsea Cook was staring at me from two tables over, where she was sitting with the Clone

Gang, which in those days included Tori. The Clone Gang were all perched prettily, avoiding their diet yoghurts, or whatever it is those guys don't eat. But Chelsea was turned entirely towards me.

The way she was looking at me made me certain that she'd been watching me for a while. She'd been watching me watch David.

Her nostrils flared and she looked away. Then she nodded in the direction of the sophomore jocks – Bryce Grierly, Jake Matthews and the rest of her adoring fanbase. They were the guy version of the Clone Gang, the main difference being the amount of food they consumed, which was vast and highly carb-laden.

After that, two things happened at once. Chelsea called out, 'Hey, new guy!' and Bryce stuck out his foot just as David, nearing their table, looked across at Chelsea.

I knew he didn't like her or anything, unlike every other guy in the world. He just looked over because she called out to him; he would have done the same for anyone.

I know it because, after David tripped and sent his tray flying into the lap of Jake Matthews, spilling gloop all over his Abercrombie sweater, Chelsea came over and chirped sweetly, 'Aw, new boy, let me help you out with the cleanup operation.' The whole cafeteria had gone silent at this point, of course, and all eyes were on

Chelsea and the fascinating lunch-time highlight of 'New Guy Getting Tripped', which I'll bet they were all hoping they could Tivo and replay at their leisure.

Chelsea glanced at me as she took a napkin and dabbed prettily at Jake Matthews's chest. Jake Matthews, of course, stared at her open-mouthed like he was in some kind of trance. He probably had no idea what was going on. He usually doesn't.

But David did. He followed Chelsea's sarcastic glance and caught my eye. And he smiled at me.

It made sugar lumps stir in my stomach.

'That's the best I can manage with this rag,' Chelsea said loudly to her audience, folding up the napkin. She smiled sweetly at David. 'Jakey will be OK, don't worry. He'll clean up real good.' She put her head to one side and coyly stage-whispered, so the entire cafeteria could still hear. 'I'm sure *you* would too. Hey, maybe ... uh ...' She twirled a lock of her blonde hair around one finger and giggled like she was shy.

Yeah, *as if*.

She took a deep, dramatic breath. 'Maybe we could go to a burger bar some time, or something.' She shot another glance at me, snapping her gum. Even that looked pretty, coming from her. She moved closer to David. 'If you want.'

There was a rumbling then – the sound of a roomful of people adjusting their assessment of the new guy from 'Total Too-New Boots Freak' to 'Possible Popular Guy'. David could have had it easy. If he'd said yes to Chelsea, he'd never have had to worry about scuffing his boots to look tough. He wouldn't have had to try any more – he'd be in, he'd have it made; no one could make his life hell.

But David, still smiling, took a step away from Chelsea.

'I'm a vegetarian,' he said in his clipped, gorgeous British accent. It was the first time I heard it and it sounded awesome, but not as awesome as what he said. 'I don't like burger bars. Besides, a burger bar is no place for a *cow*.' He plucked a fry from Bryce Grierly's plate and put it in his mouth. 'No offence, I didn't mean *you*. Necessarily. Anyway, thanks for the chip.'

The cafeteria exploded into chatter. Even Lenny on the table behind me, a loner who was rarely out of detention and basically slept all day, lifted his head for long enough to stare at David and mutter, 'He's so dead, man.'

David walked away from Chelsea, in my direction.

'I was kidding anyway!' Chelsea shouted after him. 'Ha! He fell for it. He's a joke!'

Back then, I hadn't invented what I call 'the Cookie Cutter' yet – my vast collection of comebacks for Chelsea Cook's insults, to me and to other kids. Before, I just used to take it. But after David called Chelsea a cow, everything changed for me. If I heard Chelsea say

214

anything mean – about anyone – I talked right back, every time. It didn't always stop her but it made me feel better. Never mind herbal sachets – getting at Chelsea was the best thing ever for my mental health. I wish I could explain that to Mom.

David kept right on walking until he reached my table. Then he stopped in front of me.

I turned slowly to face him as if I was doing him a massive favour even by glancing at him, when really my insides were dancing.

Until Chelsea screeched out, 'Omigod, don't sit with *her*! She's a lesbian *freak*. Everybody knows that! If you speak to her, you'll be as bad as her! Loser!'

I looked down and concentrated on shifting my stuff around as if I didn't care that David was most likely going to walk right away from me now. I couldn't blame him. I'd have done the same. High school is all about survival, and Lenny had the right idea: David was on his way to being *so dead*. But he still had a chance, with looks like his. He could scrub up good, just like Chelsea suggested. With the right words, he could still just about save this situation for himself – at least among the guys, who would probably kind of admire him for what he said. He could turn his insult to Chelsea into an in-joke for the males of the in-gang.

Right across the cafeteria, breath was bated, waiting to see what the new guy would do next.

'Hey, that's no problem,' David said idly into the rubbernecking silence. 'I think I might be a lesbian, anyway. I mean, I *really* like girls.'

He smiled at me again.

I didn't think he meant *me*, and he showed pretty soon that he didn't, though a while back he told me he'd always been attracted to me and he just didn't think *I* was into *him*. Which I find totally incredible.

He pulled out the chair next to me. 'Mind if I sit here?'

I hesitated, glancing over to where Chelsea Cook was glaring at us.

He sat down exactly two seconds before I said, 'I guess not.'

That made him laugh, which started the chatter in the cafeteria. It was official: the new guy was friends with the freak girl and not worth knowing.

'Pleased to meet you,' he said, sounding formal and ultra-British. 'I'm David, and I'm a freak. And you are?'

'Also a freak,' I replied. 'Or you could call me Rachel.'

He nodded in the direction of the Clone Gang. 'So, Rachel, I take it those guys aren't your best friends?'

'You could say that. Or you could say they're assholes.'

'I wouldn't say that,' he said seriously.

My heart sank. Was he going to defend them?

'No, I'd say they were *arse*holes,' he continued, correcting me. 'I've had it with arseholes. You know, I totally kick arsehole *butt,* only in England they call it arsehole *posterior.'*

'No they don't.' I felt the corners of my mouth twitch upward.

He nodded seriously. 'Yeah they do. I kicked so much *arsehole posterior* at my last school that I got thrown out, only in England they call it "excluded".'

'No you didn't,' I said. He was a superhero for bad-mouthing Chelsea on his first day, but that didn't mean I was going to take any macho bravado from him.

He smiled. 'You're right, I didn't. We just moved here for my dad's job. But I *was* bullied at my last school and it was hell. And I just *wish* I'd kicked their arses, but I mostly got *my* arse kicked instead.' He bunched his hands into fists. 'So we should take this lot on together. What do you reckon?' His eyes sparkled at me. 'We could get excluded together. Exclusively.'

'Shut up,' I said, and I laughed.

He looked at me, right into my eyes. 'I mean it, though. I'm not scared, and you shouldn't be either.'

'I'm not scared,' I told him. But then I ruined it by glancing nervously over at the door, where Chelsea and her clones were now leaving in a flurry of indignant hair-flipping.

'Remember they're *nothing* to us,' David added. 'Really you shouldn't even hate them.' He warmed to his theme. 'Hatred is a waste of energy. Besides, if you

217

hate someone, you're showing you care. What you need in a case like this is indifference. Says my shrink.'

I tried desperately not to sound too interested. 'You have a shrink?'

'I've got a mum who fancies herself as a shrink. She runs my life.'

'Oh.' Jesus, the way he spoke was adorable. 'Yeah, me too.' Though even then, way before I met his super-kind mom, I was fairly sure she couldn't be anything like mine. She'd have no reason to be. David was a rebel without a screw loose. I'd never met anyone saner than him.

'I mean, it's not like I ever listen to a word my mum says,' David back-tracked, which was sort of cute. 'But she could be right about the indifference thing.'

'Maybe,' I said. And then something about the way he looked at me made me want to be completely truthful. 'I mean, you're right that most of them are nothing to me,' I said. 'But the truth is . . . Chelsea Cook? The one you called a cow before?'

He smiled.

'Well, I *do* hate her. I *really* hate her. I will hate her for ever.'

He raised his eyebrows and didn't say another word about emotions or shrinks. He just waited for me to talk, to explain why I'd basically just admitted that I cared about Chelsea.

I couldn't. I'd decided long before that I'd never tell anyone, and it was ingrained in me now.

So after a silence he said, 'Oh, right. You know, she kept on looking at you just now. Helped me notice you quicker.' He smiled. 'I got the impression she's dead jealous of you.'

I came close to snorting my drink out of my nostrils. I cursed instead. 'Chelsea's not jealous of anyone. Least of all *me*.'

'If you say so.' He shrugged like he didn't agree, and then he started chatting casually about other stuff, like school and teachers and life back in England.

Five minutes into his comfortable conversation, a group of honour student sophomore misfits (though, let's face it, most of us honour students are misfits) approached our table. They were all girls. One of them asked if David was OK while the other two gazed at him in open admiration. But they were honour students so they weren't just going to stare and giggle at his hotness and his accent. Instead, they all sat down and started talking intelligently about the world economic crisis and 'how it's tackled differently by our respective countries'. A few minutes into that conversation I realized I'd totally lost David. He beamed smiles at the girls and cracked clever jokes that made them laugh and, if I was honest, would normally have made me laugh too. But instead, after everything that had happened, it made me tilt my chair back and tap the table where Lenny was snoozing into his eggplant parmesan sub.

'So, Lenny,' I said, startling his eyes into opening, 'you wanna hook up sometime?'

David looked over for a second and kind of breathed in deeply, but within seconds he was back to the clever joking.

Lenny made an effort to raise his head and slur, 'Sure.'

I leaned over and scribbled my number on a napkin for him, keeping my ears tuned to David as he asked out the prettiest of the honour students, who was now pushing her glasses up her nose, staring and giggling at him after all.

My relationship with Lenny, if you can call it that, lasted about twenty seconds, but David dated that sophomore for well over a week before the next bright, pretty girl came along. And, of course, I hooked up with a bunch of other guys too, on and off, over the next couple of years. But me and David were always there for each other: I looked out for him and he made school bearable for me again. We hung out all the time. We were always together in spite of all the others. What we had was better than any of that: we were best friends. And then we were more.

So there it all was:

1) David's hotness;

2) His boots;

3) His reaction to Chelsea Cook;

4) The way he made me laugh;

5) The way he was a perfect friend.

A few ingredients. One 'interaction'.

And I realized it in Werewolf Wilson's math class. The way I feel about David is more than a sum of its parts.

I'm pretty sure it's what some people call 'love'.

It took me nearly three years to admit this to myself. I never did manage to admit it to him.

And now I have to admit it's over.

I pick up one of David's boots and trace the outline of the cartoon I drew on it. As I turn it in my hand, I instinctively reach for the secret compartment – the coffin-shaped hole where I used to leave sketches for him.

There's something stuck in there now. I prise it out. It's a memory stick. It has to be important to him if he's hidden it there. My mind is full of David and not much else as I slip it into one of Jo's pockets.

I leave the flowers where they are, wipe a tear on Jo's arm and go find Hailey.

MORE MUD

When I emerge from the tent, Hailey's standing outside holding a bottle of water and awkwardly shifting from foot to foot.

'You OK?' she asks.

'How long have you been standing there?' I snap. I feel like being Rachel again – I mean, I don't feel like being nice.

'Long enough,' Hailey snaps right back. 'I heard you crying.'

'I wasn't crying!'

'OK, I heard you sniff, once, pathetically.' Then her voice softens. 'Honestly, Jo, if you're going to sit not-crying in a tent, why not make it ours? I could at least . . . I don't know . . . stand about feeling all helpless because you won't bloody talk to me about what's wrong. Which is what I've been doing anyway.'

This makes me smile, just a little.

'You're still not going to tell me, are you?' she asks

with an exasperated sigh. She rolls her eyes before I can even answer and holds out the water. 'For the flowers. Did you find somewhere to put them?'

I nod. I don't want to go back in there now – I don't want to think about the memory stick, or the way I'm causing trouble. I'm a discord-spreading superhero who wants to run away from the scene of the crime.

'I don't think we'll need the water after all.'

'Oh, OK. So are we going to go and tell David?' Her eyes light up. 'We're doing him a massive favour, don't you think? Heather will be so happy! And then Raj T might say— Oh my God, what are those people doing?'

I bring myself out of my daze. 'What? Why would Raj T say that?' And now *I* sound like Tori.

'Over there! Look.'

On a patch of land that's not covered by tents, probably because it's on a slight slope, are small heaps of what look like blankets. But then I realize the blankets contain people. They're rolling around on the still-muddy earth in fits of laughter, encased in sleeping bags.

And inside are some familiar-looking people. I spot some of the girls who rescued us yesterday, plus a few others, and also Clyde and Tori.

'Jo!' Tori squeals from a heap of blue.

'It's Glow-Pants Girl again!' says someone from another sleeping bag.

Tori calls over, 'Yay! I'm so glad you found us! Oh, yeah, and you, Hailey. We were looking for you when we bumped into the girls and— Aargh!' She flails about, proving that the blanket is tied around her sleeping bag so tightly that she's mummified in there. She wriggles on the ground and laughs. 'Wait – first go back to your tents and get your sleeping bags! I've borrowed Tamber's.'

I look again and see Tamber standing on the outskirts of all the action, the only person who's not joining in whatever craziness Tori and Clyde and our random rescuers from yesterday are getting up to. He sees me and waves.

We walk over to get a closer look.

'What are you doing?' Hailey asks Tori, clearly too bewildered to remember to be hostile.

'Human-snail racing, of course!' Tori giggles. 'You have to get in a sleeping bag and, you know, race each other like snails. Hurry up if you want to join in – the next race is about to start! I've already lost three times. I am caked in mud – again! And I don't even care! I'm just so rock and roll now!' She wiggles away, laughing.

Hailey scoffs, 'She doesn't care because her clothes are protected by someone else's sleeping bag!'

I snicker. 'Yeah, I think you're right.'

Then Clyde rolls towards us in his sleeping bag. 'Hey, Jo,' he says. 'And Hailey, yeah?'

'Yeah! Hi!' Hailey replies brightly. 'I love your music! Look, sorry about before, you know, outside the rehearsal barn. I was, you know . . .'

'Hey, no problem,' Clyde says easily. 'Good to see you guys are cool now.' He shuffles away towards some of the others. They all look completely ridiculous, like enormous cloth-covered slugs who have forgotten the basic principles of physical movement.

Hailey stares after them. 'So what do you reckon, Jo?' she says quietly. 'We can go and see David later, can't we? That heather's not going anywhere.'

'Yeah, I guess.' Maybe I don't want to see him after all. I don't know.

She kicks her trainers on the ground a little. 'So . . . about that guitarist?'

'Clyde?'

'Yeah. What do you know about him? You never mentioned him much.' She gives me an innocent, not-that-interested look that doesn't fool me for a second.

Oh my God, I do not believe this. 'Hailey, do you lust after *any* guy who plays a guitar?'

'Course not.' She starts counting on her fingers. 'I also fancy lots of actors, male models, TV presenters, singers . . .' She frowns. 'Well, obviously not Albie, or . . . you know. I can't think of many showbiz guys I specifically don't fancy, offhand. But, see, not just *any-one*!' She grins. 'Anyway, I don't want a relationship or

225

anything right now, not after escaping from the jealous clutches of Grant. You know?'

'Sure.'

'Right, so . . . about Clyde . . .'

I sigh. What *do* I know about Clyde, in the way Hailey means? 'OK, well, I'm pretty sure he doesn't have a girl-friend,' I say slowly.

She nods encouragingly. 'Good, good. Anything else?'

'And, well . . .' It feels highly weird saying this. 'Tamber says he had a crush on Rachel when he was a kid. But he's totally over it now,' I add hurriedly, as it makes me feel a bit guilty.

'Really?' Hailey does an excited little jump. 'Excellent. From what I've heard, I'm a lot like Rachel.'

'No you're not,' I blurt, because, seriously, that jump? So not me-Rachel. Like, at *all*.

Hailey pouts. 'Rubbish – I am! You always say she can be a bit bolshy and slightly scary and doesn't take any crap from anyone. Well, you know that's like me!' She thinks. 'I mean, obviously I'm not a Goth or anything, but then Clyde isn't either.'

'Neither is Rachel. She's . . .' Oh, forget it. 'Anyway, I thought you said you didn't want a relationship?'

'I don't. I want some harmless flirting. Come on, let's get our sleeping bags!'

I make a show of dragging my feet behind her. Though really I'm surprised by how happy I am to see

Tori and the guys again and how much I just want to hang with them all, messing around and not thinking about David or Mom or all the injustice in the world. You know, not thinking about Rachel stuff.

Hailey and Clyde flirt harmlessly with each other and I win three human-snail races in a row.

SHEEP AND GOATS

After we've dumped the muddy sleeping bags in our tents, we all wander back into the thick of the festival. Tamber, Clyde and the girls decide to head for the main stage. Tori says she'll go with them and looks expectantly at me, but Hailey says, 'We need to go and talk to David about something, don't we, Jo?'

'Uh . . .' I say.

'It's important,' Hailey says in what is actually a slightly scary way. It's probably also a bit bolshy. So maybe she's right about being like Rachel after all, except that I have a feeling her confidence is more genuine and less a result of rebuilding herself after being completely demolished in seventh grade.

I wait for Tori to fight back but she's clearly still high on giggles because she just shrugs and says, 'OK, why don't you find us later,' and then goes off with the others.

Hailey chats on and on about Clyde and Raj T all the way to the press office, where I suddenly start to panic.

Will it be a problem for David's job if Hailey barges in and starts fangirling about flowers and Topaz, right in front of all his serious press buddies?

As she goes up to the security guard at the door, I call out, 'Hailey, don't—' but she doesn't listen, and anyway, I manage to stop myself.

What am I *doing*, caring about David's image or his music journalism career? What am I doing caring about David *at all*? I'm supposed to be ErisGrrl and wreaking terrible revenge on him – revenge that I can get away with because I'm in Jo's body – and yet all I'm doing is worrying about people seeing him in a very very slightly bad light?

I remind myself that I've left heather in his tent and it makes me feel a little better. And also worse at the same time.

I stand back and watch as Hailey talks to someone at the door of the press office. He seems to know who she is – I guess because she's been hanging out with David a lot.

I spot Tori's cousin Brad leaving the beer barn next door, laughing with a group of guys.

Then David appears in the doorway and my heart lurches at the sight of him, zooming between murderous thoughts and wanting to fling myself at him right here, right now. It's *crazy*. And it's not like I can even turn to herbal sachets as a cure.

David starts talking to Hailey, not smiling and barely glancing in my direction. I take a step forward. He has new boots on. They look a lot like the ones I saw at the T-shirt stall with Tori yesterday. They don't look as cool as his other boots, and they're un-illustrated and too clean-looking: they need to be scuffed. Like before we were friends. His eyes are red-rimmed so his hay fever must be flaring up. As Hailey speaks, he's nodding with the kind of enthusiasm he shows when he's given extra assignments at school.

I get closer.

'We thought we could help you out,' Hailey is explaining. 'We collected some heather – for Heather, get it?'

Oh jeez, it sounds ridiculous when you put it like that. Though I don't know on which planet it would sound like a sane plan.

'Oh, thanks,' David mumbles, glancing at me with slight annoyance, maybe because I didn't keep his Topaz secret. 'Yeah, that's . . . thoughtful,' he adds. 'But I'm sorry, it's gone. Everything in my tent has.'

Brad and his friends move closer and stand about in a group, chatting and laughing.

'What, you mean someone nicked your stuff?' Hailey gasps. 'God, I've been thinking it feels really safe here.'

'No, not stolen,' David says dully. 'It was ransacked by an animal – a goat. I don't know why it picked on me.

I just found it there, chewing up half my tent, my clothes and even my old boots.'

'But when?' Hailey frowns. 'We were at your tent earlier and we didn't see any goat, did we, Jo?'

I shake my head. Well, apart from the field full of goats Hailey nearly went into.

Where she unlatched the gate and . . . I don't remember her fastening the latch again.

David shrugs. 'Normally I'd at least have my memory stick in, um, a safe place so it's with me all the time, but yesterday I decided I needed a change.' He stares at his feet. His new boots are all wrong. I can tell these don't have a coffin-shaped compartment. 'So, anyway, I was going off-site to visit the hospital and send some stuff, and I remembered I didn't have the memory stick, and I went back to the tent to get it and that's when I found the goat. Oh, and I saw you lot too, rolling about in your sleeping bags.'

'We were human-snail racing,' Hailey explains. 'You should have joined us.'

David frowns. 'I was busy wrestling with this goat. I managed to get it back into the field I'm pretty sure it came from. The gate was swinging open and there was a trail of half-chewed plant-life leading back there.'

Hailey shoots me a guilty glance.

Brad detaches himself from his group of friends and looks in our direction.

David doesn't pay any attention to Brad or Hailey. 'But then I wished I hadn't got the goat back in its field. Because now I don't know which one it is.'

'Yeah, but why would you need to know?' I ask. 'Are you planning on having it arrested for trespass?'

There's almost – almost – a flicker of a smile on David's lips at that, but it's gone in a split second. 'It's not funny, Jo. Yeah, the goat chewed all my clothes and my bedding and everything, but it's worse than that. I think it may have actually swallowed my memory stick. With all my work on it.'

My hand moves instinctively to my pocket but I don't say anything.

Hailey gasps, 'Oh no!'

Brad calls, 'Hey!' He stops right behind us, staring at me.

'So I thought I'd try to get it back,' David says.

Hailey's eyes widen. 'You mean . . .'

'I've lost everything. I mean, I had some scribbled notes, but half of them were chewed up too, and nearly everything was on that memory stick. So I thought it might be worth waiting and . . . you know. Sometimes you need to wade through some . . .'

'Sheep,' I suggest, but I pronounce it more with an 'i' in the middle and a 't' instead of a 'p' at the end.

'Yeah, you know. To get to what you want.'

Hailey gasps. 'Nooooo! You mean you'd wait

for the goat to . . . ? And you'd . . . ? That's revolting!'

Brad walks over, still looking at me. 'Hey, I know you! You're Josie, aren't you?'

'She's Jo,' Hailey corrects.

'Yeah, that's it. You're Albie's girl. I've seen about a hundred pictures of you at his senior prom. Boy, my cousin is crazy about you. I'm Bradford Windsor. It's great to meet you at last!'

'Good to meet you too,' I say politely as Brad introduces himself to Hailey and David as well. It's so weird, acting as if I didn't travel all the way here with him.

'So, hey . . .' Brad says. 'How's Tori? Haven't seen her for a while. And I haven't seen Albie at all. I'm supposed to be keeping an eye on them, you know. I'm the responsible big cousin here.' He laughs irresponsibly. 'Now listen, I just got to ask if I'm hearing you correctly. You're talking about examining goat crap? Is that, like, yet another crazy British festival thing, like the worm-charming I did earlier?'

'A goat ate his homework.' I'm heavy on the sarcasm and even heavier on the curse words as I explain the situation to Brad.

David looks at me, kind of shocked, but with a tiny hint of a twitch around his lips again – as if he's fighting a smile.

'Awesome!' Brad says. 'I mean, that's disgusting, but also awesome! Would you seriously do that?'

233

David shakes his head. 'It's not worth it. In fact, you know what? I've realized there's no point. My Madison Rat piece needs to be changed anyway if the lineup for the big concert is different.' The look he gives me this time is totally blank. 'And all the articles on the memory stick were finished but I can't write them again. I can't concentrate right now. On anything. It's just not working out.' His voice goes quiet. 'I'm thinking of giving up and going home.'

'You can't do that!' Hailey says. If she was in a graphic novel, there would be a thought bubble above her head right now containing a picture of Topaz, or at least of Raj T. It would be heart-shaped.

Brad looks disappointed, though he's probably still thinking about the boyish awesomeness of examining goat droppings.

'You can't,' I agree with Hailey, thinking of . . . I don't know. He just can't give up. I know this placement means a lot to him. I brush Jo's pocket with my elbow. The memory stick is still there – I could drop it near his tent, make it obvious so he'll see it. Or I could give it to him right now and tell him I found it. Why would he suspect me of anything bad?

But the thought bubble above *my* head still holds the memory of him kissing Jo. And it has spiky edges.

Yeah, I'm mixed up all right.

David sighs. 'I haven't even got anywhere to sleep. My tent's trashed.'

'You can buy stuff here,' Hailey tells him. 'I've seen it. You can't just go home!'

'I've got no money. I spent it all yesterday.' He looks at his too-new boots. 'No, I don't know . . .'

Brad pulls a key out of his pocket. 'Hey! You can stay in the room my uncle booked.' He dangles the Little Hillside Hotel key ring at David. 'Keep an eye on my baby cousin for me. I'm having way too much fun to leave the festival, and I've been crashing with my friends anyway.'

'Thanks, but—' David mumbles.

'Seriously, David, don't give up!' I blurt from my messed-up thoughts. 'Just . . . you know. You can't.' I grab the keys from Brad and press them firmly into David's hand, holding on for a second. 'Stay.'

David stares at me.

I think about the memory stick in my pocket. I should give that to him too. One of Brad's friends calls over and Brad bounds away, shouting, 'Gotta go – it's my round! Give the key back to Tori tomorrow and tell her and Albie hi! Good to meet you, Josie and friends of Josie!'

I should give David the stick.

I should.

I don't.

VELMA

The mixed-up feelings don't stop for the rest of the day. Hailey suggests that David should 'knock off for now and come and chill with us, then see how you feel'. She tells me in a noble tone of voice that she'll give up on finding Topaz for today, and I can tell it's because she's figuring out a master plan which involves getting David back in the festival mood and ready to go ahead with the interview tomorrow – inviting her.

David has been in some kind of daze since I gave him Brad's keys, and he follows Hailey's instructions and trails around after us. We locate Tori, Tamber and Clyde again, all in a crowd together with some of the girls from before, in the field nearest the main stage.

Then we all hang around for hours as a couple of bands come and go, with piped electronica blaring in between. We've sort of carved out our own space where we dance and chat (in the quiet bits) and eat bizarre vegan food that Clyde volunteers to buy for us, with Hailey running after him 'to help'.

I'm totally one to talk, though, because I keep hanging around David. I can't help it: he's my best friend and he's miserable. He has this faraway, lost look in his eyes, and I want him to laugh and totally 'take the piss' out of everything the way he normally does. I want it as much as I want revenge for the way he hurt me. I don't know how to act around him. One minute I'm all scathing, brushing off anything he says and being totally rude; the next I'm kidding around with him until he's nearly smiling. A couple of times I catch him looking at me strangely, but then he turns away and tries to be part of the crowd, still in that distracted way. I have to keep reminding myself, in the moments when Jo's prickly curls aren't falling into my eyes, that the girl he sees is Jo, not Rachel. And one thing's for sure, he doesn't seem interested in hooking up with Jo again. I don't know if that's a good thing or not. I almost feel hurt twice over.

Anyway, I already have my revenge. I touch the memory stick in my pocket. I didn't even take it on purpose – not exactly: I wasn't really thinking. But now I've ruined his summer job, his future . . . I should give it back to him. Oh God, I am mixed up like never before. So much for living perfect Jo's perfect life. Her life is as much of a mess as mine, and living it is making every-thing a hundred times more complicated. What if I really am stuck being Jo for ever? I thought it would be great – a costume of perfection, the best place to hide from myself and my problems. But being myself again is starting to feel tempting. At least my problems are *mine*, and I don't have to pretend to know how to deal with them.

It gets darker, everyone gets sweatier and the music somehow fills the air more, and soon even Tori stops talking. I'm not sure if they've turned up the sound system or it's just that we're all increasingly focused on it. Even though the rock/indie band playing are not my kind of thing, I'm carried along by the enthusiasm of the people around me and we dance together in waves, the music pulsing through us and painting smiles on our faces. It's really pretty amazing and, again, it's something I never would have done as Rachel. I'd have stood at the side and told everyone this wasn't my scene, implying *they* were lame for being into it. I'd have made a point of it. Yeah, I think I was living my own hype half the time; everyone expected me to be obnoxious, so I was.

A few people approach us, gawping. I assume it's because we're with Madison Rat until Tori nudges me and says, 'They're totally staring at *you*, Glow-Pants Girl.'

Sure enough, I hear one of them say, 'Are they glowing?'

The other one holds up a glow-in-the-dark stick and waves it about. 'Nah. Can't even see them. Oi, Pants Girl, lost your glow?' And he adds something pretty graphic about how he can help me get it back.

'Oh, that's terribly kind of you,' I start, but then I finish the sentence in a way that leaves Hailey and Tori looking kind of shocked and David sneaking odd glances at me, with that trace of a smile again.

Yeah, well, being one hundred per cent Jo is hard work, and I sort of feel like relaxing now. I feel like being me – the real me, I mean, not the one I reconstructed in seventh grade. Sure, there are plenty of similarities but there's one big difference: the real me isn't terrified of being myself.

So I'm going to dance with David. What do I have to lose? No, you know what? I'm not even going to worry about that. I'm just going to do it. I turn towards him.

Someone has beaten me to it. One of our crowd, a dark-haired girl who reminds me a lot of Velma from *Scooby Doo*, right down to the orange dress she's wearing, is dancing up close to David, playing with the ends of her short pageboy hair. She leans towards him and makes a show of laughing loudly at something he says to her – something I can't make out.

Velma is totally David's type. He dated a whole Mystery Machine full of Velmas before we got together. A surge of red-hot anger swells in my ears and I wouldn't be surprised if steam started to come out of them, like I'm some cartoon human kettle. Oh no – being Jo hasn't stopped my raging jealousy at all. And I'm scared again – I can't let these feelings out, especially now. It would be even crazier than when I was Rachel.

I turn away – I can't look. I won't look. I will flick the switch on those feelings.

Tamber, Hailey and Clyde are standing near me, and a little way in front of them Tori is rocking out. Amazingly, she has completely stopped looking out of place. Her designer clothes have been beaten down by snail racing through mud, but that's not biggest change in her. It's like she's let herself go, in a good way.

Tamber's watching Tori with such a hopelessly lovestruck expression on his face that I can't believe he had to drunkenly confess his crush to Clyde the other day. Surely it was blindingly obvious? Though I bet it was worse after he admitted it. Sometimes talking about feelings can do that – intensify them. I swear that all the time I spent yakking at professional listeners about my 'anger issues' only made me hate my father more. And that is one reason I can never tell David the truth about why I'm so messed up. I think I might explode.

I'm also terrified he won't understand. Or he'll be disappointed in me. Or horrified. Or all of those things.

But we're through anyway. It's too late for us.

Maybe I can help Tamber, though.

I go over and tug at his arm, feeling girlie and Jo-ish because I have to look up to talk to him. He leans his head down and I say in his ear, 'Hey, Tori totally can't see the stage and it looks like she's loving this band. Why don't you offer to, you know, lift her up?' It wasn't on the list, but then Tori probably never expected to get so transported at a music festival.

A look of horror crosses Tamber's face but I ignore it, and the next thing I see is Tori climbing on his shoulders, giggling as she clings to his beanie to get her balance. Tamber shoots me a grateful look, as if I'm responsible. Like 'matchmaking' was up there on my list of desirable superhero skills. Which it so isn't.

What am I doing? I have to stop this! I'm supposed to be the opposite of a matchmaker! I'm ErisGrrl, not Cupid – discord, not love! According to my research, Eris was thought to influence every fight on earth. That is way cooler than anything stupid Cupid ever accomplished with his lame-assed love-arrows.

I look back at Velma, who's now punctuating every other burst of over-the-top laughter at David's jokes by touching his arm. My cartoon human kettle reaches boiling point and clicks off.

And it's time to channel my inner Eris. I'm not prepared to turn my back on this after all. No, I am going to trash it. I will find a way to ruin David's chances with her, and preferably with all girls. I have to do something terrible, like accuse him of something . . . I don't know what. Something to make her stay away from him. Saying he's a player won't work – girls actually go for that in this double-standard world. It has to be something that will properly put her off. Like . . .

Maybe I can send David away somehow, to get a drink or something, and then I can talk to her.

I can tell her some stupid lie to make her think he's gay.

Room 121, The Clarence
Saturday

Rachel's Diary Therapy
by Jo in Rachel's body (IF THIS ISN'T PRIVATE I'M
GOING INTO HIDING AND DISGUISING MYSELF
IN ONE OF MY REAL MUM'S TIE-DYED HATS!)
Conversations with my so-called mother, Part 5

Jo-in-Rachel's-Body: Hey, fabulous, a present! Wow,
    thanks! (*Opens plastic bag*) Oh.
My So-Called Mother: I thought it would be good for
    therapy, you know? It's a stress-reliever. I know
    you have all the others I bought you at home, but
    you don't have one here. And it has sort of an
    eighties or early nineties retro, festival look, don't
    you think?
JIRB: Oh yeah, yeah, it's great. Squishy bright-
    yellow smiley faces are great. Just, you know –
    there wasn't, like, an HMV or something nearby, or
    a second-hand movie memorabilia shop with an
    eclectic collection of . . . Never mind. It's great!
    Thank you.

MSCM: You hate it.

JIRB (*starting to spontaneously roll eyes, Rachel-style*): I don't hate it.

MSCM: You do. You hate it. (*Turning head away in near-tears drama*)

JIRB (*starting to sympathize with Rachel a whole lot more*): Oh God, I just said I don't hate it, OK? God!

MSCM: No, it's OK. You can hate it. I just thought it would help.

JIRB (*misses own, relatively sane mother*): Hey, listen, it's really nice of you to buy me a present. Just, you know. Does it have to be a therapy thing? Can't it just be a nice present? I mean, it doesn't even have to be a poster of Spike from *Buffy*, though that would be cool and you should always consider it an option. But they do some great deals on box sets nowadays, and I'm sure we can persuade Foxy – I mean, Dr Boxtree – to let us have a DVD player, and we could just sit and watch things, maybe have a bit of a sob together. I mean, yeah, that's therapy too, in a way, but it's just a lot more enjoyable, don't you think? Than, you know. Squishing something. Even something with an eighties retro smiley face. (*Does good impression of eighties retro smiley face*)

MSCM: Oh, Rachel. Oh, Rachel, I'm sorry I made such a mess of things.

JIRB: Er . . . You haven't . . . (*Wonders*) I don't think. (*Becomes unsure*) Have you?

MSCM: Yes, I have. I sent you to all those therapists, I put you in those personal relationships sessions at school, I encouraged you to talk to experts about your anger towards your father, but back at home I was silencing you. Constantly.

JIRB (*slightly scared now*): Silencing me? What do you mean?

MSCM: You know. About your father's affairs. I kept telling you they weren't happening because I wanted to believe it. But it meant you couldn't talk about it to me. That had to be bad for you.

JIRB (*nodding*): Actually, that does sound pretty bad.

MSCM: And it's been going on for years. Since before you were born. Well, as you know.

JIRB: That sounds even worse.

MSCM: I know. I know. I believed him, though, that it wouldn't happen again. Over and over. I figured it was good for us as a family, pulling through. Getting past it. And there were times, you know – years even – when everything was great. But then it did happen again. It kept happening and . . . I started worrying about you. Even before your breakdown in seventh grade, I worried. But I think children adapt amazingly well, and you were too young to really understand. I'm right about at least some of that, aren't I?

245

JIRB (*stifling gasp*): Hold on. Breakdown? That doesn't sound like me.

MSCM: OK, *school refusal* – whatever you want to call it.

JIRB (*relieved*): OK, that sounds more like me. I think I was still refusing school last year even though I was there.

MSCM: You always make it sound like it was no big deal but, Rachel, I know you were suffering. I'm your mother! I'd do anything to make things better for you! (*Close to tears*) But you never told me what exactly went wrong. It can't just be because you stopped hanging with those sweet little girls.

JIRB: Ha ha, I used to *hang* with *sweet little girls*?

MSCM: You know what I mean. Suddenly you seemed to have no friends. It wasn't like you.

JIRB: *Really?* I mean, I can be great when you get to know me, but most people find me a bit scary. I mean, I think. I'm sort of intense and hard to get close to. Don't you think?

MSCM: Yes, you've always been intense, but you didn't used to be so withdrawn, did you?

JIRB: Oh no, I wouldn't say I was withdrawn! I'm just . . . tough. I mean, you should hear the way I stand up to Chelsea at school, for example, even when it's my friend Jo she's having a go at, not me. And I'm all, like, *women's rights* this, *men should respect*

246

women that. It can be pretty cool. Sometimes.

MSCM (*silence*): That poor girl. (*Near-invisible shudder*)

JIRB: Poor . . . ? Who? Me? Jo?

MSCM: You know. (*Pretty visible shudder*) Chelsea.

JIRB: Chelsea? Poor? Girl? (*Does not compute*)

MSCM: Well, yes, don't think I don't know what's been going on. I know it's all a massive secret in Milltown but I heard a fair amount of it from Mike Cook himself – he used to email me. We used to be friends, of a sort. He thought I'd agree with him but I didn't – not all the time, at least. I didn't realize how ill he was getting – I thought it was all just pure anger. I should have guessed when he threw that poor girl out of her own home. Though maybe it was the best place for her – no wonder Iliana made those arrangements.

JIRB (*remembering*): Oh yeah, didn't Chelsea's dad go nuts or something? I mean, have a breakdown. When Chelsea went to live with Jake Matthews. So what, he actually kicked Chelsea out?

MSCM (*gives JIRB a strange look*): Yes, I know everyone heard about Mike Cook being hospitalized for a while. But I'd say he's recovered now. He's back with Iliana, keeping the family together, as he should. If only he didn't still have those issues with, you know, your half-sister. (*Winces*) They had

247

another huge crisis a couple of months ago, I heard. He needs to get over himself – there are children involved. I've tried to be bigger than that, you know. Well, of course you know. The way I turn a blind eye when your father sees ... his other daughter.

JIRB: Half-sister? Other daughter? What? You mean ... no *way*!

MSCM (*stern look*): Rachel. You don't have to do this, you know. I'm admitting it, OK? You've made me realize I need to. We can talk about it like adults, like you said earlier. It's probably better therapy than everything else I've provided for you. (*Deep breath*) Yes, your father cheated on me, on and off, for years. Yes, he had an affair with Iliana Cook after we were married but before you were conceived. Yes, Chelsea Cook is your half-sister. I'm accepting it, and I don't want you to deal with it alone any more.

JIRB (*squishing smiley-faced stress reliever*)

'End of log. Actually this probably completes the analysis. If this isn't the cause of the family argument Albie witnessed at the Cooks' house that Sunday, if this isn't the secret Albie and Chelsea were talking about that day when it all started to go wrong for me and Albie, I'll eat my mum's tie-dyed hat.'

DADDY'S GIRLS

It all blew over amazingly quickly, for Mom. She made Dad move out for a while, but then he charmed his way back and she was all: 'Your dad's sorry. Give him a break, Rachel. We can get through this as a family. Besides, if I can get over it, so can you.'

Mom didn't understand, though – she wasn't the one who had to live with the consequences every day at school. The only good thing was that Chelsea was keeping it as secret as I was. At the start, when Mom had that horrible phone conversation with Chelsea's dad – the one she thought I wasn't listening to, complete with repetitions of 'Are you sure?' and sniff-filled silences that wrenched my gut – I wasn't even sure that Chelsea knew anything about it. I avoided her at school as usual – it wasn't difficult. We were in seventh grade and we ran with different crowds, anyway.

Then one day Chelsea pulled me aside and whispered furiously at me. Her dad had demanded a paternity test but could I please persuade my father to refuse? In fact, would my whole freaky family just *butt out of her life*?

Believe me, I wanted that too, but my father hadn't even mentioned anything about any paternity test to me. Probably because he was never at home, and when he was, I didn't feel like talking to him anyway, not since his incriminating emails to Chelsea's mom had been broadcast to *my* mom.

I waited a few excruciating weeks, willing the test thing to go away or at least come back negative. But it didn't, and suddenly it was official: my dad was now also Chelsea's dad. I found out from Mom, who was sobbing to her friend on the phone and saying things like 'No wonder he didn't want any more babies. He already had two!' And later I had a mega-awkward conversation with Dad where he tried to explain things, which somehow ended in the worst idea in the world. He suggested going for dinner together, me and him and Chelsea, to 'smooth things over'. I don't know why Chelsea's dad was the one who was labelled 'crazy' when I had a dad who thought *that* was a good idea. Though I also can't believe Chelsea's parents let her go. I found out later that her father bullied her into going – that it was all part of his rejection of her; that her mother stood by and let it happen because she didn't know what else to do. As for me, I mostly only went to get my mom off my case for five minutes. (*I think it could*

help you come to terms with things, Rachel. Your father's try-
ing to make amends for something in his past that he realizes
was a mistake.)

Well, the whole thing was a mistake. I wish I'd stayed
home and let Mom pseudo-psycho-nag me instead.

Chelsea was hostile, then she was rude, and then she
was running off to the restroom looking like she was
about to hurl.

'Can you check she's OK, please, Ray-bunny?' Dad
asked me after a few minutes. It was probably the last
time he called me 'Ray-bunny', but then it was also one
of the last times he really spoke to me at all – which was
partly my fault as no way did I want to speak to *him* ever
again for putting me through that night and what
happened afterwards.

But at the time I was still kind of sweet (for me) and
twelve and, although I didn't really want to chase the
tearful, cheerleading result of something that had made
Mom cry, I still loved my dad enough to listen to him.

I could hear Chelsea retching in a stall of the other-
wise empty restroom. I stood by the door and picked at
my nail polish – it wasn't black polish then, but it also
wasn't anything like Chelsea's regular French
manicures. We've been poles apart all our lives; we've
never had anything in common. Except this.

Chelsea retched again. I wondered idly whether she
could be bulimic. I'd heard that girls like her often were.

I didn't say anything because I wasn't sure what to say. If she'd heard me come in she must have thought I'd left after a while, because when she opened the door she looked shocked – then horrified – to see me.

'Are you OK?' I asked in a dutiful, Daddy's-girl voice.

'Do I *look* OK?' she snapped.

She didn't. She looked terrible. Her makeup was streaked and her eyes were bloodshot. I might have been young and naive, but I wasn't stupid enough to answer her honestly. Instead, I asked, 'Are you sick?'

'No,' she said. 'I thought I was going to . . . but I didn't. I'm sick of *this*, though.' She glared at me with her bulgy eyes.

'I know. It sucks, doesn't it?' I said. 'It sucks the big one. And then some. It's the suckiest thing in Sucksville, Suck-achusetts. In Suck-merica, the Sucky Way, the Sucky-verse.'

I thought she'd agree with me then, or call me a freak, or walk off, or some combination of those. What I didn't expect her to do was what she did.

She laughed.

It totally shocked me.

Then she surprised me even more by throwing her arms around me and sobbing in my ear. 'You're right!' she said between sobs, holding me tightly as if I were one of her cloney perfect friends. 'It so sucks! I can't believe Mom!'

'I can't believe Dad,' I said. I kind of put my arms around her awkwardly and we stayed like that for a while, until her sobs died down. Then I said, 'Come on, let's get back and get this night over with,' and she nodded. But first she made me wait about a hundred hours while she touched up her makeup, and that's when she told me all about what had been going on at her house, and how her dad was totally mad at *her*, which made no sense. I made lots of sympathetic noises.

We went back to the table together, and my dad mouthed *Thanks* at me, and we all got through the rest of the evening somehow. By the end of it, I even thought me and Chelsea might be, well, not exactly friends, but people who kind of understood each other. I was still mad at Dad for putting me in this position, but at least the secret half-sister part wasn't as bad as I expected.

The next day at school I smiled at her in the hall in front of her friends, and three seconds later it all started.

It was the usual stuff. I'd seen similar things happen to other people. It seemed like my case was worse, but maybe I only think that because it was me at the centre of it. And I must have been a super-softie or something because it hit me hard. *Real* hard. There was name-calling, whispering, pointing, notes stuck to my locker, people refusing to sit near me: the works.

And my old friends? They made awkward excuses if they made excuses at all and they vanished overnight. It was a very long time before I had a female friend again, and even then I had to fight for it. Girls like Chelsea have that kind of power. If she says a girl 'made a move' on her in the restroom at school, that the girl, like, must have been stalking her for weeks and dying to get her alone, that the girl practically 'worships' her, that this girl is clearly *disgusting*, then that's it – she did, she is, and it's a junior high school crime punishable by social death. No one forgets – ever. Chelsea told her friends she'd decided not to 'report the attempted assault' and no adults should be told – it was 'too upsetting' for her and she hoped they understood. And they sure did. It became gossip gold for a really, really long time. And I knew I'd be with the same kids in high school, year after year, and I was seriously sure it would never end.

So I pretended it wasn't a big deal and I retreated, first into schoolwork and then into myself, further and further, until I was getting lost inside my own head. After a couple of weeks of that, I refused to go to school, which was a relief at first, but then I had to cope with Mom. I hadn't told her what had been going on because I didn't want to set off the worry machine, and anyway she'd had a rough enough time as it was. I didn't want her to blame herself any more than she already did, or watch her stick her head any further in the sand.

But refusing school meant Mom had to get involved, even if she didn't know why. She just saw me staring into nothing, wanting to disappear so bad that it was taking over all my thoughts.

She called in the shrinks and I went along with it, and I guess it must have helped because I talked and talked, and eventually I pulled myself out of it and toughened up. It took weeks, months, years, but I rebuilt myself, snark by snark. I even managed to stand up to Chelsea eventually. Yeah, after I met David, the boy who insulted the most popular girl in school on his first day; my hero.

All that talking might have saved me, but it put nails in the coffin of my murdered relationship with Dad. I tried telling him not to meet with Chelsea again; I tried telling him she was evil. He said she was having a tough time and I should try to understand. He said he'd speak to Mom about my anger issues. He said it would be great if I could 'find it in my heart to forgive him' for 'a mistake from such a long time ago'. He said he loved me. He didn't have a clue.

If I have one regret about what happened, though, it's not about all the catch-up schoolwork I had to do, or the so-called friends I lost, or the father who let me down. It's the fact that I gave Mom a mental health focus that made her blind. She uses it to bury herself ever deeper in denial with every single 'business trip' my dad goes on. I can't make her see it. I used to try, especially after one of the shrinks told me to discuss it with her, and she'd say, *It's behind us now, Rachel. If he says it's a business trip, then that's what it is. I've learned to trust him again, and you should too.* I've given up trying. I know you can't trust anyone, but I can't make her see it.

Well, the world is full of guys like my dad, and all good caped crusaders find a way to fight back. It's called a vendetta if you're the villain, but when you're the hero, it's called justice.

Room 121, The Clarence
Saturday

Rachel's Diary Therapy
Jo in Rachel's body: quick update

Persuaded Rachel's mum to watch TV movies with me all afternoon in patients' lounge. Both sobbed enough to leave behind a cloudy Ben Nevis of tissues. I think she needed it. I think I needed it too. Foxy Boxy walked past, brow furrowed in a mildly concerned TV-doctor way. Wondered whether anyone would ever make a film based on the true story of Rachel's mum's life. Think it would be a perfect TV movie. Would be called something like *Misguided Daughter Love*. Felt sad about that. Sent my so-called mother to get more tissues, preferably those posh ones with the sooth-ing balm.

CHELSEA LOW

I could do it. I could say something to make Velma think David was gay: it would be easy. At school, lies spread and rumours escalate and the truth counts for nothing. I could tell a well-timed lie to the right person and I could make everyone look at David differently for years. Course, Chelsea added an 'assault' element when she trashed me, but lots of kids in school latched onto the 'gay' thing far more, however totally wrong that is. I've seen how it works.

Then my heart sinks as low as I've stooped, thinking of doing something like this. *Chelsea* low.

I'm as bad as Chelsea. Yeah, it must be in our blood.

That thought makes me seriously nauseous.

Anyway, this festival isn't school. People here are older, or just cooler, and . . . yeah. Why is it even a big deal? Some of those girls we're hanging with are clearly in couples together and nobody is paying any attention. And why would they? Who would care if I tried to spread a rumour like that about David? Well, maybe Velma would, if she wanted to hook up with him, but still.

I'm not saying it. It would be stupid and wrong.

Behind me, Velma's giggling and David's voice is low and gorgeous, and there's nothing I can do. No, there's nothing I *will* do.

It can happen. It can happen and it has nothing to do with me.

But I don't have to be here to see it.

I start to walk away.

I haven't even taken two steps when Hailey appears beside me. 'Where are you off to?'

'I'm leaving.'

'Already? But Wondrous Jenny are on next! You love them!' She lowers her voice. 'Plus you have to stick around to see what happens with me and Clyde. I might not tell you about it, you know, as payback for not telling me *your* stuff.'

I manage another step away as I say, 'Hailey, I'm sorry, I have to—'

'Josie!' Tori calls out really loudly, making Tamber nearly lose his balance. All our crowd turn towards her as she climbs down in an amazingly elegant way, leaning against Tamber to steady herself. 'Josie, where are you going?'

Everyone's eyes are now on me. Tori keeps leaning

casually against Tamber and his hand hovers near her head as if he's not quite sure where to rest it.

'Uh . . . back,' I mumble. I hadn't planned on this. I'm always leaving when things get tough, storming out before I get hurt any worse – no one ever stops me. Now what? I stand there uncertainly.

David smiles at Velma and says, 'Listen, it's been a weird day. I think I might head off too.' He turns to us. 'Hey, Tori, I'm staying in your cousin's room at the hotel tonight.'

'Are you serious?' Tori asks in surprise. Then she lets out a huge yawn. 'Why?'

'It's a long story. But Brad insisted, and he's crashing here.'

'Omigod, you're totally reminding me how tired I am. Jet lag's a killer.' She rubs her eyes. 'Hey, this is perfect! Josie and I can get a ride back and you can tell us that long story on the way.' She detaches herself from Tamber, who looks disappointed, then she waves to him. 'Night, C.'

The three of us are at David's car before I let the crazy thought creep through my head, bringing all-body shivers along for the ride. I don't know if they're good or bad shivers, though.

Did David leave because he wanted to be with me?

GLITCHY STREETLIGHT

Tori falls asleep within seconds, so David doesn't get to tell her the story of the heather trail leading to the goat that ate his tent, his memory stick and his fledgling music journalism career.

I'm exhausted too but I can't relax enough to fall asleep. I'm riding shotgun and David's just ... *there*, right beside me, driving in silence, his sad expression showing every time we pass a streetlight. I keep touching the memory stick in my pocket and wondering whether I should tell him that his work isn't lost after all.

But why would I do that? What kind of superhero am I, if I give in to the villain?

We're about halfway to the hotel when David surprises me by saying, 'Jo, so ... did something happen? You know, just now at the festival?'

Yes, I thought seriously about trying to convince some random girl you were gay just to stop you hooking up with

261

her and then I was disgusted with myself, I think. 'No. I'm just . . . you know. Tired.'

'OK. Only I thought you might be upset. And if you want to talk again . . . or anything . . .'

What exactly does he mean by 'talk again'?

What exactly does he mean by 'or anything'?

'I . . . no.' Or possibly *I . . . yes*, depending on what the question really means.

'OK.'

'OK.'

He goes quiet, staring straight ahead. Which is good, I guess. I mean, he's driving, isn't he? Staring straight ahead is good.

That lost, tragic air about him is less good.

'So are you sorry you didn't get to hook up with Velma?' I blurt. Oh no, why did I say *that*?

I can't believe I even said *Velma*!

David frowns. 'You know, not that it . . . but she was just being friendly.'

Yeah, right, I think. David's always had an odd definition of 'friendly'. There is no way he can be that clueless about the effect he has on girls.

'I mean, I think . . . not that it matters, but I'm pretty sure Velma was there with someone else anyway.' He gives me a quick look. 'I mean, with her girlfriend.'

Nah, come on. 'No way.'

'Yeah, I really think so. But anyway, you know . . . I'm

just saying.' Then he surprises me by laughing. 'I thought she looked like Velma too!'

After that he kind of relaxes and starts talking about the bands he's met and the things he's done since he got here. I join in and make him laugh with my observations about the festival, and he makes me laugh right back, and it's almost like we're ourselves again, together again, even if he still doesn't take his eyes off the road for a second, even at red lights. That's what reminds me we're not.

He pulls into the hotel's tiny parking lot and kills the engine. So now he can look at me, and when he does, our eyes lock and I swear there's a spark.

Or maybe the streetlamp he's parked under is glitchy.

From the back, Tori mumbles, 'Help me up, will you, C? I was having the nicest dream about you . . . and me.' She turns over and goes right back to sleep, mumbling, 'Thanks, C. Mmm.'

David raises his eyebrows at me. 'C?'

I remind myself I'm supposed to be the authority on Tori, my best friend. 'Christopher. Her ex,' I explain.

'Really?' he says. 'I've only really heard her call him Topher and complain about him.'

'Me too,' I realize. Something else dawns on me. 'Hey, didn't she call Tamber "C" right before we left? She must have been so tired she was mixing him up with Clyde.' Behind us, Tori starts snoring softly. 'You don't

263

think she meant Clyde just now, do you?' Hailey will freak.

David laughs. 'Probably not. In, er, the kind of *situation* it sounded like she was dreaming about, I reckon she'd call Clyde by his first name, don't you?' His eyes sparkle at me. 'And maybe she wouldn't call Tamber by his nickname, either. It's kind of his Madison Rat name.'

'So you mean it *could* be Tamber? But how would we know? No one knows their real names!' I temporarily forget that Jo almost certainly does.

David doesn't notice, or he doesn't know. Anyway, he's busy looking smug. '*I* do,' he says.

'What? How?' David was never close friends with them!

'I wrote an article about Madison Rat, remember. I did loads of research.'

'Wow!' I jump up and down a little in my seat. 'So what are Tamber and Clyde's real names? You have to tell me!'

'Oh, I *have* to tell you, do I?' He gives me a slow smile. 'What's it worth?'

'David!' My stomach stirs, like this morning only soundlessly. I swear he is flirting with me.

'I mean, seriously,' he says, though he's not looking serious at all. 'Why do you want to know?'

'Why d'you want to know why I want to know? Just tell me!'

He shakes his head at me and smiles even more.

'Please,' I beg.

He nudges me. '*Please* answer my question.'

I give an exasperated sigh. 'All right! I want to know because Tamber would *die* if he knew he had a chance with Tori. I mean, in a good way. He's liked her for ever. I could tell him! Or talk to her! I could make it happen for them.'

'Right.' David nods seriously. 'Well, since that's a selfless cause, Ms Reilly, I shall tell you. Clyde is Eric Clyde Junior. Pretty simple.'

I try to ignore the way my heart sank when he called me 'Ms Reilly'. Jo's last name, not mine. 'OK. Boring.' No wonder I forgot. 'And?' I prompt.

'Tamber's is a bit more interesting.' He folds his arms as if that's all he's going to say.

'David!' I fight a sudden urge to tickle him until he tells me. The silence crackles between us.

'OK, OK,' he says at last. 'It's Caesar. Caesar Tambs, which became Tamber. Get it?'

'Oh wow! She's not even just calling him by his *initial*, is she?' I breathe. 'I mean, Tori could be calling him "Cee". Like she has her own nickname for him!'

'Sounds like it.' David smiles. 'Sounds like he's *well* in there. Speaking of which,' he says, pointing to the main door of the hotel, 'we'd better get well in *there* before they bolt the doors for the night. Come on, Eros.'

I freeze. 'Eros?'

'You know, like that statue in Piccadilly Circus. Cupid. Look at you, matchmaking for your friends.'

I lean back in my seat. Oh, wow – Cupid is *Eros*? I didn't see that in my research. Well, I totally focused on the females, and Cupid is a typical man, messing with people's hearts.

Anyway, I can't believe David said that! I am *Eris*, not Eros. Discord, not love.

ELECTRIC STARS

The hotel is quiet. Mrs Pernickety has gone to bed and left the light on for her wayward festival-going guests.

I use the key she gave me for the main door and then wedge it open with a nearby fire extinguisher before we go back to help the very drowsy Tori out of the car and into the hotel. This means a lot of whispered negotiations with David about how exactly we're going to prop her up. I end up choking back laughter as we struggle up the stairs with her, and then I make things worse by pointing out the hotel decor to David and kidding around about it. It's not long before he's stifling laughter too, joining in with my jokes and making me want to laugh even harder. Finally we get Tori into the room I'm sharing with her, where she collapses into an instant deep sleep. At last we can laugh without disturbing anyone, but suddenly neither of us seems to want to.

David takes out Brad's room key and stares at the number on it. 'Just down the corridor, right? It'll be ace to sleep in a proper bed again. Well, goodnight, Jo.'

He starts to leave.

'Wait!' I say, and he does, but I have no idea what to say next. I stare out of the window. It's a clear, moonlit night and it miraculously hasn't rained all day. 'Want to go for a walk?'

His reaction's pretty strange. He sighs like he's struggling with something, then he says, 'Yeah, OK.'

I follow him down the stairs and out of the back door into the hotel garden, wondering what I'm doing. There's a bench at the far end of a dark stretch of grass and I think David's heading towards it, but then he stops in the middle of the garden and lies on the ground. David never likes to be conventional.

I hesitate, then I lie down next to him, ignoring the beads of damp tickling my back. I stay like that for a few minutes, listening to a light wind blow through the trees, staring at the stars, wondering what he's thinking. Until I can't bear it any longer.

I edge closer to him – I don't exactly mean to but I'm just so drawn to him. I reach for his upper arm, right where the short sleeve of his T-shirt ends. I brush his skin with my fingertips.

It. Feels. Electric.

I know he thinks so too because he shuts his eyes in *that* way. I recognize this expression, even in the moonlight. I know him so well.

I shut my eyes as well and keep my hand on his arm. His biceps flex slightly but he says nothing. His silence blares like a foghorn: a signal for me to continue. All my nerve-ends are jangling. I work my hand up his sleeve. He seems to tense and relax at the same time. I shift nearer, press my thigh against his, let the shivers climb deliciously up my spine, breathe him in.

He sighs.

I roll onto my side and reach for him with my other hand, losing it in his wild hair and pulling him towards me. I want his mouth, his lips. Closer, closer. My whole body turns to liquid. I whisper his name.

He jumps away from me, sitting up. My arms snap back into place at my side.

He murmurs, 'Can't.'

I want to scream, but my voice is low and calm. 'You're kidding, right?'

'No.'

I curse.

Some cats howl in the distance, joining in with me. Then there's silence.

He runs a hand through his hair, clears his throat. 'Are you OK, Jo?'

No, I want to shout. *No, I'm not OK, and can't you freaking tell I'm Rachel?*

But I'm not, of course, not exactly. The body he was melting was Jo's. The lips he nearly kissed were Jo's.

Well, it wouldn't be the first time.

My heart thuds. I flatten my back against the grass. The stars blur together in loose patterns.

'I'm sorry. I shouldn't be here with you. I should have stopped you sooner,' he says. 'I don't understand what's going on.' He sighs again. 'Look, we've been friends long enough, Jo.'

'Long enough for what?' My voice is full of bitterness.

'Long enough for honesty.'

'Honesty about what?'

'Everything. Stuff that matters.' He lies down again, back at my level, resting one elbow on the ground and his chin on his fist. 'On Thursday it was just . . . well, you know. But now . . . There's something about you right now. For the last day or so, in fact.'

He reaches over with his free hand and pushes a spiky curl out of my eye. He touches my face.

I want to pull myself away then, like he did to me before, but I can't. I'm caught, frozen in the moonlight. I want him to want me. Who cares which body I'm in? *I want him.* I stay as still as I can. His hand moves to cup my chin.

He's so close. Now won't he kiss me?

He takes his hand away. 'But it wouldn't be right.' His voice gets smaller. 'You know, I miss Rachel. Too much to . . . you know, move on. It's too soon. Way, *way* too soon. And I know you're the same.'

I breathe in sharply. I was not expecting this. He's supposed to be like that guy from Troy who brought down the whole of his city because of some random beautiful woman. Yeah, like every guy.

I'm beautiful now. I'm Jo. Why won't he kiss me?

He says, 'Let's face it, we're a mess. Rachel, Albie . . . they broke up with us and neither of us are doing a good job dealing with it.'

OK – inventory time. A mess? Check. Confused? Check.

'They broke up with us?' I say aloud, not hiding any of my shock. It's not true! I don't know for sure about Albie and Jo, of course, but I – Rachel – did not break up with David.

Well, not properly.

But if he isn't telling Jo this because he wants to hook up with her, then why *is* he saying it?

'I know. I can't believe it either. We're so great. They're so losing out.' He starts off sounding like he's joking but then his voice cracks and he rubs his eyes furiously.

I remember we're sitting on grass. 'Oh, hey, this can't be good for your allergies,' I say, sounding amazingly concerned for a person who earlier left heather in his tent, which was chewed up by a goat.

'They pretty much cleared up when I got to England,' he says. 'Dad swears it's because I've been eating locally sourced honey, but I think I'm naturally growing

271

out of it or something.' He sniffs. 'I didn't know you knew about my hay fever. I had it pretty mildly this year, even in Boston.'

'Rachel told me,' I mumble.

He's quiet for a while. Then he says, his voice thick, 'God, Jo. I don't understand why she won't see me. We've broken up before, you know. Well, you must know. You've probably heard her shouting at me, telling me it's over. She's done it in front of the whole school.'

'Uh, yeah,' I say. I guess I have. When I see red, I don't even notice who else is around. I need to strike out, so I do.

'Usually we make up really quickly,' he continues. 'But this time . . . Well, I suppose the distance didn't help, and she was so weird on the phone. I even stopped telling her stuff, you know. Things got so awkward – like, I didn't tell her about the driving course Dad got me on, and the fact that I passed my test first time. I kept willing her to ask what I'd been doing, and she didn't. All she talked about was how well she was doing without me.'

I'm too entranced to be angry with him. What is he saying? Is he trying to blame *me* for the way things were after *he* upset me enough to – temporarily – break up with him? For the way he never seems to notice how upset I am in the first place? Or why?

'But then I heard she was here and I thought, you

know, she might have come to see *me*. But she didn't. And this time . . .' He takes a deep breath. 'This time something's different, you know. She's in hospital and she doesn't even want me to visit.'

'She's probably just confused,' I say, thinking of Jo in my body. She can't be having an easy time of it, not with Mom on her case 24/7, and missing the whole festival and her favourite bands and everything. And, yeah, whatever is going on with Albie.

Plus David kissed her. That's confusing enough for anyone.

'No, I mean something's different for *me*.' He sighs deeply and sits up. 'It's like I've come to my senses. I've realized it's really over, you know, between me and Rachel. It's over.' He repeats it as if he's convincing himself. 'And I know it, I *know* it, but I feel like I need to hear it from *her*, you know. And until I do, I'm in some kind of limbo. Only it feels like hell.'

I'm stunned. Completely stunned.

He looks at me with that super-serious expression I'm starting to get used to. 'God, sorry. Really. I didn't mean to go on like that.' He turns away again. 'I just wanted to explain why . . . you know.'

I feel weird – like I'm totally not myself and never will be again – as I say, 'But on Thursday you' – *betrayed me, cheated on me, killed me* – 'kissed me.' Kissed *her*.

I don't realize I'm holding my breath until he gives a

light, wry laugh and says, 'Jo, come on. You know it wasn't like that.'

I breathe out, and then I want to storm out. The only thing keeping me here is that I'm supposed to be Jo and she wouldn't do that. How can he deny he kissed her? I *saw* it! I was there – whichever body I mean by 'I'!

'And don't worry,' he says, 'I understand why it happened. That moment on Thursday when you reached for me, um, like *that*, I mean. And just now. I know it doesn't mean anything – I know you don't mean it that way. You're upset, and mixed up. And we're friends, you know. I hope we always will be.'

He puts his arms around me in a hug and my heart beats so fast I think it might explode. But he breaks away quickly, like he really doesn't want to be close to me.

So Jo kissed *him*? And he didn't want her to?

Yeah, *right*.

It sounds like an excuse. A bad, sorry excuse for an excuse, like the ones my father spouts at my mother. *It's a business meeting that's dragged on . . . The flight was delayed . . . I can't find a cab . . . I have a breakfast meeting nearby . . . I may as well stay over . . .*

But it doesn't make any sense right now. David doesn't need to lie to Jo.

He picks at the grass and neither of us speak, until Jo's phone beeps in my pocket. I'd forgotten it was there –

I've gotten so used to having no reception at the festival. I take it out, narrowly missing taking out the memory stick with it.

I frown. 'It's from Albie,' I say out loud, even though I meant to keep that sentence in my head.

David looks instantly ultra-sympathetic. 'Told you he'd get in touch! What does it say?'

I read it to myself twice. It says: S5 E15. Pls forgive me.

I can't read it to David. He might ask me what it means, and I don't really know.

'It doesn't matter,' I mumble. 'I'm not replying.'

'But maybe you should? You should talk things over.'

'Maybe,' I say, though it comes out sounding like 'No way'.

David stands up. 'Well, I need to get some sleep. I've got a long drive in the morning.'

My heart sinks. Even further. 'You're really going home? You're really giving up on that job?'

David shrugs and nods. He starts to walk off but he hesitates. 'Listen, though, about Albie. You two are made for each other. Albie loves you, Jo.'

'Rachel loves *you*, David,' I tell him, just like that, out of nowhere. I've never said it before, not out loud and barely even to myself. But now I'm not myself and it wasn't that hard to say.

And anyway, it's true.

275

I turn away, shut my eyes and listen to my heart pound in my ears.

When I look back, he's already at the door. 'Yeah, I wish,' he says. He pushes the handle down. 'Bye, Jo. Thanks for the chat.'

He goes into the hotel, leaving me alone with the stars and my thoughts.

I think and think.

I think about Thursday. That kiss I saw that I thought was the tail-end of something bigger – well, what if it wasn't? What if it really was a confused Jo reaching out to David in a mixed-up way while he tried to make her feel better in his typical David way?

And after I switched places with Jo, David wasn't even there. He arrived later, and he didn't exactly behave like he and Jo were together. He didn't behave like he wanted to deny a passionate hookup and run a mile, either. He just turned up, with tea.

Like a friend.

Then I think of the way David acted when he thought Rachel was injured; the way he was determined to find the hospital. The visits he made, only to be turned away, more than once. The heartbreak in his body language – the red eyes that were not due to allergies after all.

Also just now on the grass, when we nearly kissed – it was after I was being *Rachel* with him, saying things *I* would say, making him laugh with *my* jokes. I

276

might have been in Jo's body but I wasn't Jo. I was me.

Yeah, I can boil water in a foreign country, sing with gas for Madison Rat and play Cupid for my friends, but I can't see what's right in front of me. I feel so stupid.

It doesn't matter how 'friendly' David is with other girls.

He only wants me.

At least, he used to.

I stand up and shake the grass off Jo's dress.

You know, a goddess of discord is still a goddess, and goddesses have power.

I don't see why I shouldn't have the power to set things right. Or at least damn well try.

You should talk things over, David said.

Well, right now, there's only one person in the world I can talk to about this.

And it's Jo.

CODE

My brain's so full of all this stuff that I don't sleep much. So it's easy to get up mega-early and dress quietly while Tori snores. I choose a total rock-chick outfit that will work for the gig later, in case I'm delayed and/or this whole plan fails miserably. I figure I can carry off another of Jo's super-short dresses, especially now that Enchantment is celebrating my underpants. I sneak out of the room.

Mrs Pernickety is already up and she jumps a little when I turn up in front of her.

'My goodness,' she says. 'Burning the candle at both ends?' She tuts and then seems to remember she's a professional. 'Will you be wanting the full English? Only the kitchen's not open yet, but if you wait half an hour we can sort you out.'

'Uh . . .' I'm half tempted because of Tori telling me not to. Then again, I have a lot to do before she wakes up. 'No, thanks, I have to be somewhere. If it's all right with you, though, I'd like to use the computer for a while. It's OK to send files, isn't it?' After all, David did it.

Mrs Pernickety nods like she doesn't really know what I'm talking about, and pretty soon she disappears into the office behind the reception counter. Meanwhile I sit down at the twentieth-century cream-coloured chunky monitor and open up a browser. I find the details I need and scribble them down. Then I take out David's memory stick and make things right.

I still have the contact page open on the website for David's magazine when I notice a link on the sidebar to an episode guide for one of Mom's favourite hospital drama shows. I absent-mindedly click on it, thinking about how I'm about to go to the hospital myself. And then I stare and stare, but I'm not too sure why I'm staring, so I stare some more.

It has a list of links and they go like this: *S1, E1*; *S1, E2*; *S1, E3* until the end of Season 2, which is as far as that show has gotten.

I stare some more.

Oh. My. God.

It can't be that simple – can it?

I enter '*Buffy* episode guide' into the search engine. There are loads of them. I click on the first one and my screen fills with hot-looking vampires. Plus a list. Just like the first guide, there are letters and numbers, but this one has some additional information. It has episode names. The list goes from Season 1, Episode 1 to Season 7, Episode 22. From *S1, E1: Welcome to the Hellmouth* to *S7, E22: Chosen*.

I think about Albie's messages. I scroll through the texts on Jo's phone.

There's last night's message. S5 E15. Pls forgive me.

And before that is the one from Freaky Thursday: S5 E2? S5 E13. Sorry.

And before that, just the damning: Sorry yes am seeing her.

I pull my finger down the online *Buffy* index. I know Jo would never need to do this. She knows this stuff, just like Albie does. He bases half his song lyrics on it.

I check the earlier messages against the list:

S5, E2: Real Me.

S5, E13: Blood Ties.

Oh. Well, even if I've cracked their Nerdish code, this is still useless. I'm no closer to knowing what Albie was talking about. Maybe I should just call him? Yeah, and say what? *Hi, it's your girlfriend, or probably your ex, and I just want to ask what exactly you meant by your cryptic messages. Also David says you dumped me. Could you just remind me why?*

I check last night's text. It actually makes a little sense. S5, E15: I Was Made to Love You.

It's almost exactly what David said last night about Jo

and Albie – that they were made for each other. Yeah, so much that even their messages to each other aren't understandable to anyone without a *Buffy* guide or a serious retro vampire habit.

I'm running out of time now. I move away from the text messages and tap in the number from the card in my pocket, the one Tori left by her bed.

I switch off Mrs Pernickety's computer, slip David's memory stick and Jo's phone back in my pocket, and wait for Mr Zeta-Jones to arrive in his cab and take me to Jo.

Room 121, The Clarence
Sunday

Rachel's Diary Therapy

This is my last entry in the loon-diary. If things work out, I'm outta here. If things don't work out, I'm outta here. Either way, I'm ... yeah, you get the picture, dear little blue scribbles on a white background: making things right one ramble at a time.

So yeah. One reason I'm out is because on his dawn rounds this morning, Foxy Boxy declared me to be of sound mind. Ha! He must never see this diary. He must also never ever see the internal workings of my actual mind.

But yeah, we had a big family-counselling type session yesterday after Foxy Boxy witnessed the therapeutic TV movie sob-athon. Rachel's mother did most of the talking and the Foxy One listened hard and started to shape his decision that I was basically sane but of insane family. This morning he declared everyone's family to be quite insane and discharged me on that basis. Though he also said that

I'd shown no signs of head injury in seventy-two hours and the American insurance people wouldn't cover more time than that.

I have another theory, though, about why he discharged me. I couldn't help but clock the way Foxy Boxy was checking out my so-called mother. I actually think he needs me to stop being a patient so as not to breach the code of conduct that demands that doctors don't fancy the pants off their patients' mothers.

This was proved by the fact that, after he said I could leave in a couple of hours and left me to pack up my room, I overheard him talk to Rachel's mother just outside my door. He said he was off work in a while for the rest of the day, and would she and her daughter like to go with him to this local music festival? He had some day passes for the final day, and he knew how much I liked music – I must have been sad to miss the festival – and wouldn't she consider it?

And Rachel's mum sounded particularly embarrassed when I yelled out, 'Say yes, Mum!' from my room. I mean, maybe I didn't want to go and face my friends, but I could wait in the car or something while Rachel's mum went in with the hot doc. I knew this was an important moment for her. Foxy Boxy could be just what she needed.

Then, just after this, everything changed when Rachel came to see me.

Yeah, as in Rachel-in-my-body. And yes, it was freaky. There's a very good reason those three films and one book were called 'Freaky' Friday. (*Three films, I swear, with the sad, neglected middle one being my favourite.*) The fact that it happened to me and Rachel on a Thursday did not lessen the freakiness quotient by even one freak-notch, or whatever the received unit of freakiness is in the world freak-onomy.

Right, if Rachel were still here she would tell me to stop nerding and start explaining. So I will. Herewith follows the transcript of Rachel's visit.

Conversations of Freakiness

My-So-Called-Mother (*at the door*): Rachel, someone's here to see you.

Jo-in-Rachel's-Body: God, it's early! Is it even visiting hours yet?

MSCM: Dr Boxtree said he could make an exception because you've effectively been discharged, once we've done the paperwork in his office.

JIRB (*rolls eyes at Foxy Boxy's obvious MSCM-fancying behaviour*): Well, tell David I still won't

284

see him. (*Thinking MSCM will have gone to do her bidding and is no longer present*) Tell him I'm really touched that he's so determined to see Rachel, but really it's the complete devotion he displays to his beloved that got me into all this trouble in the first place.

MSCM: Rachel, what are you talking about?

JIRB (*jumps*): God, Mother, are you still here? Grr! Oh, er, don't listen to what I said, I was just . . . practising for a play. (*Snorts lightly at the unlikeliness of ever being on stage again after Baskervilles-gate*)

MSCM: OK. I've always thought you would be great on stage – all that drama. (*Smirks*)

JIRB (*thinking she preferred the sobbing over-attentiveness*): Hmm.

MSCM: Anyway, it's not David this time. It's that British friend of yours from school.

JIRB: You mean Jo? (*Thinking: Rachel! Oh God, oh God, oh God! Does she know about David? Even though she finished with him, she might still want to kill me!*)

MSCM: Yes. Should I tell her she can come in?

JIRB: No way! No way, no way, never never never!

MSCM: Oh. Only she's behaving quite strangely and . . . I don't know. I think you should talk to her.

JIRB: Strangely how? (*Wonders about weapons*)

MSCM: She, uh, was very affectionate to me. She actually hugged me for quite a long time. She seems nice, Rachel. I think you should see her. In fact, you know, I'm going to let her in. I've realized it's important not to run away from other people. To reach out rather than push people away. You've taught me that. (*Kisses JIRB on the forehead and leaves quickly*)

JIRB (*Aaaaargh!*)

MSCM (*outside*): Here you go, Jo. Through here. Bye, girls, have a good chat.

Rachel-in-Jo's-Body: Thanks, Mom . . . uh . . . I mean, Rachel's mom. (*Appearing at the door as MSCM walks off*) Hey— Oh! OMG!!! (Bleeep bleep bleeeeeeeeeeeeeep! Bleeep! Bleep!) What the (bleeeep) have you done to my hair? Why are my lips so (bleeeping) pale? And what the (bleeeeeeeeeeeeeeep) are you wearing?

JIRB: Hey yourself. The hairband's just to keep your hair out of my – er, *your* – eyes. I don't really do bright red lipstick. And I'm wearing a jumper.

RIJB: OK, I don't even know what that is but from where I'm standing it looks like you are WEARING AN ITEM OF MY MOTHER'S CLOTHING!!!! (*Bleeeeeeeeep!*)

JIRB (*offended*): I was cold. She offered. She's lovely, your mum.

RIJB: (Bleeeep! Bleeeeeeeep!) My mother's (bleep) *clothing*!

JIRB (*sniffy*): Anyway, you're totally one to talk. Why are you only half dressed?

RIJB (*calming down, actually looking sheepish*): What do you mean? It's one of your dresses. I've worn a couple of them over the last few days. (*Sits on edge of bed*)

JIRB: It's one of my *tops*, you mean. You're supposed to wear leggings with them. (*Realization dawning*) Oh my God, have I been walking about half naked? Oh my God! Just promise me you didn't wear the one that was unravelling at the hem!

RIJB (*short silence*): What the hell happened to us, Jo?

JIRB: Freaky Friday, of course. I wished I was you and you worked your weird magic—

RIJB: There is no way you wished you were me.

JIRB (*hiding eyes, wishing could hide whole self under the bed*): I did. I was with David and he was just listening to me and being so kind and . . . well, *uncomplicated*, and I just wished . . . Well, something vaguely happened between us (*winces*) but it was all because of me and I know he was too hurt about *you* to . . . and I thought if I was you . . .

RIJB: I know you kissed him, Jo.

JIRB (*looking for self-defence items and wondering*

287

whether MSCM's latest gift could act as a shield): I'm sorry! I'm sorry! Rachel, I'm sorry! It wasn't supposed to happen, but Tori once told me that after someone dumps you, you have 'slut exemption' so you can snog whoever you want, and . . . And I know that doesn't make it right, I *do*! I wasn't thinking straight. I was just so cut up after Albie finished with me and David was so understanding, and I just wished I could have a relationship as perfect and easy as yours is with David. (*Pauses*) Er, before you dumped him, that is.

RIJB (*frowning*): So it's true? Albie finished with you?

JIRB: Yes, about an hour before . . . you know. I was just wandering crazily around the site, and I found David moping in a tent and I talked to him. I was in pieces, Rachel!

RIJB (*sitting down, surprisingly calm*): I don't understand. What happened with Albie?

JIRB: We had an argument about . . . something. He never wants to see me again. (*Sniffs*)

RIJB: (Soft bleep.) Oh, I'm sorry.

JIRB: Oh God, don't be sympathetic! You're supposed to hate me for evermore. I'm so sorry about David, Rachel.

RIJB: Never mind that now. I mean, yes, you're a (bleeping bleeeeep) but never mind that now. Why didn't you tell anyone about you and Albie? Because I get the impression you haven't talked to any of your friends, except David, which doesn't make sense, with all these fantastic female friends you have. You haven't told Hailey—

JIRB: I was *going* to tell Hailey! Eventually, probably. But she's been so busy lately with her own boyfriend troubles and it was just too . . . complicated to bother her with. Plus Albie's been so secretive, I wasn't sure how he'd feel about me telling even Hailey. Anyway, then he finished with me and we switched places, and I couldn't exactly call her.

RIJB: And you haven't told Tori—

JIRB (*gulps*)

RIJB: Why are you making that face?

JIRB: It's your face. You tell *me*.

RIJB: Funny. Listen, Jo, you need to talk about stuff. You can't keep big things like relationship problems to yourself. Your friends have been telling me that non-stop for the last couple of days.

JIRB: That's what I've been telling your mum too. In fact (*whistles innocently*) don't be surprised if she's wanting to divorce your dad soon. Er, sorry.

RIJB (*tiny smile*): (Bleep) your 'sorry'! I've been dying for her to do that for years! How did you (bleeping) manage that?

JIRB: By talking to her without swearing.

RIJB: (*Bleep*) that.

JIRB: OK, first she confessed that your dad had a billion affairs.

RIJB: She admitted it? That's a breakthrough!

JIRB: But then she said your father means well, and so does she. They just want to keep the family together. Or something.

RIJB (*rolls eyes*): So she still forgives him for (bleeping) around, yeah?

JIRB: Rachel, ssh! She didn't say that. She said it was over for her and your dad a long time ago, but now she thinks about it, what she really can't forgive is the way he hasn't been a proper father to you for years.

RIJB (*deadpan*): Oh, wow, she noticed? (*Stares into space for a second*) Yeah, anyway. Whatever. Let's talk about you. What I want to know is how Albie has the balls to finish with you when *he's* the one sneaking around, and then you sit talking about keeping his secrets? What's up with that? I mean, are you turning into my mother now?

JIRB: Your mother is cool. And . . . (*avoiding my own eyes*) Albie had his reasons. He asked me to keep a secret for him and I did, but I kept telling him not to keep it secret, and I was pushing him and pushing him until I gave him an ultimatum and . . . he took it. He finished with me. (*Aargh, lip quivering*)

RIJB: No, wait, this really makes no sense. He was seeing some girl in secret and told you not to tell anyone . . . ?

JIRB (*sharply*): Some girl?

RIJB: The hot chick from the photo. (*Looks guilty*) Oh, sorry, those are Clyde's words, not mine. I'm sure she's a total—

JIRB: Don't finish that sentence! Don't! Oh God, Albie didn't know anyone had seen his photo.

RIJB: Jo, stop keeping secrets. You can't keep them from me, anyway. You *are* me.

JIRB: Well, technically . . .

RIJB: Jo, tell me. Tell. Me. Now. (*Picking up MSCM's latest gift from where it was laid out on the bed and dangling it out of the window*) Tell me or the vamp poster gets it.

JIRB: Nooooo! Not William the Bloody! Not Big Bad! OK, OK, I'll tell you.

RIJB (*withdraws Spike poster*)

JIRB (*deep breath*): OK. The photo? Of the 'hot chick'?

RIJB: Yes?

JIRB: Well, I didn't see it, but, you know. I bet she *was* good-looking.

RIJB: Huh?

JIRB (*chews nail*): It was an old picture of his

mother. Albie's birth mother. At the time when she gave him up for adoption.

RIJB (*speechless*)

JIRB: Yeah, I know. I always thought Albie was fine with all that, you know. He always said he was. But something happened a couple of months ago and it really affected him. He started to track his birth parents – you know, in secret. He didn't want his parents to know – or Tori – or even me, though he told me in the end, when I was already in England and had less contact with Tori. He told me he had an address here for his mother. He made me swear not to tell anyone. It made things so strained with Tori . . .

RIJB: I'll bet. I'll bet you had to avoid her calls.

JIRB: Um, yeah, exactly.

RIJB: Wait a minute – so Albie was adopted from England? Albie's British?

JIRB: No, no, he was born in the States, adopted there too. He's American. But his mum was a student from England, and she didn't tell anyone from home – she just went to this private agency, apparently . . . And the Windsors knew – in fact, I think that's what made them so obsessed with British things.

RIJB: Wow. Wow, seriously?

JIRB: Yeah. Well, anyway, so Albie had this address in England, and he arranged for Madison Rat to go to a festival right near it, and he said we could go together, me and him, to find his birth mother. He said he would tell the band he had to go somewhere and he needed to speak to me first, and then when we both disappeared they'd just assume we were having a little honeymoon thing – I hadn't seen him for weeks: they'd understand if he missed some rehearsal time to be with me.

RIJB: That doesn't sound completely . . .

JIRB: Sane? Rational? It wasn't. *He* wasn't. You should have seen him, Rachel – he was a wreck. It's like he got a bit worse every day, the closer he got to seeing her.

RIJB: But what about his band – surely he wouldn't do that to his bandmates?

JIRB: He said he'd get back in time for the big gig. But then we had that enormous argument, and now I don't think he's coming back at all.

RIJB: What kind of argument?

JIRB: The worst kind. It was a proper grown-up argument, you know – not like some little row at school. He told me I wasn't supporting him, that I hadn't been for a while. He told me I didn't under-stand what he was going through. I mean, he's right! I didn't. Maybe I should have tried more, you know, but I was getting so fed up with it all! He'd kept this secret from me for ages, which felt weird in the first place. Then he told me and put me in an impossible position with Tori, and he was being so stubborn about not telling his parents – it was like he felt *guilty* about it all or something! (*Thinks*) Well, I suppose he did.

RIJB: Yeah.

JIRB: But it was like he'd opened some kind of Pandora's box, you know, and unleashed all these deeply scary feelings that just kept getting worse. He couldn't deal with them . . . and neither could I. And he said . . . in the argument he said there was no point. In anything. He said he didn't even care about the band any more. He said nothing mattered to him now because he didn't even know who he *was*, and he couldn't be with me any more because I clearly wasn't with him. He was really low, Rachel. I've never seen him like that. And maybe he was right to finish with me. I mean, I really thought I was doing the right thing by insisting that he told his parents. But maybe it was exactly the wrong thing – I pushed him away. (*Swallows hard*) Anyway, there's nothing I can do about it now because I made things a hundred times worse and I can't ever face him again after . . . you know. David.

RIJB (*staring at me for ages and then weirdly ignoring that*): So is Albie near here? Where exactly did he go?

JIRB (*miserable*): I don't know. He didn't tell me – he just said he'd find his mother without me. I kept telling him not to see her yet – I told him not to even look for her until he'd spoken to his parents, or at least Tori. Tori's great, you know – she'd be on his side, she wouldn't have felt betrayed. He shouldn't have shut his sister out like that. In fact, that was one of the things that set off the argument, when I said it was wrong that he was planning on disappearing and not even telling her he was OK—

RIJB: She's heard from him. He told her he was OK.

JIRB (*surprised*): Really?

RIJB: That's all he said, but still. (*Chews lip*) He sent you messages too. (*Takes phone out of pocket*)

JIRB (*resisting temptation to bite off RIJB's hand*): Oh my God! You've got my phone! Oh God, but he said we were through – why was he texting me? Did you read the messages? What did he say?

RIJB: He wrote to you in code, mostly. *Buffy* code.

JIRB (*almost-almost smile*): Oh. Can I see? Er, can I see my own phone?

RIJB: Yeah, but I cracked the code anyway. He said, 'Real Me? Blood Ties. Sorry.'

JIRB (*sad pause*): Oh. He's still trying to explain it to me – how much it means to him to find his roots, like it's some clue to who he really is. He said something like that before. I didn't understand. I still don't understand, really, and I'm not sure whether he does either. But it's like once the thought gripped him, he couldn't let go of it. (*Goes into bit of a daydream*) He started really tentatively at first, you know, Rachel. Little enquiries, so it barely even mattered that he hadn't told me or his family. He started searching after he went to Chelsea's house for work one day. Now at least I've worked out what happened that day that made him start looking. He overheard an argument at Chelsea's house, which I'm pretty sure was Mr Cook yelling all kinds of horrible stuff at Chelsea, probably about her not being his real daughter. Albie was talking about it with Chelsea at school the next day. It must have got him thinking about non-biological parents. Even though Albie's situation is completely different from Chelsea's . . . Oh. (*Shifty glance at RIJB*)

RIJB (*nearly falls off bed*): OMG, you know about Chelsea? So Albie knows? Did he tell you? I can't believe Chelsea didn't threaten to kill him if he told anyone. Sometimes I'm tempted to announce it at school just to ruin her life, if only I wasn't so sure it would ruin mine too.

JIRB (*biting lip*): Albie didn't tell me. I don't think she threatened him, she just asked him not to say anything. Albie's loyal like that . . . even to her.

RIJB: So who told you?

JIRB: Er, your mother.

RIJB: No way. No (bleeeping) way. My mother admitted *that*? You're a miracle worker.

JIRB (*pointing at top of head*): Plus maybe I would have suspected anyway, now I know you've got blonde roots. *Chelsea* blonde.

RIJB: OK, I take it back. You suck. Plus your hair is way spiky. So what do you think that evil witch told Albie to make him turn his back on his entire family and his girlfriend?

JIRB: She's had a hard time of it, you know.

RIJB: Don't *you* start.

JIRB: Yeah, sorry. (*Little laugh*) But your mum told me some of the stuff that's been going on – for years now. Chelsea's dad – I mean, Mr Cook, not your . . . (*Coughs*) Er, anyway, *he* keeps trying to throw Chelsea out, and he's said some terrible things, like calling her a 'cuckoo in the nest', and worse. Your mum said she might try to talk to Chelsea's mum about all this, even though they're total sworn enemies now. Apparently they used to be best friends at school, and they both had divorced parents and swore they'd never do that to their own kids . . . But your mum thinks Mrs Cook might need someone to talk to.

RIJB: You know what? I almost feel sorry for Chelsea too now. (*Frowns*) (Bleep!) It's the influence of being you!

JIRB (*smiles*): Nah, it's totally *you*. I still think she's a total—

RIJB: Jo! Don't turn into me!

JIRB (*smiles and shrugs*): Why not? I love being you, especially now it's over for me and Albie and I know I messed things up so badly. At least, being you, I can hide from all the mess, and be strong and sure like you are, and not just keep making everything worse. Although I've not felt all that different, really. Maybe this is nothing like those *Freaky Friday* movies – didn't the characters learn lessons from being each other? Well, I think I might have helped your mother, but nothing's really changed for me. I feel as terrible as ever, and Albie doesn't want to see me any more and, you know, neither do I. I think I should stay being you for ever . . . (*Continues like this for a while until RIJB interrupts*)

RIJB: He sent you another message you know, Jo.

JIRB: Yeah?

RIJB: Yeah. I didn't finish telling you before. Probably because you've been rambling on and on in a self-pitying, solve-nothing kind of way.

JIRB: Shut up!

RIJB: OK. I won't tell you what it said, then. I won't tell you that it said, *S5 E15. Please forgive me.*

JIRB (*thinking*): Actually, that's quite creepy. *I Was Made to Love You?* That episode was about a robot love-slave built by evil nerds. Wait a minute – how did you even understand Albie's messages? Are you a closet *Buffy* fan?

RIJB: Give him a break, Jo. He loves you.

JIRB (*thinks*)

JIRB (*thinks*)

JIRB (*thinks*): So can we work out how to switch back now?

'Here endeth the loon-diary. Over and out.'

GODDESS OF LOVE

After Mr Zeta-Jones drops me back I sneak into the room and I'm relieved to see that Tori's still sleeping. I lie on the bed and think about everything, starting with how completely off-this-planet weird it was to sit and chat to myself (well, myself wearing Mom's sweater – *shudder*) in that hospital room, eating bizarre British cookies that Mom brought in for us after we'd talked for a while. And how strangely fantastic it was to see Mom, and how much I wanted to hug her and tell her how proud I was of her for admitting that stuff to Jo (or to me).

But I didn't, of course. She left us eating the cookies, and we sat and tried to figure out how to swap back. Jo appointed herself as the expert, having read and watched all those *Freaky Friday* stories, plus various other helpful TV movies. It all sounded kind of crazy to me, but then again, so was the whole situation, so I listened carefully. Apparently it's all about what the people who swap learn from their experience, and how they finally 'do the right thing'. But it can be only *one* side that has to do this – only one person has to use what they've learned to make everything right and cause the switch back.

Jo told me that since I was the mystical one who'd clearly caused the swap in the first place (here she gave me a semi-scared look, like I'd done spooky things to her before), combined with the fact that I was the only one who'd learned anything (according to what I'd told her about David not actually being after every girl in the world after all, plus some stuff about friendship and seeing Tori as more than a Chelsea-clone), then it had to be *me* who did the right thing.

But I was the one who decided what that should be. And after everything that's happened, and everything David said last night when we were lying on the grass, it was obvious.

I have to finish with David.

Properly, for real, and not in anger. I have to set him free, like Hailey said she wanted Grant to do to her. It's the right thing to do, however much it's going to hurt. I realize that now. I haven't been fair to him at all, and it has to stop. For ever.

The trouble is that Jo has to finish with him for me, to make us switch back. But then that will be it – we'll be ourselves again, and hopefully Jo can find Albie and talk things through with him, and at least they have a chance to be the perfect couple again. She seems to think that'll never happen – she refused to even reply to his messages from before, saying, 'It doesn't matter what he says – I blew it, Rachel. It's too late for us. Maybe when I'm me again I'll try to talk to him, but only in a few months' time or something, when I have the guts to face him. Maybe me and Albie can be friends.' Then she looked like she wanted to cry.

Yeah, I don't know. I think she's being too hard on herself. She's just been through a bad patch with Albie – it's not like me and David, where we were doomed from the start.

I think about this until I'm drowsy, and the next thing I know Tori is standing over me yelling, 'Josie! Wake up! You have to get up NOW or you'll miss the gig!'

I groan. Oh no, the gig, where I get to stand in front of thousands of people hoping they've forgotten I'm Enchantment's own Glow-Pants Girl. I didn't tell Jo about that part. If our plan works, at least she might be able to get over her performance phobia.

Tori's screeching now. 'Josie! It's time to get up! David managed to sneak in for the last breakfast downstairs, and he's said he can give us a ride to the festival afterwards.'

'He's definitely going there?' I feel the need to check. 'He's not going home or anything like he said

302

yesterday?' Jo and I sent him a text from my – from Rachel's – phone earlier, asking him to meet Rachel at the Temple of Diana. It turns out that some doctor at the hospital invited Mom and me-Rachel to the concert today, only because he was going anyway and had some spare tickets, and Jo talked Mom into saying yes. Jo said that when they get there she'll tell Mom she needs to meet David somewhere, though she won't tell her where. She says Mom seems to like David so much that it shouldn't be a problem. I agreed with Jo on that.

Tori shrugs. 'All I know is that David offered us a ride. And I think we should accept it, because I can't stand talking about Hollywood Boulevard and Route 66 to that cab driver again.'

She should try talking about 'traffic jams on the A38' and ten different types of rain instead, which is clearly Mr Zeta-Jones's standard conversation for passengers with British accents.

'So come on, Josie! David said he'd be leaving in a couple of hours!'

I get out of bed and then I realize what she said. 'Wait – in a couple of *hours*? That's loads of time. You made it sound urgent!'

'What do you mean? I left it until the last possible minute. How can you get ready in less time than that?' Tori asks. Then she looks me up and down and says, horrified, 'Wait – did you go to bed *dressed* again?' She

303

shakes her head at me. 'And I will never understand your British fashion sense. Anyway, you've missed breakfast, not that I would have let you touch that Full English stuff today. I guess you'll have to try the pub, but you're on your own. I need to, uh, do something else, as soon as I'm ready.'

'OK, I'll go ask the pub for a banana or an orange.'

Tori grins. 'Yeah, very funny. Get yourself some of those scratchy porkings.'

'Actually, I think I'll skip breakfast, Tor.' I ate all those British cookies at the hospital with Jo, anyway.

I wait for Tori to take a year in the shower and a decade doing her makeup. When she heads downstairs, I take out Jo's phone. I've been thinking. Jo shouldn't keep hiding from Albie. She should start putting things right, right now. She's better than that – stronger than that. She's a fighter. She's a superhero. We both are.

And besides, I'm some kind of matchmaking goddess of love. I can totally do this.

Albie doesn't answer his phone, but I leave a long message on voicemail, in Jo's voice, using words I'm sure she'd say if she stopped worrying for five minutes.

When Tori comes back I've only just put my phone away, but she seems to be in a world of her own anyway, and she doesn't notice the guilt that must be all over my face. In fact, she's acting kind of guilty herself, shifting about a lot and looking everywhere except my eyes.

She wiggles some more. 'Look, when I was downstairs just now I . . . uh . . . left a message for Albie,' she confesses, thankfully just before her movements can make me seasick.

'Oh,' I say. Well, if we're being truthful . . . 'So did I.'

'Did you get a reply?' Tori asks.

'No.'

'Neither did I. But I hope he gets the messages. Also . . .' She hesitates and then takes a deep breath. 'Josie, I think there's stuff you're not telling me about Albie. And I just want to say that it's cool with me, OK? I mean, I could be kind of hurt about you not telling me, but I've given it some thought and . . . I don't think I am. I think I understand. Under special circumstances it's OK not to tell your best friends everything. And these are special circumstances. Aren't they, Josie?'

'Uh . . .'

'I know they are. I've worked it out from some stuff Albie said before he left. I should have known it was weird, the way he kept insisting our olds shouldn't come to the festival – it's so unlike him, and he's been so distant and weird with all three of us for weeks . . . Anyway, look, you don't have to say anything. And I don't want to say any more either in case I've got it all wrong. But if I haven't, then you and me need a good long talk when all this is over, OK?'

'Uh, OK.'

'Good.'

There's an awkward silence which seems to go on for ever, and then Tori blurts, 'Omigod, Jo, I think I'm finally in love!' Then she says, 'Shoot. I didn't mean to tell you that. I just wanted to change the subject away from Albie!'

I laugh. Wow, I actually do *like* Tori. 'Why wouldn't you want to tell me? I'm your friend, aren't I?' Well, in a way. Though maybe I am now, whichever body I'm in, even if I'm keeping weird secrets from her.

'Yeah, but it's all sort of' – she puts her head on one side – 'scary. It's someone I've known for ever. In fact, I don't think I should do anything about it. What if he doesn't feel the same about me? It would be a mistake. Yeah, forget it. In fact, pretend I never said anything.' She picks up her purse, jangles the room key and heads for the door. 'We should go. David might be ready soon.'

'Tori, I think Tamber likes you too.'

She stops and stares at me open-mouthed. 'You're kidding me! That's incredible. I knew you and me were on the same wavelength but— Whoa! How did you know I was talking about Tamber?'

I shrug. 'We talked about you. He's crazy about you.' I probably should admit this part. 'I told him the list of what you look for in a man.'

She screeches, 'Shut *up*! Get *out*! I can't believe you even remember that! Wow, I was telling Rachel about that on the plane, but I told you, like, months ago! Is that what all the chocolates and apologies were for?' She smiles sheepishly. 'He's so sweet, following the instructions like that. But you seem to have forgotten the part where I said that if any guy actually followed the list, I'd probably run a mile in the opposite direction! And I'm no Hailey-style runner, you know, but I might even break a sweat in this instance.'

'No, you didn't tell— I mean, I don't remember that!'

'It's true! Anyone who comes close to following the list is automatically deeply unattractive to me, and anyone who doesn't is usually bad for me. It's a fatal flaw in my life plan.'

Oh no! My heart sinks. I can't play Cupid even when I try.

Tori looks thoughtful. 'Weird that it hasn't worked in this case though. Maybe I should just forget it. Go off-list. You know, I've kind of liked him for ages, but I've always thought he was too, you know . . .'

'Fugly?'

She laughs. 'Josie! I think he's totally hot. Omigod, I saw him try on some T-shirts yesterday . . .' She clears her throat. 'No, I've always thought he was too *nice* for me.'

'What the flock, Tori! You deserve someone nice.' I think about the guys I know that she's hooked up with. 'You've basically dated a string of losers.' Well, it's true.

All those jocks, pre-approved by Chelsea. Tori dated one who was constantly getting jealous and sulking about it at parties. Actually, that sounds a little like how Hailey describes her ex too.

And possibly a little like how David could describe me.

'See, I don't know,' Tori says. 'It's what I'm used to.'

'Well, maybe it's time for a change.'

'But won't it just be weird? Won't it wreck every-thing? What if we date and then break up, and . . . We'll ruin our friendship!' She waves her manicured nails about in a frenzy. 'And he likes shopping more than any boy I've ever met but he has *zero* taste in clothes! It's a total disaster!'

'So you'll shop with him. You'll probably influence each other's taste. Look at you in that top anyway – grungy much?'

'Shut up!' She grins, pulling at the T-shirt. 'It's classic D&G, you know.' Her face falls as she remembers her calamity. 'He's a *drummer*, Josie! Drummers are, like, famous for being weirdos with personality disorders!'

I go over and give her a hug. I do this spontaneously and it doesn't even feel weird, which in itself is off the weirdness scale.

'Lead singers aren't exactly known for their stability,' I point out to her, 'but your brother is pretty damn reliable.' I decide not to add the word 'usually' because

Tori's starting to look shifty again. Instead I say, 'Not all drummers are the same.' *Not all men are dastards*. 'Anyway, people latch onto this stuff, but it's never completely true, not in real life. You have to get to know the person behind the costume they choose to wear. No one's really a hero, no one's really a villain.' I'm not really an angry Goth; Tori isn't really an airhead; David isn't really a typical cheating man; Jo's not really perfect; Chelsea . . . I don't know. 'We're all just muddling through.'

'Omigod, Josie, is that a speech from one of those lame TV movies you love watching?'

I smile and ignore that. 'Look, dating a friend is awesome. You'll work it out.'

You know, like I *didn't*.

MUD UNITED

There's an excited buzz at the festival entrance when we arrive, even though it's only recently stopped pouring with rain (again). I should find the Madison Rat boys and prepare for the gig, just in case Albie doesn't turn up. (But surely he will after that message I left?) I know there are only two live bands today, probably because 'this ain't bleedin' Glastonbury', and the festival ends in the late afternoon. Madison Rat are on first in an hour or so, supporting Topaz, the headliners. I bet Hailey can't wait.

Tori seems to be thinking about it too. 'Are you interviewing that big important band today?' she asks David. 'Is that why you changed your mind about coming here?'

David hesitates. 'No, I'm not. I'm still going home.'

'Because I think it's great you're not giving up . . . Oh. You *are* giving up?'

'Well, yeah. The memory stick's still gone, isn't it?

310

Most of my stuff is lost, even if I do this interview. Anyway, you know, it's not important.' He looks distracted, nervous. I want to reassure him but I can't. I know what's going to happen.

Hailey appears, flinging herself at me. 'Thank God you're here! And you, David! Today's the day! I'm so excited! So should I collect more heather for Heather?'

'Er . . .' David says.

Behind Hailey, Tamber and Clyde are coming over, bickering among themselves.

'I'm, er, sorry, Hailey. I'm not here to interview Topaz.' David squints in the direction of the enchanted Temple of Diana. 'I'm meeting someone in a while and . . . Anyway. Maybe I'll go now and wait for . . . Sorry. See you. Have a good gig, guys.'

Hailey stares after him. 'Aw. No! Jo, do something! Make him come back!'

'I can't,' I say. And I wouldn't want to. Whether the swap back works or not, we need to do this for David's sake. Set him free, like Hailey said. Ouch.

The guys reach us and Clyde hovers shyly near Hailey. 'Hey,' he says.

'Hey,' she replies, staring approximately three inches to the left of his eyes.

From where I'm standing, it looks like they're both displaying a classic case of post-hookup awkwardness.

So much for harmless flirting. I wonder what happened after we left last night?

But Hailey and Clyde's behaviour is nothing compared to the way Tamber and Tori are totally avoiding each other.

God, these guys need help. But I can't play Cupid now. I have problems of my own. I glance up towards the Temple of Diana. I try to imagine David walking up there, retracing the steps I took on my first day here when I was so upset. He'll probably walk past the Topaz band members, sulking around and complaining about confines.

Oh.

Hey.

Everyone's still shifting about when I say, 'Hey, Hailey. How would you like to meet Topaz right now? I think I know where they hang out.' Watching her fangirling has got to be better than this nervous, nerve-racking silence. I mean, these guys have to be on stage in less than an hour. They need to relax if possible. (Oh no. So do I.)

'Oh my God, Jo!' Hailey gasps. 'And you're telling me *now*?'

'I didn't think of it before,' I admit. I had other things on my mind.

'Hey, don't talk to my friend like that!' Tori jumps to my defence.

'I'll talk to *my* friend how I want,' Hailey tells her.

'Come on, guys, this way,' I say quickly, and everyone starts following me towards the hill, but Tori and Hailey have not stopped fighting.

'She is so my friend!'

'I don't think so.' Hailey's building up steam now, glaring at Tori as we trudge through the mud. 'Anyway, where do you get off, coming over here, flashing your cash about and making Jo stay in some posh hotel instead of in the tent *her* mum saved up for?'

'I didn't make *Josie* stay with me. She *wanted* to stay with me.'

'Come on, guys,' I say half-heartedly. 'Don't fight. We're nearly there.'

'She started it!' Hailey booms.

'No way! *She* did!' Tori squeaks.

Hailey opens her mouth to say something equally childish. Luckily the guys are a way back from us, having a some kind of word-fight of their own, so they don't have to witness their potential girlfriends totally acting like kindergarteners.

'Look,' I say. 'Hailey, Tori. You know, you're both my friends, and I think you're both great. You shouldn't be jealous of each other.' Ugh. This trying-to-make-every-one-happy thing is hard work. Actually, I think discord was way easier.

Tori stares at me. 'Omigod, what are you talking about? No way am I jealous of *her*!'

'Yeah, Jo. You're talking absolute rubbish! Why would I be jealous of her? At least you can actually talk to me about proper things instead of just warbling about clothes like you do with *her*.'

Tori widens her eyes. 'Josie, have you been telling Hailey all that stuff about Albie?'

Hailey narrows her eyes. 'What stuff about Albie exactly? She keeps refusing to talk about it to *me*. And I've known her for ever. We're like sisters.'

'Yeah, well, she's going out with my brother so she really *is* practically my sister and anyway—'

'She's not going out with your brother. Albie dumped her.'

Tori's jaw drops. 'He – what? No way!'

Two sets of eyes turn on me, waiting for me to explain.

Now what?

'Uh . . .'

'Don't worry, Tori, Jo didn't tell *me* that either.' Hailey's face shows a mixture of hurt and triumph. 'But she told David, and he accidentally told me because he expected me to know.'

Oh.

Oh no.

'I've been waiting for her to tell me, but she hasn't.

She just ran off with you,' Hailey continues. 'And it turns out she hasn't told you either.'

Tori frowns. 'Josie?'

'Listen, guys, she'll explain later,' I blurt suddenly. Oops. 'I mean, *I'll* explain later.'

You know what? I'm so tired of being Jo. I wish I could be Rachel again. Life was crazy, but it made more sense. So much for walking a mile in someone else's shoes. My own old battered boots were way more comfortable.

I realize that Hailey and Tori aren't fighting any more. In fact, they're kind of giggling together as we approach a large bank of swampy mud.

'Why are you guys laughing?' I ask.

'Nothing,' Tori says innocently.

'Yeah, nothing,' Hailey echoes.

Then they start whispering. Honestly, I think I preferred it when they were at each other's throats.

'Seriously, *what*?' I ask.

'Well, you know . . .' Hailey says. 'I was considering doing something to make myself feel a bit better. You know, about the way you've totally blocked me out of your life.'

Before I register what she's said, she's picked up a handful of mud and thrown it at me.

It lands with a splat all over Jo's shoes.

'Hey!'

'You deserved that.' She smiles, but then yelps as a heap of mud lands on *her* shoes.

Tori's smugly wiping her muddy hands together. 'And, Hailey, that's for what you just did to my friend.'

'But you encouraged me!'

'I agreed that it would make you feel better.' Tori smiles too. 'I didn't say I'd let you get away with it. I used to be friends with a girl who was a total bully and I hated myself for it. I'm not going to let you attack another girl, not without a fight.'

'Oh my God, I can't believe you!' Hailey bends down to scoop another handful. 'Right!'

But before she can aim, a ball of mud hits Tori squarely on the shoulder from behind us.

'That's for throwing mud at Hailey!' Clyde calls out.

I look questioningly at Hailey and she lowers her eyes guiltily. Ooh, those two have *so* hooked up!

'Oof!' Clyde shouts, and we turn to see Tamber laughing.

'That's for throwing mud at Tori,' he says. 'Ouch!' he adds as a mud bomb hits him on the shoulder, thrown by Hailey.

'Revenge is sweet,' she says. 'And also quite sticky.' She aims another handful squarely at Tori. 'That's for . . . well, for fun.'

Then Tamber starts pelting Hailey with mud. Hailey

throws mud at Tamber, Tori throws mud at Hailey, and Hailey gets Tori back.

I shrug and scoop up a handful of mud, aiming it at Tori. 'That's for snoring!' I call, but really, like I care about that. It would have been good to say: *That's for standing by Chelsea Cook when she trashed me in seventh grade.* But I'm over it now; I really am. And I really think Tori has changed. I might never forgive Chelsea, but I can forgive her. It feels good to let go of at least a small part of the anger I've been carrying around for years.

More mud lands at my feet. It's Tori, saying, 'That's for putting my brother before the sisterhood!' But she's smiling.

I manage to forget all my worries as I throw myself, literally, into the Great Mud Fight of Enchantment.

At some point Tori and Tamber break away from the rest of us and the next time I see them, they're kissing, Tamber bent low over Tori and both of them covered in mud and looking like they've never been happier in their lives.

Clyde notices and says, 'I don't believe it, man!' so I pelt him hard.

Hailey's staggering up the hill with a handful of mud, ready to get me back for that, when we hear some raised, argumentative voices and two familiar figures appear in front of us.

Hailey releases the mud in shock.

And it lands right on the famous head of Stumpy Braids herself.

We all freeze.

Hailey stands there, stunned. She whispers, 'Topaz!'

Stumpy Braids glances at her. Then she turns to me and says calmly, 'Hey, I know you.'

'She's Glow-Pants Girl,' Clyde supplies helpfully, though I kind of suspect Stumpy Braids is referring to the day I questioned her by the ambulance, something I'd rather she didn't mention right now.

I decide to throw mud at her. You know, in solidarity with Hailey. Also so that she doesn't say anything about me not recognizing her celebrity status before. And anyway, she deserves it for not telling me-Rachel not to go into the ruins that day.

Splat!

It goes ultra-quiet. Everyone looks kind of shocked, especially Stumpy Braids, whose filmy white dress is kind of less white now. Also less filmy.

'We were having a mud fight,' I explain.

'Oh.' Stumpy Braids bends down and scoops a handful of mud. 'OK.'

Hailey and I duck.

She throws it right at Heavy Lids – uh, her brother Raj – at close range.

'Ouch!' he says.

She smiles. 'Hey, that was quite liberating. In fact, I

think I feel it unlocking my creativity.' She gathers more. 'Yeah. That feels great.'

'Oh yeah? Then you won't mind this,' Raj says, gathering some ammunition. But he throws it at Hailey and me. 'That's for throwing mud at my sister,' he says.

The mud fight starts up again, complete with celebrity guests, and it only stops when Stumpy Braids – I mean, Heather T – announces, 'OK, I feel released now. Let's go and catch some of the support act from backstage. I don't know much about them.'

I gesture at Clyde, who's covered in mud, and Tamber, who's covered in mud and also covered in Tori.

'Oh, hey, you know, it's actually . . . us.'

SWAPPED BY A BREAKUP

From the main stage, the crowd looks vast. A sea of people that spreads so far and wide that they all blur together. They're all here to see Madison Rat.

Us.

Aaargh.

Tamber and Clyde, standing in the wings, look like they want to die. They're not even fighting with each other – that's how scared they are.

As for me, the original Glow-Pants Girl?

I am terrified.

And where is Albie? He should be here by now! He must have got the message I sent him. Surely he didn't ignore it?

Up the hill I can see the Temple of Diana. Jo will be there with David there by now, like we planned. There are giant screens at the side of the stage and they've been turned outward to cope with today's larger crowd. I wonder if David and Jo can see the screens from up there.

I hope not. If Jo sees me in ten seconds' time, she might not go through with it. What if she doesn't carry out her part just because she doesn't want to end up onstage?

No, she will. She *has* to.

An amplified voice rings out and fills the air. *'Ladies and gentlemen, all the way from Milltown, near Boston in America, to our very own Enchantment festival, we're proud to present . . . Madison Rat!'*

This is it. This is it, and Albie's not here.

Albie's not coming.

And I'm the lead singer of Madison Rat.

There's some whooping and applause and we walk on. Clyde plugs in his guitar and taps his foot, looking really nervous. Tamber settles behind his drums, looking like he wants to disappear. And as for me – I have nowhere to hide.

'Oh my God, it's Glow-Pants Girl!' someone calls from the crowd.

Oh no, I totally forgot to put Jo's leggings on! She will kill me. If it works.

I take the microphone and hit the top like I've seen people do a million times. I cannot believe I'm here.

Clyde looks at me. 'Say something,' he mouths.

'Ah, hello—' *Screeech!* 'Hi, we're, ah, Madison Rat,' I say. 'But there's been a change in our lineup so bear with us, ah—'

'Yay! Madison Rat!' a familiar voice calls from the audience.

I look down.

Oh. My. God.

Mom?

Yes, it's Mom. She's standing in front of Tori, Hailey, Brad, Velma and the rescue girls. She's as close to the stage as she can get without being a security guard – not that they seem too worried about her. She's wearing one of her tailored Mom-suits and she doesn't look any kind of threat, standing next to a man who's way younger than her and has a Patrick Dempsey thing going on. In fact, I think I saw him at the hospital – he was Jo's doctor. And he has his arm around my mom. I don't believe it!

Suddenly I feel it again: a weird rush of affection for my mom. I want to body-surf into the crowd and give her another hug.

'Go, Madison Rat!' she shouts. She was a cheerleader in high school, together with her ex-best friend Iliana, Chelsea's mom. She sure can make her voice carry. 'They're from our hometown. Rachel knows them,' she tells Dr McSwoony more softly, but I still hear her because the crowd's gone quiet, waiting for us, and also I am always astoundingly tuned in to the sound of my own mother's voice.

Then Mom whoops. She actually *whoops*, like she's

322

not one hundred and thirty-seven years *old* and wearing a *suit*.

'Oh my *God*, Mom!' I say, forgetting the microphone is right in front of me.

But then I notice it's not, and Albie is standing beside me. He's whisked the microphone away without me even seeing and he's saying, 'Hey, everyone! I've been away in hiding a while but I'm back now, and it sure is good to be here!'

Clyde strikes a chord on his guitar, thoroughly relieved but grumbling, 'You're dead, man. So dead.'

'Shut up and play, Clyde dude,' Tamber calls from behind us, crashing at his drums, a huge grin all over his face. 'It's good to see you, A-Man.'

'Yeah, wait till I tell him about you and *his sister*,' Clyde says. 'Then you're dead too.'

Albie just laughs. 'I've missed you guys.' Then he gives me a really intense look. 'And you, Jo.'

Uh-oh. I look up at the temple. *Jo! Come on!*

There are restless murmurs from the crowd.

'One second, Enchantment!' he calls. Then he covers the microphone with his hand and turns to me. 'Thanks for the message – it really meant a lot to me. And I also can't believe you'd do this for me – the singing, I mean, when I know how you feel about being onstage. You're amazing. Listen, I'll tell you everything later, but I overreacted before. I haven't been myself. I haven't known who I am – I've been a mess. I really am sorry.'

'No,' I mumble. 'She – I mean *I* overreacted. I think. *I* haven't been myself!' Help, we didn't practise things from this side at all. *Come on, Jo.*

Jo's Notes: What Rachel wants me to tell David: a script to practise from:
'David, it's over. It's really over between us. That's it, we're through, and I'm telling you calmly and I'm not angry. I mean it.'
Ugh, Rachel, do you really want me to say that? How will I say any of that to him when I just know the way he'll be looking at you? How am I going to do this? How?

Albie puts the microphone back on the stand. He holds me real tight and the audience – oh my God – the audience cheer. Because he's going to kiss me.

'David, it's over. It's really over between us. I mean it. That's it, we're through.'
Bloody hell, Rachel, why did I agree I'd say this?

Oh, no. He really is. Help! Albie is so going to kiss me.

'David, this is it. I'm finishing with you. It's really over between us.'

I can't say it. I won't say it.

Albie leans in close. I feel his breath on my face – Jo's face – and Albie . . .

'David, it's over. It's really over between us.'
   I have to say it.
   I'll say it.
'David, it's over.'

Albie kisses . . .

Swirling, swirling. Darkness. That feeling of spinning, out of control. Then I open my eyes.

'Rachel, I don't believe you!' David says to me. To me. To *Rachel*. I am wearing my black dress and I am at the Temple of Diana and I am Rachel again.

Which means I have just finished with David. For ever.

'David?'

In the distance there's a cheer from the crowd and the big screen at the bottom of the hill zooms in on Albie sweeping Jo into a huge, passionate kiss.

'David?'

'Don't, Rachel! I mean, *don't*! You blank me on the phone and then you fly to England and you won't see

me for days, and then you ask to meet me here' – he
kicks hard at the ground – 'and then you tell me calmly
that it's over between us? I mean, seriously, Rachel.
What's the matter with you? *Are you crazy?*'

SWAPPED BY A KISS

His eyes are blazing at me, and all I can think about is that I want to kiss him and I never will again.

But it's the right thing to do – the proof is that it worked. Jo and I swapped back.

And all I had to do was break up with him. For ever.

I did the right thing. I used the stuff I learned when I was Jo. I set him free.

God, it hurts.

'Yeah, you know what, David?' I tell him, trying to keep the wobble out of my voice. 'I probably *am* crazy. Mom's been telling me I am for years, ever since . . . I can't tell you why.' I steel myself. 'Never mind. There's been freakiness, let's leave it at that.'

His expression softens a little. 'You never tell me anything.' He takes a step towards me. 'I just have to guess what goes on in your head. I end up pretending there's nothing wrong, acting like everything's fine when I know that's not true.'

'David.'

'Tell me now.'

'I can't.'

'Tell me.'

I really can't. I've been visualizing telling people since seventh grade, since the hellish situation with my family and Chelsea's family started. I worked out that, if people knew I was related to Chelsea, their reaction would totally depend on where they stood in the school hierarchy.

The Clone Gang would laugh at me and say, 'In your dreams, freak!'

The Chelsea Cook Fan Club, the absolute majority of the school, would say, 'You're connected to Chelsea Cook? Like, OmiGOD! Can we have your autograph?'

Chelsea Cook herself would destroy me. I'm as tough as David's old boots now, but I know she'd find a way.

David? I don't even want to think about how it would change the way David sees me.

Even now – now I have nothing to lose with him – I still couldn't stand to see his reaction. He'll think I was ashamed or something, which I know is ridiculous. But I think I *have* been ashamed on some level – I'm ashamed that I let Chelsea get to me so badly. It's all just a mess, and I do not want David to know that his so-called superhero girlfriend is actually weak and powerless.

Ex-girlfriend.

He's still waiting. 'I think you owe me an explanation, Rachel.'

I don't owe him anything.

I might possibly owe him everything.

So I tell him. All of it.

He doesn't look at me any differently. He's still angry with me, but not any more than before. He says, 'God, Rachel.'

I mumble, 'Yeah.'

'I knew Chelsea had it in for you, and it's not like I hadn't heard some of those stupid rumours about you stalking her, or whatever. But I never would have guessed the rest of it.'

I shrug and stare at the ground.

'You should have told me.' He runs a hand through his hair. 'Anyway, you know I went through something similar – I mean, not the dad stuff, but you know I was bullied at my old school and I took it pretty hard. You knew that the day you met me.'

'Yeah, but you're tough. You coped.'

'So are you. So did you.'

I force myself to keep my eyes on his. 'It doesn't change anything. It doesn't excuse the way I've been with you. The way I haven't trusted you.'

David kicks at the ground with his still-too-new boots. 'Yeah. True. Though you know what? I'd almost rather have you yelling at me in the cafeteria than what happened after I left for England. All that silence on the phone, and you refusing to see me when you got here – what was going on, Rachel? It's like you suddenly stopped caring about me *at all*!'

'I didn't. I haven't. But . . .'

He glares at me. 'And what are you doing now, breaking up with me *for my sake*? What the hell is that? Since when did you get all sensitive about my feelings?'

'Since I realized I was treating you like you didn't have any,' I say. 'Since I noticed you're not some typical cheating man, like . . .' Yeah, admit it. 'Like my dad. You're a typical caring, non-gender-defined you.'

'Yeah, OK, about that . . .' David says coldly. 'Since we're being brutally honest. You should know something . . .' He hesitates and some of the warmth comes back to his voice, mixed with guilt. 'You should know that I kissed Jo at the start of the festival. And—'

'No you didn't,' I interrupt. 'She kissed *you*, and when she tried it again you pushed her away.'

He stares at me. 'How did you know that?'

'Never mind. But while we're all about the confessions and while you're angry with me, which you totally should be . . . I took your memory stick.'

'What?'

I take the stick out of my pocket, where Jo put it. Like

I asked her to. I hand it to him. So now he has to understand.

'But you were in hospital! That's impossible.'

'Yeah, it should have been impossible, but it wasn't. I . . . I guess someone else might have – you know – had a hand in it. But it was all down to me,' I add quickly. 'Blame me.'

'I don't get it. You wanted to ruin my work placement? Why?'

'Because I saw Jo kiss you and I was insanely jealous.'

He says in a really low voice, 'Shit, Rachel.' There's a silence.

'See what I mean, David? I'm in love with you but I can't go out with you. I'm all wrong for you. You should have a normal relationship with someone . . . you know. Sane.'

David's turning the memory stick over and over in his hand. 'I don't even care about the work placement,' he says.

'Yes you do.'

'Well, yeah, I did. But I thought I'd lost it and I got used to the idea. It was easier than getting used to the idea of losing' – he steps towards me – 'you.'

I press myself against the stone wall, horrified. 'Oh no! Oh my God, David, you can't be like this. You have to be angry with me.'

He shrugs. 'Yeah, well. I am.'

'You don't sound it!'

'It was a horrible thing to do, Rachel, and you'd better never do anything like that again. Is that better?'

'No!'

'It was a *really* horrible thing to do, Rachel, and . . . Oh, forget it. Look, I think that's the angriest I can get over this. It helped me make up my mind about something important, so, you know, it had its uses. Besides, one of us here has to be a soppy, love-struck idiot. That's what makes our relationship work.'

'David, it doesn't work. There isn't a relationship.'

'Oh no?'

'No.'

'I disagree. But anyway, I was telling you about the important decision you helped me reach.'

'David, I didn't *help* you. I messed things up for you.'

'Nah, I was doing a good enough job of messing things up for myself. I was dropping out of school, you know. I wasn't going to go back for senior year. I was going to try and get a job instead. That's why work experience was so important to me. I, er, didn't tell you that.'

'You were *what*? Why?'

He shrugs. 'You know I don't rate school much. Mum and Dad are OK with it – you know what they're like. They said they'll support me as long as I'm taking steps to support myself too. Which I am. I was the star pupil on that driving course, and that was just the start of my plans for sudden adulthood.' He pushes his hands through his wild hair. 'I'm eighteen in a couple of months. It's not so freaky, really. Lots of people leave school at sixteen in England.'

'Seriously, though? You were dropping out of school? Without even telling me?'

'By the time I decided, you weren't talking to me.' He shrugs. 'And Rachel, you've lost all rights to lecture me about not telling you stuff.'

He sits on the ground right by me, against the wall. I sink down next to him and he puts one arm lightly around me and I shouldn't – I *shouldn't* – but I let him. It feels so good.

'Anyway, I changed my mind,' he continues, 'and the memory stick thing helped me. I wasn't even enjoying that placement, and any paid job I could get would probably be ten thousand times as boring. I'd end up in a burger kitchen or something. I just liked the idea of . . . you know. Shocking people by dropping out of school.' He thinks. 'No, shocking *you*. Making you realize you want to be with me because you miss me so so much.' His lips twitch in a half-smile. 'OK, I admit it. I'm an idiot. But at least I admit it. Plus I realized what I was doing, and I'm going back to school to become a *qualified* idiot who will end up in a burger kitchen after failing his summer work placement.'

He moves his arm so his fingertips brush my back and I fight to stop myself melting inside.

'I sent your articles in for you,' I tell him quickly. 'The people at the magazine still think you're great. You could even interview Topaz later, but you might have to take Hailey with you.'

'Seriously?' He grins at me and thinks for a while. 'You're terrible, Ray. You're totally messing up my chances of a future in the burger kitchen.'

'David, I—'

'No, come on, it's your turn,' he says. He takes his arm off my shoulder and shifts away so he's looking right at me. 'Admit that you don't really want to finish with me. That you're just trying to shock me and make me miss you. Which, by the way, I already am.'

'But, David . . .' I can't believe he doesn't get it. 'No, I meant it. We. Are. Broken. *Up!*'

'Maybe. For now.'

'No, *definitely*, for ever!'

'I don't think so. I thought this time was different, but it isn't. It's still just you being you.' He gives me a look that makes my stomach twist. 'You know what, Rachel? I love you.'

My heart pounds. I screw my eyes shut. 'David, stop it!'

'No, I won't! Because, OK, now I've decided I'm soppy and love-struck but I'm not an idiot after all.'

I open my eyes. 'What are you talking about?'

'I mean, I'm not wrong about us.' He's looking at me so intensely. 'You said you're in love with me. I know you mean it. I can tell. I should never have doubted it.'

Now *he* sounds crazy. The only time I've said anything like that was when I was Jo, which can't possibly count. 'I said it? When?'

'Just now, about two minutes ago. You didn't even notice – that's how naturally you said it. Like you've been thinking it for ever. Ha! You can't fool me. I know I'm right.' He grins at me. 'Did you love me from the first moment you saw me? Were you already planning how to decorate my boots that day I stood up to bloody Chelsea in the cafeteria?'

'No!' I protest.

'You were, you were, I *knew* it! Did you ask Lenny out because all those girls crowded around me?'

I can't believe he remembers. We were fourteen! And self-centred much? But also true. 'You loved all the girls surrounding you!'

'I loved you surrounding me more. I fell for you right away,' he says, and he stops smiling. 'It was like being hit repeatedly by a ten-ton truck, and about as much fun too. I only asked that girl out because of you and that spotty boy. I couldn't even remember her name on our first date. It was embarrassing. I only wanted to be with you.'

'Lenny did not have zits!'

'OK, but half of the five million other boys you got off with that year did. I was starting to think I had to develop acne to get your attention.'

'David! You were just as bad with all those girls!' I can't believe I've just terminally broken up with him and he's digging up old memories and making me laugh. 'It doesn't change anything. We're still broken up.'

He reaches towards me, pushes my hair roughly away from my face and leans in, burying his fingers in it. It's so unfair. He knows that drives me crazy.

'We're still broken up,' I repeat like I'm in a trance. But I don't move and neither does he.

'Oh yeah?' he whispers, lowering his eyes and sweeping them over my body.

I stand up, tearing myself away from him. 'Yes! God! What is the *matter* with you? How I feel about you doesn't count, anyway. I am *wrong* for you. I . . . I have proof.'

A smile plays on his lips again as he stands too. The lost look he's had for the past few days is completely gone. 'Oh, you have *proof*?'

'Yes, I do.'

'Let me guess, this is some superhero sixth sense, isn't it? What's your proof, RachGrrl?'

'Hey,' I say, indignant. 'I stopped writing RachGrrl, remember?'

'Oh yeah. What did you pick instead? A Greek goddess, wasn't it?'

'Yeah, actually, it was. Eris, Goddess of Discord.'

He puffs out his chest, totally kidding now, not at all like someone who's just been broken up with. He is infuriating. 'Well, OK. Eris, meet Eros, God of *Luurve.*'

Oh, him again. 'I can't believe their names are so similar when they're absolute opposites.'

'It's probably because being in love is a total pain,' David says. 'Especially when you're in love with someone who's a total pain.' He raises his eyebrows at me.

I swat him lightly on the arm, even though touching him a little makes me want to touch him more, which was not the point at all.

'So go on, Eris, where's your *proof* that we shouldn't be together?'

'It's here,' I say, aware that nothing I say will make any sense. 'These ruins. The Temple of Diana, Goddess of the Hunt. It's enchanted. I had to . . . to put everything right. I had to do that by breaking up with you properly, so you can move on.' I sigh. 'Never mind. I can't explain.' Not without sounding even more insane.

'Oh, this is all about a *goddess*, yeah?'

'Kind of! David, stop teasing me, it's true.'

'Well, OK. So what if I asked the *gods* for a sign?'

'What kind of sign?'

'You know, like a sign from the heavens that we're meant to be together.'

'That's garbage.'

'No more than what you said. Besides, I'm an elementalist. I know all about signs from the heavens.' He laughs.

Strains of Madison Rat carry up the hill from the concert. I think of Jo and Albie and how their onstage kiss filled the giant screen and probably cured Jo of her performance phobia for ever. I think about how awesome it is that they're back together.

And then I wonder. Jo told me this *Freaky Friday* stuff only needed to be one-sided: one side had to make things right. Why was she so sure it was *my* side? It could well have been *her* side. What if Albie and Jo's kiss was the thing that made us switch back, not me breaking up with David? Her getting back together with Albie seems way more 'right' than me and David breaking up. Love, not discord. Besides, I've always thought there was something weird about Jo. Something freaky happened around her in our first semester of junior year too. I never managed to work out what it was, but it was definitely nothing to do with me.

'All right, goddess, I'm going to use my powers right now,' David announces, stretching his leather-clad arms out dramatically. 'So here it is. If it starts raining in three seconds then it's a sign we're meant to be together. *One . . .'*

'David – no, wait. I don't treat you right. I get so angry when I see you with other girls—'

'Yeah, well, I understand that better now. You should have said. I'll watch out for you more. I won't try to brush it off when I sense you getting angry. Probably. *Two.*'

'But . . .'

'Or you'll get over it. You're the only girl for me, anyway. I'll find a way to remind you. *Three.*'

I hold out my hand, though I have to admit the sky's gone very dark. 'See? Nothing. We're not meant to be.' I can't believe I'm actually disappointed, like I believed in his craziness.

'Don't give up on me,' he says seriously. He looks up. *'Three and a half.* I felt a raindrop. There! We've always been a bit different, you and me.'

'You're making it up.'

'I'm not.'

A wet splash lands on my head. Then another, then another. Then it starts pouring. 'OK, you got lucky,' I say, wiping the rain off my face. I'm starting to smile too, despite everything.

'A bit. I also saw the black cloud approaching. Besides, it's a music festival in England. Rain is part of the package. You should have seen the Glastonbury pictures from last year.'

'This ain't bleedin' Glastonbury,' I say, pleased to hear that my British accent is way better than it used to be.

He laughs. He closes the gap between us, and this time he holds me tightly. The sound of Madison Rat carries through the air and settles into our silence. The crowd is going wild. Out of the corner of my eye I can see them on the giant screen, jumping and swaying together in the distance.

I feel David's heartbeat quicken against mine, and when I shiver it's not because I'm getting soaked by the rain.

He says, 'Doesn't matter how I got it right, though, and whether I'm an elementalist or you're a mentalist or both of us are both things.' He puts on a super-deep voice, sounding like the man who does the upcoming attractions at the movies. 'In a *world* of *rainy-ness*, *two people* come together . . . against all the *gods*.' His voice goes back to normal. 'But who needs ancient deities? We're in love. You know I'm right.' He shuts his eyes and showers kisses on the raindrops on my face.

'OK,' I breathe in the after-shock. 'You're right.'

Then we're back together, united in a heart-shaped bubble in the graphic novel of our lives, kissing in the rain, lost in each other and our perfectly crazy relationship.

SCRIPT

Enchantment – During and After

(NOT QUITE) A GRAPHIC NOVEL SCRIPT BY RACHEL
GLASSMAN

1.

PICTURE: Festival-going crowds drenched in torrential
rain and covered in mud.

CAPTION: *Everything was back to normal at the Enchantment
festival.*

2.

PICTURE: Madison Rat rocking out.

CAPTION: *Madison Rat totally outplayed the headliners.
Ha!*

3.

PICTURE: Clyde onstage with his guitar. Hailey fangirling
at the front of the crowd.

CAPTION: *No one really knows what went on between
Clyde and Hailey, but everyone's pretty sure it was
something.*

4.

PICTURE: Old-fashioned photo of 'hot' girl in a smiley-face T-shirt.

CAPTION: *Albie's birth mother wasn't at the address he had for her and no one knew where she'd moved to. Albie spent half the festival sitting in a B&B (with patchy cell-phone reception), writing love songs about throwing away the girl who was made for him. Then he got a message from her that made him race back – just in time – to face the music.*

5.

PICTURE: Skinny rock god holds hands with perfect-looking curly-haired girl.

CAPTION: *Jo kissed Albie in front of a huge crowd without wearing leggings and can never suffer from stage-fright again. She later confessed to Albie about the David stuff, which caused a difficult moment and several 'long talks' between her, Albie and Tori, but they all got through it. Jo and Albie are sooooo back together now. Listen out for Madison Rat's latest hit:* Robot Love-Slave.

6.

PICTURE: Social networking site.

CAPTION: *Jo enjoyed brief fame on several websites as Glow-Pants Girl, Enchantment's mascot, and she'll receive free tickets to next year's festival for herself and a friend, with thanks from the publicity team. The question is: will she take Tori, or Hailey?*

7.

PICTURE: Tamber and Tori, shopping for T-shirts in the mall, surrounded by hearts.

CAPTION: *Tori and Tamber meet regularly for fashion consultations, maybe more. Sometimes Rachel even goes shopping with Tori, which was a surprise for Tori the first time Rachel suggested it. They are – gasp! – kind of friends now. Like, totally.*

8.

PICTURE: of evil in a designer dress.

CAPTION: *Rachel might make more of an effort not to be rude to Chelsea next year. Maybe.*

9.

PICTURE: of a herbal sachet.

CAPTION: *Rachel will* definitely *make more of an effort with her mother. She will also offer medicinal drinks before every date with Dr McSwoony.*

10.

PICTURE: blank.

CAPTION: *Rachel isn't sure what will happen with her father. Might talk to him again, might not. But the divorce has to be a good thing, doesn't it?*

11.

PICTURE: Rachel in the school halls.

CAPTION: *Rachel is still fighting everyday injustice in high school. She's careful when contacting Jo, even over the phone, as that girl possibly has mystical powers.*

THE END

12. – ALTERNATIVE ENDING BY DAVID McCOURT

PICTURE: Rachel and David. Together.

CAPTION: *Superhero (who happens to be female) Rachel is still fighting everyday injustice with the aid of her super-hot side-kick David (who happens to be male). This often ends in super-steamy passion.*

RACHEL'S NOTE: *Yeah, OK.*

THE REAL END

EXTREME KISSING

By Luisa Plaja

Two best friends. One extreme adventure.
Too many secrets…

Bethany is the sensible one with a long-term boyfriend, Carlota is the rebellious one with the wild past. All is fine in their world – except Carlota hates her stepdad and longs for her ex. And Bethany is worried that her boyfriend is about to dump her – and she's 'late'…

Carlota has a plan to put their troubles behind them on a crazy day out in London. She uses her favourite magazine to guide them on a life-changing adventure – setting real challenges from the glossy pages that lead to exclusive shopping, exciting snogging and … explosive secrets.

The magazine will take them everywhere they need to go – but will it make them reveal the truths they are keeping from each other?

SPLIT BY A KISS

By Luisa Plaja

I'm two different people. Literally. I'm split.

Jo has never been one of the popular kids . . .
until she moves to the USA. Suddenly the
coolest girls at her new high school adopt her,
and the hottest boy, Jake Matthews, notices her.
But when Jake picks her as his partner in the
kissing game Seven Minutes in Heaven, it's
not half as heavenly as she imagined!

Jo has a choice: should she carry on with Jake
for guaranteed popularity – or should she
tell him where to get off and risk losing
her new friends . . . ?

At this moment, Jo splits. She's Josie the Cool –
girlfriend of Jake, member of the in-crowd.
But she's also Jo the Nerd – rejected by the
It girls, single . . . ordinary. Will her two halves
ever come together again?

'A cute, sweet and funny read. Fans of
Louise Rennison will love it.'
Meg Cabot